DEATH OF A

"Terry." I stopped him. "Do you know what happened? Was it a hit-and-run?"

"I can't give a whole lot of details right now, Sugar." He rubbed a knuckle across his chin. "But it doesn't look like a hit-and-run. It looks like Alma was run over with her own car."

"With her own car?" Holy Moly, how could that even happen? "Still an accident though, right?"

"We're treating it as a suspicious death..."

Books by Mary Lee Ashford

GAME OF SCONES

RISKY BISCUITS

Published by Kensington Publishing Corporation

Risky Biscuits

Mary Lee Ashford

LYRICAL UNDERGROUND
Kensington Publishing Corp.
www.kensingtonbooks.com

LYRICAL UNDERGROUND BOOKS are published by

Kensington Publishing Corp.
119 West 40th Street
New York, NY 10018

All Kensington titles, imprints, and distributed lines are available at special quantity discounts for bulk purchases for sales promotion, premiums, fund-raising, educational, or institutional use.

Special book excerpts or customized printings can also be created to fit specific needs. For details, write or phone the office of the Kensington Sales Manager: Kensington Publishing Corp., 119 West 40th Street, New York, NY 10018. Attn. Sales Department. Phone: 1-800-221-2647.

First Electronic Edition: July 2019
ISBN-13: 978-1-5161-0506-9 (ebook)
ISBN-10: 1-5161-0506-0 (ebook)

First Print Edition: July 2019
ISBN-13: 978-1-5161-0507-6
ISBN-10: 1-5161-0507-9

Printed in the United States of America

Dedicated to all the lovers of biscuits and books. Your love of both keeps me going.

Acknowledgments

As always huge thanks to my awesome editor, John Scognamiglio, for his insight and expertise. Also, many thanks to the rest of the crew at Kensington Books and Lyrical Press in editorial, production, and marketing who lend their unique magic to the effort.

A big shout-out to my agent, Christine Witthohn, for her ongoing support and guidance.

Huge hugs to my critique group, Tami, Cindy, Christine, and Anita, for hours of listening to story ideas and plot twists. I owe you guys a round of coffee drinks and bushels of biscuits.

A special thanks to my family for their love and understanding. It takes a unique bunch to discuss methods of murder at family gatherings.

And to my best friend and biggest fan, my husband, Tim, a big thank-you for his all-in attitude and his scone and biscuit testing stamina.

And finally, to my readers and Facebook and Twitter friends, your support and friendship mean the world.

Mary Lee
@MaryLeeAshford
MaryLeeAshford.com

Chapter One

Home. Some people can't wait to leave home. Some believe you can't go home again. Some long for home.

That would be me. I believe I've been longing for home most of my life. Growing up with a series of moves after my parents' not very messy but very final divorce, I'd never felt a true sense of home until I moved to St. Ignatius, the small town that had adopted me. Or maybe I'd adopted it. I mulled over the concept as I let the sounds of the Red Hen Diner wrap around me and a warm buttermilk biscuit melt in my mouth. Comfort food.

Rosetta Sugarbaker Calloway here. But you can call me Sugar, everybody does. I'm not from anywhere near St. Ignatius, but the locals had embraced this southern gal and most of the time totally ignored that I was a transplant. It helped that I was in business with life-long resident Dixie Spicer. Dixie and I had a friendship and a partnership formed when we had both needed a new start. Her roots in town gave me street cred.

Chicken and biscuits had been today's special and I'd been reading the table while I waited for my order. You heard that right, reading the table.

The Red Hen had clippings from the *St. Ignatius Journal* sealed under glass atop the diner's wooden tables. A *Notes from Memory Lane* column about a bank robbery that had happened in 1932 had captured my attention. That would have been during the time when there were a number of Depression-era gangs and I wondered if the crime had ever been solved. Could St. Ignatius have been hit by the likes of the Dillinger Gang, Pretty Boy Floyd, or Bonnie and Clyde? I'd never considered that the sleepy midwestern town I'd come to love might have been part of a history-making crime spree.

When I heard the word "bank" from the booth behind me, I whipped around, wondering if I'd been seated by a mind reader or if I'd said something out loud about the tabletop story under glass. The two women continued talking and didn't appear to notice me peering over the booth.

"Do you think he's planning to stay?" The brunette stopped midbite, a biscuit dolloped with butter and strawberry jam halfway to her mouth.

I felt I'd shown great restraint by swiping only a smidge of butter on mine, but I've got to confess that her biscuit toppings looked tasty.

"I can't believe he's back in town after all this time," a second voice responded.

I couldn't see the other woman because we were back to back, but the strong scent of her hairspray had tickled my nose when I turned. Grabbing a napkin, I held it against my face to keep from sneezing.

"Sounds like you ladies have already heard that Nick Marchant is back in town." Another voice joined the conversation. I didn't need to look to identify this one. I recognized the bubbly chirp of Tressa Hostetter. Tressa spotted me and swooped by my booth.

"Sugar, look at you!" Tressa exclaimed.

It always seemed like the redhead spoke in exclamation points.

"Hi, Tressa." I braced for the big hug I knew was coming.

I didn't mind. Who can't use a hug, right?

"Love that top!" Her long arms enveloped me in a bear hug. I appreciated the compliment but seriously, it was my gray Sugar and Spice T-shirt. "It brings out the gorgeous gray of your eyes!"

Tressa leaned back and held me at arm's length. "So jealous of you, Sugar, your porcelain skin [yes, I'm pale] and that rich sable hair! [it's brown]. What I wouldn't give for such natural beauty." She gave me a big smile, but I suspected that last comment meant any makeup I'd started the day with was long gone.

With her colorful and creative commentary, Tressa could have been a writer of ads for beauty products, but she wasn't. She was the proprietor of Tressa's Tresses, the hair salon on the town square. I know, not a very imaginative name, but what she lacked in imagination she made up in good nature. The girl was beyond sweet, though at times not the sharpest knife in the drawer.

Tressa moved on and sat down with the group behind me and said something to the two women that I couldn't quite catch. I shifted in the booth so I could hear better and then told myself I needed to MYOB. That's mind your own business, according to my Aunt Cricket back home in Georgia. Aunt Cricket used a lot of acronyms, but she had a bucketload of pithy sayings so I guess it was kind of handy to have a shortened way to remember them.

Marchant, Tressa had said. The name sounded familiar.

"I hear he's driving a red Jag and that he's still a hottie," the dark-haired woman noted.

"I heard…" I couldn't catch the rest and didn't turn around because I didn't want to risk a noseful of hairspray again.

"Sugar, do you need a box for that?" Toy George, the owner of the Red Hen, and "Head Chick" according to her apron, interrupted my eavesdropping.

"Yes, please." The chicken and biscuits special had been a generous portion, and I'd barely made a dent in the chicken. Of course, that might have been because I'd started with the warm-from-the-oven biscuits.

Toy hustled back behind the counter, pulled out a to-go box, and brought it to me. The diner had begun to hit the lunchtime rush and I felt guilty tying up a booth, so I quickly packed up my leftovers.

Standing, to-go box in hand, I headed to the register to pay. The door chimed its signature "cluck." I'm telling you, the Red Hen Diner went all out with the chicken theme. I glanced up as Nate from the bank ducked in.

"Nate, I hear your brother's back in town," one of the brood back in the booth called out to him.

Nate Marchant. That was why the name sounded familiar. The Nick who the women had been discussing must be Nate's brother. Nate not only worked at the bank, he was also a city council alderman. I knew this because he'd recently asked to put a reelection poster in our window at the shop. I hadn't even realized he had a brother.

Handing the ticket and my money to Toy, I couldn't hear his response, but I could hear the laughter from the booth. Toy handed me my change and just as I dropped it into my bag, my cell phone rang. I glanced at the display and saw it was Greer Gooder, my landlady. The eighty-something dear had decided to rent out her house and move to a retirement complex just as I'd been looking for a place to live. I'd snapped up the well-kept Victorian right away. Greer's friendship had been an added bonus.

"Hello, Greer," I answered as I nudged open the diner's door with my hip.

"Cluck," the door chime announced as I went out.

"Sugar, Bunny is missing." Greer's voice was excited.

"Bunny?" I asked and started walking back toward the office.

I ran through possibilities in my mind. Had there been a bunny statue? Greer had left a slew of boxes behind at the house and was prone to asking me to bring various items from the attic. No, I couldn't recall a bunny. Had there been a real live bunny she'd talked to me about?

"You know. My friend Bunny." She sounded out of breath. "You met her at the meeting about the breakfast club cookbook."

I searched through my memory for Bunny. I'm usually pretty good with names, but I'd met quite a few new people when we'd had our first meeting with the Crack of Dawn Breakfast Club. The group of retirees were very excited about their plan to raise money to refurbish the aging shelter house at the St. Ignatius City Park. And Dixie and I were very excited to have a paying client.

"Oh, yes, Bunny." Now I remembered the stooped white-haired Bunny because her last name was Hopper. I mean, really? Still the moniker did seem to fit her. She'd reminded me a bit of the actress in the Miss Marple series I loved to watch on PBS. "Why do you think Bunny is missing?"

"I don't *think* she's missing." Greer's irritation crackled through the phone. "I *know* she's missing. She was supposed to be at pinochle and she's not. Bunny knows we don't have enough people to play without her and she's always on time."

"Where have you looked for her?" I asked. I didn't want to rile Greer any further, but it would help to know where she might be.

"Her apartment and around the grounds," Greer replied. "As far as we old ladies could walk anyway."

"Okay, I'll come and help look. Do you think she might have fallen?" I picked up my pace as I headed across the town square. "Does Bunny have a cell phone?"

"She does but she doesn't always turn it on. Besides, it was sitting on her kitchen table when we looked in the window at her place."

"I'll be right there." I hung up as I unlocked the front door of the office and stepped inside. "Dixie, are you here?"

As I mentioned before, Dixie is the other half of the partnership in the business that brought me to St. Ignatius, Sugar and Spice Publishing. We publish community cookbooks. Dixie's the food talent part of our partnership, the best cook hands down I have ever known, and a great friend to boot. She'd passed on lunch with me at the Red Hen because she'd had some groceries to pick up and errands to run. I'd thought she might be back since I'd spent so long reading the news clippings.

I jotted a note telling Dixie I'd gone to see Greer and stuck it on the counter where she'd be sure to see it. I'd fill her in later on the missing Bunny part of the story when we met up.

Walking around the counter and through to the back door, I fished my car keys from my bag. I made sure the door was locked and then hopped in Big Blue, my Jeep Cherokee. Turning the vehicle toward the Good Life retirement center, I wondered what could have happened to Bunny. The Good Life was an independent living complex and was on the western edge of town but truly nothing in St. Ignatius is very far.

The weather was nice but fall was in the air. If Bunny had fallen at least she wasn't lying somewhere out in the elements or in drifting snow like we'd have in just a few short months. I turned the corner at Jefferson Street. Dixie's Aunt Bertie owned the Jefferson Street Bed & Breakfast a bit farther down. I slowed as a mother with two small children had just started to cross and then I looked both ways before continuing. As I did, a figure on the opposite corner caught my attention.

Walking along the sidewalk, straw hat square on her head, big decorative daisy bouncing with each step, was Bunny Hopper.

I pulled around the corner, stopped my car, and got out.

"Hello, Bunny." As I got closer, I looked her over. She seemed to be okay and didn't look like she'd taken a tumble or anything.

"What?" She didn't seem to have heard me.

"I said, hello." I spoke louder.

"Oh, hello." She nodded.

"I don't know if you remember me—"

"What?" She leaned closer, the daisy on her hat coming very close to smacking me in the face.

I tried again, this time even louder. "I don't know if you remember me or not but we met at the cookbook meeting."

"'Course I remember you. You make cookbooks with Dixie Spicer." She smiled up at me. I'm not terribly tall myself, but Bunny was so petite I suddenly felt like a moose.

"The ladies who play cards with you were worried when you didn't show up for today's pinochle game."

"Wasn't my fault." She shrugged thin shoulders. "Alma dropped me off at the post office because I had some things to mail to my daughter in Indiana. She never came back for me so eventually I started walking."

"I see." I wasn't sure I did see. There must have been some confusion about Alma coming back. I guessed the main thing was that Bunny was found. "Can I give you a ride back to the Good Life?"

"Oh, yes." She immediately headed toward my Jeep. "I was afraid I was going to have to walk the whole way. I was getting pretty worn out."

I glanced back at the post office. Bunny had only made it a block so I truly don't think she could have walked the whole way. Dialing Greer's number, I let her know that Bunny was found and that I'd explain when I got there. And then I helped Bunny into the Jeep. Big Blue was great for travel and especially good in Iowa snow, but it was not a great choice for ferrying tiny elderly people.

Once she was in, I helped Bunny get her seatbelt buckled and then headed once again toward the retirement village.

* * * *

"I can't believe Alma forgot Bunny." Greer poured tea into my cup, although she'd just asked if I'd like more and I'd said no thanks. She sloshed some in her own mug and came to sit across from me at the table.

I'd taken Bunny to the community center, where the residents had various activities. The group of pinochle players had finally dispersed after determining that Bunny was okay. Bunny seemed less upset than the rest about being abandoned at the post office. She'd apologized for missing the game and then was ready to get on with her day.

Greer and I had walked back to her place, and I'd accepted her offer of tea, thinking that preparing it might give her a chance to calm down.

"Do you think Alma's dealing with some memory issues?" I asked. "Could there maybe be a problem with medication she's on or something like that?"

"The woman is normally sharp as a tack but lately she's had the attention span of a gnat." Greer added sugar to her tea and pushed the container of honey in my direction. "I asked her for her recipe for Better Than Sex cake and she said she'd email it to me as soon as she got home. I still don't have it."

"Her what?" I very nearly spat my tea across the table. "What kind of cake?"

"You know, Better Than Sex cake or some call it Better Than Robert Redford cake. I don't call it that, because I'm not so wild about him. I mean he's okay, loved him in *All the President's Men* and *The Natural* and that one where everybody is after him."

"*Three Days of the Condor*?" One of my favorites. I love old movies.

"Right." She took a sip from her cup. "I mean he's okay but I don't love him like I love that cake." She paused. "Or George Clooney."

I'd have to ask Dixie about this cake. I hadn't heard of it, but if Greer thought it was that good, it sounded like something we definitely should try.

But back to Alma. "I'm sure it just slipped her mind."

Greer leaned back in her chair. "You're probably right. I don't mean to be griping. I know she's a busy woman with being in charge of the cookbook and carting us old ladies around, but I'm kind of worried about her."

"I know you are." I patted her hand.

"She's been on edge. Like the other day we were going to the bakery over in Marston and she turned the wrong direction on the highway. When I said, 'Hey Alma, wrong way!' she slammed on the brakes so hard that poor Freda Watson's wig ended up in the front seat on top of Nellie's pocketbook. It's lucky we didn't all have whiplash."

Glad that I didn't have tea in my mouth this time, I tried not to snicker at the visual of Freda's wig flying through the air and landing in Nellie's lap. Stopping in the middle of the highway was serious and could have caused an accident. "Maybe when you see her, you can talk with her about what's going on."

"I'll do that." Greer set her cup down. "She's probably okay. I just hope it's not a medical thing. We ladies of a certain age worry about that kind of stuff, you know."

I could imagine they might.

"Bunny seemed to be having problems hearing when I picked her up." Standing, I carried my cup to the sink and then returned to the living room. "Is that usual or something new?"

"That's been going on for a while." Greer rolled her eyes. "We've been trying to get her to have it checked out, but she thinks she hears just fine. We'll nag her until she gets to the doctor."

It's true what they say about old age not being for sissies. These ladies, and Greer especially, were proof of that, and I loved how they took care of one another. I could see why Greer had moved to the Good Life and why she enjoyed living there.

Picking up my bag to leave, I gave Greer a hug. "I need to talk with Alma about all the recipes she's collected for the cookbook. I'll see if I notice anything peculiar when we get together."

"Thank you." She hugged me back and hung on for a bit. "You're a dear to come and help me with things."

* * * *

Back at the shop, Dixie had arrived with a bunch of supplies. I talked while she put things away in their places. My cinnamon-haired, no-nonsense business partner knows exactly where she wants things and I've found it's best not to get in her way.

"Greer seemed to think Alma had been distracted lately." I handed her a large bag of pecans, wondering what tasty thing she was going to make with them. Pecan pie? Pralines? There were so many possibilities.

"I'm thinking if Alma is having problems maybe she shouldn't be driving the rest of those women around, even if it is mostly in town." Dixie pushed a red curl off her forehead, placed several cans of soup on a shelf, and then shifted a few items around.

Just then we heard a ding as the bell at the front door announced a visitor. Not as fancy as the "cluck" sound the door at the Red Hen Diner made, but an attention-getting ding. We'd found our bell sound handy because often I'm in the office at the back, and Dixie is in the kitchen. Since we weren't really a storefront operation, we could have just kept the door locked but that seemed kind of unfriendly. Though, I have to tell you, there were times.

We looked at each other. "Disco," we said in unison.

I handed the last of the baking flour to Dixie and poked my head out so I could see the front entrance. Sure enough, it was Disco, the guy who owned Flashback, the record and memorabilia shop down the street, and he was in fine form today. His real name was Dick Fusco but everyone in town called him Disco. An appropriate nickname, because it seemed like he was stuck in the seventies: his vocabulary, his hair, and especially his clothes.

Today it looked like a rainbow unicorn had upchucked on Disco's shirt. The eye-bruising colors were in no way toned down by the tan suede vest he wore, or the white bell-bottoms that completed the outfit. I felt like I should shade my eyes.

"Be right with you," I called out. "We're just putting some things away."

I popped back into the storage area. "We were right. Do we have anything to feed him?"

Dixie turned to look at me, hands on her hips. "It's not our job to feed him."

"I know, but..." I smiled at her.

"You are such a sucker for people." She shook her head. "Okay. I tried a recipe for cherry-chocolate chip cookies and they didn't turn out the way I wanted them to."

"Where'd you put them?" I looked on the shelves under Dixie's work area. No cookies.

"They're over there." She pointed at a shelf near our large trash container.

"Looks like Disco rescued them just in time." I grabbed the plate of cookies, transferred a few to a paper plate, and snagged one for myself.

"Hey, Sugar, what's shakin'?" Disco stood near the front counter looking at his cell phone. Even his modern technology had a seventies vibe as the phone cover was a psychedelic tie-dye pattern.

"Hi, Disco." Not really sure how to answer the "shakin'" question, I moved on. "How are you?"

"I'm cool." He looked at me over blue-tinted wire-rimmed glasses, but only for a second as his eyes slid immediately to the cookies. "I stopped by to ask if you've been having any problems with your deliveries."

"Not that I know of." I placed the plate of cookies on the counter. "Help yourself to a cookie. I'll check with Dixie. Why do you ask?"

"I had a shipment of brains that should have been delivered, but I never got them."

"I'm sorry, hon, I thought you said 'brains.'" Maybe, like Bunny, I needed my hearing checked.

"That's right." Disco reached for the plate and grabbed a cookie. "Brains. The zombies came last week, just fine, but the brains…" He lifted his hands toward the ceiling, the fringe on his vest swaying, "…missing."

"Well," I didn't know how to respond to the dilemma of missing brains, "I guess that is a problem. Do you think they were lost in transit?"

"Maybe." He munched his cookie. "But the tracker says they got here and were delivered so I think maybe somebody snatched them."

Hmmm. Brain snatchers. Story at ten.

"We don't have many things delivered here and haven't had anything shipped lately." I picked up another cookie for myself. They were amazing. Whatever Dixie had thought was wrong with them was beyond me.

She walked out of the backroom just as I took a bite of my second cookie.

"Disco's been telling me he's had a problem with packages missing. Have you heard anything like that from others around the square?"

"I ran into Tressa at the grocery store last week, and she said she'd had a box of hair products go missing. They'd been delivered, and she'd left them at the back door and gone to take care of a client. When she came back the box was gone." Dixie sat down on a stool at the counter, tore off a paper towel, and picked up one of the cookies. She crumbled it between her fingers and onto the paper towel.

Ah, apparently the texture had been the thing she'd thought needed improvement.

"Tressa probably shouldn't have left the box out there unattended," I noted.

Her salon was a few doors down from the Sugar and Spice Cookbooks office, the other direction from Disco's Flashback shop.

Dixie walked to a nearby wastebasket with the crumbs in her hand. "No, probably not, but this is St. Ignatius and we all do that kind of thing all the time." She dropped the cookie remnants into the trash and came back to sit at the counter. Disco watched her with a look of disbelief on his face.

"I guess my big-city paranoia is showing." I pushed the rest of the plate of cookies toward Disco. "You should probably take those with you."

He latched onto the plate and moved it out of Dixie's reach. Something on his face told me it wasn't just Tressa leaving boxes outside, but that he had undoubtedly done the same thing.

I pulled up a stool and sat beside Dixie, and as I did I caught her expression. So, not just Tressa and Disco. Add my business partner to the list.

"I'm not naming any names here, but I'm afraid you all are going to have to change your ways." I really wanted another cookie but wasn't sure I wanted to battle Disco for the plate of treats.

Neither of them would make eye contact with me. I sighed.

Disco started to leave with his plate of cookies and then turned back. "Oh, the other reason I stopped by—Nick Marchant stopped in the store yesterday."

"Nick Marchant?" Dixie's face immediately flushed. One of the drawbacks of having red hair and the fair skin that went with it: there's no hiding your emotions. "Nick Marchant is back in town?"

I wondered at her reaction. Usually it took a reference to our local sheriff, Terry Griffin, to get her riled up so quickly.

"What's up with this Nick?" I looked from one to the other. "They were talking about him when I was at the Red Hen earlier."

"He was really into finding out what you were up to." Disco slid his wire-rimmed sunglasses back up. "I guess he'd stopped by here and nobody was here. He asked me about your hours and I told him you didn't have regular hours. You don't, right?"

"No, we don't." Dixie pushed back her stool and stood, brushing her hands on her denim skirt. "And if he stops by again tell him…" she paused. "Never mind, it's not your job to tell Nick Marchant anything. I'll tell him myself."

"Okey dokey, catch ya later." The door dinged as Disco opened it to go. "If you happen to hear anything about my box of brains, let me know."

I waited and let the door shut completely (which I thought showed great restraint) before I asked. "Okay, spill. Who is this Nick guy?"

"The other son of Stanley Marchant, Marchant's Savings and Loan," Dixie answered. "Local boy made good. Came back after college, then left town, and never looked back. A successful Wall Street broker, according to his father."

"So that's why the Red Hen was all a-buzz." I tried to recall the details of the conversation I'd overheard. "Apparently, according to the gossip, he's 'still hot' and drives a Jag."

"No doubt." Dixie pushed a curl off her forehead. "He always was hot. I was one of many who was enamored with him in high school. We dated for a bit. Nick never dated anyone for very long. Actually, my going out with him was sort of the beginning of the problems Terry and I had. Ancient history."

Ah-ha. I had been trying for months to figure out the friction between Dixie and our handsome sheriff. I knew they'd dated years ago and then each had married someone else. The sheriff divorced, Dixie was widowed. But neither had been forthcoming about what had happened between the two of them.

"Is he just back in town for a visit?" My eavesdropping hadn't provided any further details about this guy other than his hotness and the cool factor of his car.

"I have no idea." Dixie shook her head, red curls bouncing. "I hadn't heard a thing, I must be out of the gossip loop."

"Wonder why he wants to see you." I brushed a few remaining crumbs off the counter. "Maybe he wants to pick up where he left off," I teased.

"No idea on that either." She headed to the backroom.

I understood there was always a stir when someone who'd been away for a while came back for a visit. But there seemed to be a bit more to it with this particular visitor and there was definitely more to the story with Dixie and Sherriff Terry.

Where there's smoke, there's fire. Another Aunt Cricket idiom. And in this case, there was definitely something still smoldering between my business partner and our handsome county sheriff. It would be interesting to see what the returned Nick Marchant brought to the bonfire.

Chapter Two

Two hours later, I pulled Big Blue into my driveway and sat in the Jeep a few minutes, gazing at the house in front of me before getting out. I was glad to be home. I loved the white Victorian house. Stately, yet homey, it welcomed me at the end of a busy day. One day I hoped to be able to buy the house from Greer, but in the meantime I would simply enjoy it. It was a bit like fostering a pet: you could love it but you shouldn't get too attached. I kept reminding myself it wasn't mine, but held out hope it might be.

We'd moved a lot when I was growing up. My parents had divorced when I was five, and my mother and I had moved to an apartment. I had vague memories of the clean but small impersonal space. We had taken with us only a few personal belongings. Nothing to remind me in any sense of the only home I'd known. We had simply left it all behind. The four-poster bed with the pink-sprigged quilt, the small white tea set, the big dining room table, and Daddy. Or at least that's how I remembered it. Most of the memories I had of Daddy after that time were of visits with him at a restaurant or ice cream shop. Those visits had always seemed magical and full of fun.

Now I know in retrospect that my young view was extremely unfair to my mother. Cate Sugarbaker, nee Calloway, was practical and, in many ways, much more driven than Daddy had ever been. "Fun doesn't put food on the table," she'd say. And she had worked hard to take care of us. Though we'd started out in that first tiny apartment, after that the moves were always upward. Up to something bigger, something better, something in a nicer neighborhood. Still, I'd never call any of those places "homey."

Enough wallowing in the past, Sugar Calloway. Don't let yesterday eat up today.

If you guessed Aunt Cricket again, you'd be right. The woman had a saying for anything and everything.

I grabbed my purse and the bag of groceries I'd picked up. Better get inside before my neighbor, Mrs. Pickett, came to complain about my loitering in the driveway. I wasn't sure why, but the woman didn't like me. I was convinced I could eventually win her over, but I sure as shootin' hadn't made much progress lately. With Mrs. Pickett, it was always something.

Collecting my mail from the metal box on the front porch, I unlocked the front door and nudged it open with my hip. "Ernest, I'm home."

Now I bet you're thinking I forgot to mention a roommate or a family member. Well, Ernest is both. The six-toed tabby-colored feline had arrived on my doorstep shortly after I moved in, and after I'd confirmed that he didn't belong to anyone in the neighborhood, Ernest and I had become family.

Most days when I came home he was asleep, either in the window seat or some other slice of sunshine, but today he was parked on the stairs with an expectant look on his face. Obviously, I'd taken too long at the grocery store.

Not that Ernest was worried about me. More like he was worried his dish was empty. He stood and stretched, and I was sure I was in for a scolding. But before Ernest could make his way downstairs, my cell phone rang. I put the mail aside and glanced at the caller ID. It was as if my earlier reminiscing in the driveway had conjured up a phone call. It was my mother.

Adding the new mail to the top of the stack already on the table by the door, I carried my groceries through to the kitchen.

"Hello, Mama." I pulled items from the bag and set them on the counter. Ernest joined me and wound around my legs as I worked.

"Hello, Sugar. How are you?" Her soft drawl remained. Many a corporate rival had been lulled into a false sense of security not realizing that gentle siren voice belonged to a shark-like business mind.

"I'm wonderful, and how are you?"

"I'm doing well. I'll cut to the chase." She always did. "I'm calling because your father's agent has discovered some personal items of your daddy's and I thought you might like to have them."

"Of course, I would." My father had been a writer before his death. A premature death caused by his lifestyle, according to my mother. I wasn't sure how his agent had ended up with some of Daddy's personal things and couldn't imagine what they might be, but whatever they were I wanted them.

"I thought that would be the case but wanted to make sure. Do you want me to have Barry ship them here or directly to you?"

Even though I was renting, my residence was far more permanent than my mother's. I knew she'd been in her current condo for a while, but who knew how long she'd stay?

"Have him send them to me here." I thought about Disco and his missing brains. "Would you ask him to ship them with a signature required? You have my address, right?"

"My assistant has it on file."

I had long suspected the birthday and Christmas gifts I received were signed by my mother, but probably selected and mailed by her trusty assistant, Jocelyn. A very nice lady and one with excellent taste based on the style and quality of the gifts.

"Tell Jocelyn thanks from me."

I asked about the aunts. My mother's sisters Cricket and Celia were forces to be reckoned with. I sent them my love and silently thanked my lucky stars I was thousands of miles away from the family trio of Steel Magnolias back in Georgia.

After we hung up, I finished unpacking the rest of my groceries and then started water boiling for pasta.

"Italian is on the menu for tonight," I told Ernest. "Don't tell Dixie the sauce is out of a jar, okay?"

He didn't seem interested in what I was having and pointedly walked to his dish, which was empty.

"All right, buddy." I went to the small pantry where I kept his food and pulled out the bag of cat food. "I hear you loud and clear."

Once Ernest was taken care of and I'd finished my own dinner and cleaned up the dishes, I grabbed a book off the stack I'd checked out from the St. Ignatius library a couple of days ago.

Settling into my favorite overstuffed chair with an iced tea, I opened it. *The Silver Gun* was a mystery set in the 1930s and got me thinking about the article I'd read earlier at the Red Hen that mentioned the 1930s-era bank robbery. My next trip to the library I'd have to check and see if they had any information about that robbery. I usually browsed the fiction section, but I'd be willing to bet there was a collection of town history among the nonfiction shelves.

I'd just gotten into the story and Ernest had settled into his place on my lap, when there was a knock at my front door.

"Sorry, Ernest." I moved him to the ottoman and stood, leaving my finger between the pages to mark my place as I carried the book with me.

I opened the door, but when I saw who it was I had to fight the urge to close it again. Mrs. Pickett stood on the threshold, arms crossed. Her gray hair was tucked into a scarf, her floral cotton dress was covered by a clashing flowered apron, and her expression said I was in trouble for something.

Oh no, what now?

"I have thistles," she pronounced.

Why, yes ma'am, you do.

I didn't say that, but I wanted to. But knowing she wouldn't get my reference, or probably worse, would get it, I figured either way I'd be two steps back from any progress we'd made toward friendliness. Not that we'd really made any.

"And…?" I waited for her to explain.

"And they came from the thistles you have in your yard." Her mouth turned down in a frown. "You gotta get them under control or they'll take over."

"But—"

"You also have Creeping Charlie."

"Who?"

It was too late. She turned on her heel and left.

I closed the door. Well for cryin' in a bucket, I didn't put those thistles in her yard. I had seen them in mine and thought I probably should do something about them, but I wasn't sure what to do, so I'd just mowed right over them. And I had no idea who or what Creeping Charlie was.

Remember. Apartment or condo dweller all my life.

I put my book aside and went to Google thistles and Creeping Charlie. Or maybe I'd start with a search for tips on how to get along with your neighbor.

* * * *

The next morning, I waved good-bye to Ernest, who had already selected his sunny spot for the day. He raised his head in acknowledgment, but apparently lacked the energy to comment.

I climbed into the Jeep armed with a large cup of coffee and a printout of different ways to get rid of weeds in your yard. The Internet had advised a white vinegar solution could do the trick. If that didn't work the plan was cutting the stem at the ground. I was rooting for the vinegar.

It was a short trip to the office. I parked in the back and went in. Dixie was already there with a good start on what smelled like cinnamon rolls.

"Good morning," I called, stashing my bag in the office. "This place smells like heaven."

"It's my Granny Ruby's recipe." She wiped her forehead with her wrist.

"Don't worry about taste testers for this one." I grinned. "I've got you covered."

"I hadn't thought I needed testers for these, I've made them so many times." She set the bowl with the dough aside and grabbed an oven mitt to check the batch that was already in the oven. "But I'm experimenting with the glaze, so it's good to know that I have a volunteer."

"I meant to ask you yesterday about Better Than Sex Cake, but then Disco showed up and you got all riled up over that Nick guy."

"The what? Wait—" she interrupted herself. "I did not—"

I heard my cell phone ring from the other room. "Hold that thought. I'll be right back."

Hurrying to the office so that the call didn't go to voicemail, I grabbed it from the front pocket of my purse. "Hello?"

"Sugar, it's Greer. I'm sorry to bother you again, but we've got another problem."

"What's wrong?" I straightened papers on my desk and laid the printout about weeds on my chair so I wouldn't lose track of it.

"Alma is missing."

I was feeling a sense of déjà vu all over again with Bunny missing and now Alma.

"How long has she been missing?" I asked.

"Since last night." I could hear the worry in her voice.

Shoot. That *was* concerning. Though it wasn't long, the four women kept pretty close tabs on one another, and if she'd gone somewhere overnight, she surely would have mentioned it.

"You've called her phone?" I assumed they had, but I had to ask.

"Sure have. And knocked on her door real loud. Then we called the county sheriff's office, but they said she's not officially missing until she's been gone for forty-eight hours."

"I'll be right there," I was already gathering up my keys and bag. I was pretty sure I wasn't going to find Alma walking along the street like I had Bunny, but maybe I could do something to help look for her.

I stepped into the kitchen area and explained the situation to Dixie.

"Do not give those cinnamon rolls to anyone else. If Disco comes by, he may have one and only one."

Then I headed to the Good Life retirement center for the second time in two days.

Chapter Three

I felt a little funny about breaking into Alma's place.

Okay, we weren't really breaking in because Nellie knew where Alma kept her key. But still I wasn't sure I should have allowed myself to be led astray by a group of silver-haired hooligans.

We'd discussed where Alma could be and decided—well, actually the hooligans had decided—that we should check her home first and make sure she wasn't ill and not answering the door.

"Just open the door and put the key back where you found it," Nellie whispered, turning up the collar on her tan trench coat and looking around.

"Why are you whispering?" Greer said in her normal voice.

Nellie held a finger to her lips. "Shhh."

"Well, for Pete's sakes." Greer shook her head and turned back to the front door.

It opened with a loud squeak and Greer handed the key to Nellie, who slipped it back into the pot of bright red geraniums beside the patio.

Greer stepped through the doorway. Bunny and Nellie crowded in behind her. I waited until they were inside before I followed. Alma's place was the same all-on-one-level floor plan as Greer's. Living room, a kitchen/dining room combo, and then bathroom and bedrooms down the hall.

Her taste in decorating, however, was far from Greer's simple and homey style. Where the furnishings at Greer's place fit the rooms, Alma's space was bursting at the seams. Sort of like I felt after too many of the Red Hen Diner's famous biscuits and gravy. I imagined she must have taken pieces of furniture from her former home and stuffed in as many of them as she could. A large walnut armoire stood just inside the door. At its base was a grinning gnome holding out a "Welcome" sign. The sofa, a deep green velvet, was sandwiched between a huge bookshelf and a curio packed with ruby-colored glass pieces.

"What are we looking for?" Nellie whispered.

"Stop that." Greer pointed a finger at Nellie. "Right. Now."

Nellie shrugged, picked up a pair of binoculars from the bookshelf, and peered into them.

"We're looking for anything that might tell us where Alma has gone," I responded.

Nellie turned the binoculars toward the front window like she might find Alma there.

Bunny stepped through the doorway into the kitchen and began opening and closing cupboards.

Yeah. Not sure what clues she expected to find in there.

"Do you know if she kept an appointment book or a calendar?" I opened one of the doors of the armoire. There were files and papers packed into the compartments, but I didn't see anything that looked like an appointment book. "Maybe we could figure out where she was before she went missing."

"She always wrote things in her book, but she kept it in her purse," Greer commented as she stood in the midst of the clutter and continued looking around the room. "I'm going to check her bedroom."

As Greer headed determinedly down the hall, I had an awful thought. Though the ladies had said Alma's car was missing too, what if it had been stolen? What if someone had broken in, killed her, and taken her car?

I know. Morbid thoughts. But having once (okay, twice) had a terrible experience with finding a dead body, I didn't want Greer to find her friend's perhaps lifeless body.

I started down the hallway after Greer.

Just as I reached the end of the corridor a siren-like sound bounced off the walls. Thinking at first it was the smoke alarm, I started for the kitchen, but quickly realized it wasn't an alarm, but a scream.

Good grief, Alma *was* dead.

"Greer?"

"What?" She poked her head around the corner and I suddenly realized it hadn't been Greer screaming. "For crying out loud, Nellie. What are you shrieking about?"

We both hurried back to the living room. Bunny leaned against the door jam, her hands over her ears, her eyes closed.

Nellie pointed at the front window and kept the scream going. The woman had amazing lung capacity for an eighty-year-old.

Finally, she stopping screaming and took a breath. "There. Is. Somebody. Out there." Her hand shook as she pointed again. "Look!"

Greer and I stepped toward the window to look, but a squeak stopped us.

The doorknob turned.

Squeak.

I picked up the item nearest me, which happened to be the welcome gnome. Ready to protect the ladies from whoever might come through the door, I held the heavy statue aloft.

The door flew open and just as I started to bring Gnome Guy down on the noggin of our intruder, I realized it was actually the noggin of Sheriff Terry Griffin.

"Is everything okay—" The sheriff stopped midsentence.

I stopped midstrike.

He looked at me, looked at the gnome, and then took in the rest of the scene. Bunny with her hands over her ears and eyes scrunched shut. Nellie gasping for air after that prolonged scream. Greer, arm extended, hand wrapped tightly around a can of what looked to be mace.

The sheriff is a handsome guy. All-American, boy-next-door, sort of good looks. Right now, however, his brown eyes were serious. He shook his head.

"What in the Sam Hill do you ladies think you're doing?"

"We're looking for Alma." Greer looked like she still might spray him with the mace if he made a wrong move. "You folks said you couldn't look for her because she couldn't be declared missing unless she'd been missing for forty-eight hours."

"That's true." Sheriff Griffin moved out of Greer's direct line of fire. "But we also said we'd keep an eye out for her." He glanced around the room.

"Well, she's not here." Greer noted.

"We thought there might be something to indicate where she'd gone." I reached over, took the mace from Greer, and slipped it into my pocket. Better safe than sorry. "Maybe an appointment book or a note."

Bunny suddenly opened her eyes, spotted the sheriff, and gasped. Dropping her hands from her ears, she slid down the wall. "Are we under arrest?"

The sheriff turned stern. "No, but you really shouldn't just break into someone's house."

"We didn't." Nellie had finally regained her speech. "I had a key."

"Okay, I won't arrest you this time." A smile tugged at the corner of his mouth. "But how about we leave the investigating to the professionals?"

"What have you found out so far?" Greer was not to be deterred.

"We've checked with her daughter and—" The sheriff's phone rang, interrupting him. "Sheriff Griffin," he answered.

Suddenly his expression turned even more serious.

"Excuse me." He opened the door and stepped outside.

Obviously, he was hoping for some privacy.

Obviously, we followed.

The sheriff's long legs took him away from the building faster than any of us could keep up. He stopped at the end of the sidewalk, but we reached him too late to hear anything more than, "Okay, I'll be right there." The sheriff turned on his heel and headed directly toward his car.

"Wait a minute." Greer started after him, but he was moving fast. He got in and sped away. I helped the ladies lock up at Alma's and headed back to the shop.

Famished after their excitement, the Golden Girls were headed to Greer's for coffee cake. Also famished, I remembered those cinnamon rolls Dixie had been baking.

* * * *

I filled Dixie in on what had transpired at the Good Life while she washed up.

Her last batch of rolls were still warm and I loaded one onto a plate and prepared to dig in.

"Leave it to you, Sugar." She set aside a large mixing bowl. "To get yourself into trouble with a rowdy crowd of little old ladies."

"Don't let them hear you say that." I licked frosting off my thumb, and then searched for a napkin. "Those ladies, and especially Greer, would be insulted. Not about the rowdy part, about the little old lady part," I clarified. "Actually, we were doing pretty well until your sheriff arrived."

"Not my sheriff." Dixie whipped around to give me a glare.

"So you say." I shrugged.

Dixie rinsed a group of utensils and picked up a dish towel to dry them. I finished off my cinnamon roll, washed my hands, and grabbed a towel to help. Picking up the colorful mixing bowls, I carried them out front to put them away on the shelves where she kept them.

As I slid the last one into place, I heard a tap at the door. We usually unlock it when we're in the office. Dixie must have forgotten. Or was avoiding visitors. I wondered if this was about Nick Marchant. She truly had seemed agitated about talking to him.

Sugar and Spice Cookbooks isn't exactly a walk-in business so our visitors are often other merchants around the town square. Or even more frequently, Disco, looking for samples, aka free food. Today's visitor was Tina Martin, one of the local realtors who had an office down a few doors.

"Hey, Sugar," she greeted me when I flipped the lock on the heavy glass door. "What's cookin'?" She slapped her bright pink spandex-clad knee at her own play on words. "Get it? What's cookin'?"

I chuckled politely. "What brings you out today, Tina?"

"I just finished my morning power walk and thought I'd stop by and say hello." She ran perfectly manicured bright pink nails through her perfectly highlighted blonde hair.

The color of the day was definitely pink. I'm sure it wasn't just pink, though. It was probably Passion Pink, or Pink Lemonade, or some fancy name like that. You see, in additional to being a realtor and fitness enthusiast, Tina was also a Looking Pretty cosmetic consultant. One of those in-home party deals. Dixie and I had fallen for it only once.

Okay, I'll admit, it was me that had caved. Dixie was more seasoned and had avoided hosting a Looking Pretty party. So far anyway. Tina was nothing if not persistent.

Dixie stepped out from the back, carrying the plate with the remaining cinnamon rolls. "Hi, Tina."

"I just asked Sugar what's cookin' with you two," Tina guffawed and slapped her leg again.

Okay, mildly funny the first time but now it was getting old.

"Hmmm." Dixie's expression said she wasn't all that amused and she was hearing it for the first time. "I guess if you're out power-walking for fitness, you probably don't want to take a cinnamon roll back to the office."

"Is that the luscious smell I'm smelling?" Tina lifted her nose and sniffed. "I could be convinced."

"I'll get a bag for you." I hated to see any of the cinnamon rolls leave the premises but it was probably for the best. Though I tried hard to stay in shape, I'd neglected my morning run for too many days.

I quickly found our box of plastic bags and carried a couple of them out front. Maybe Tina would take two rolls and save me from myself.

The real estate maven, aka fitness enthusiast, aka makeup lady was bent over tightening the laces on her—you guessed it—pink running shoes.

"Tina was just telling me about how things are going with her new guy." Dixie looked at me over Tina's head. Her expression said, "All right, here's your chance."

Dixie and I had just had a conversation about Tina's new boyfriend and whether or not he really existed. Tina'd had extreme bad luck in the relationship department and I was on the side of she'd totally made up this new guy.

He came on the scene out of nowhere, no one in town had seen him (she claimed he was Canadian), and he seemed too perfect (constant flowers and other little gifts). Dixie said I was too suspicious of people because I read too many mysteries. She feared I was on my way to becoming a cynic.

Life will do that to you, but I didn't think I'd reached that stage. It was just that something about the whole thing seemed fishy.

"How are things with…what's his name again?" I asked.

"Rafe," Tina responded with a smile.

And that name. Rafe? Really?

"Well, I'd better get going. Thanks for this." She held up the bagged cinnamon roll and hurried out.

I followed Dixie to the back, where she continued her clean-up. She pulled open a drawer and tucked away her freshly washed measuring cups.

"What do you think now?" I asked.

"I had thought you were exaggerating, but now I'm kind of thinking you could be right. He does sound too good to be true. But why would Tina make up a fake boyfriend?"

"I don't know. Maybe her previous luck with a married man and a murder investigation made it hard to get a date."

"Could be," Dixie agreed. "Did she ever say why she stopped by?"

"Oh, yeah." I'd forgotten to mention it to Dixie. "She slipped me this." I pulled a folded-up piece of paper from my pocket. "She's doing a Looking Pretty makeup thing with her doing makeup and Tressa doing hair. She thought we might like to come."

"Figures." Dixie glanced at the flyer.

"Did you want me to sign you up for that?"

"Do I look like I've lost my mind?" Dixie pulled a face. "Don't answer that."

We finished putting things away and I headed to the office to finally get to work on what I had planned for the day.

A few minutes later, Dixie walked in, purse in hand.

"I've got some errands to run. Should I pick up lunch somewhere while I'm out?"

"I'm sure not hungry right now. Not after that huge cinnamon roll, but I will be by the time you get back."

"Preferences?"

"Not really. Maybe something light?" I figured I'd probably consumed a full day of calories in that one roll.

"I'll surprise you." She headed out.

I got busy reviewing my list of potential clients, aka my notes on anyone who'd ever mentioned they might want to do a cookbook. This Crack of Dawn Breakfast Club project was a nice but small project. We'd had some inquiries about other projects, but didn't have anything firm lined up after it. I had questions for Dixie on a couple of the possibilities. She always had good advice.

Advice. Shoot. I'd been going to ask Dixie what she knew about Creeping Charlie and if we had any white vinegar. I went to look in the supply closet and found a half bottle on the shelf. I also found a bowl that belonged on the shelf out front.

It was a vintage mixing bowl that I'd found at an estate sale and bought for Dixie. Her grandmother's bowl, one she'd used for years, had been smashed when we'd had a break-in earlier in the year. I hadn't been able to find the exact pattern, but this one was from the same era. I loved estate sales so I'd keep looking. Hers had scattered autumn leaves on it and this one a smattering of daisies. I knew a replacement wouldn't be the same as the one her grandma had used when they made cookies together, but she'd been so heartbroken over its loss that I had to try.

I ran my finger across the smooth rim, which was somewhat worn. I'd bet some grandma had made cookies in this one. I'd never had that experience. Daddy's family was totally unknown to me and my maternal grandmother had passed away before I was born. I'd made cookies with my Aunt Cricket a few times when I was a kid. She was the oldest of the sisters and while I loved her to pieces, I sure wished I'd had the grandma experience.

Carefully carrying the bowl to the front, I placed it on the wide shelf with the other bowls.

I looked up as the bell over the door chimed. I didn't know the handsome guy in navy dress pants and a crisp blue dress shirt who walked through the door. Maybe I was totally wrong about Tina's beau and this was the elusive Rafe. For her sake I hoped so. Barring that, I hoped the guy had a potential cookbook project up those crisply starched sleeves.

"Welcome," I stepped forward. "What can we do for you?"

"Hello," he said with a smile and the view got even better. Tall, lean, model good looks. As he came closer I could see that the shirt was custom tailored. You didn't get that fit off the rack. And I suspected the deep blue shade had been specially selected to match his eyes.

Tina's guy or… it hit me just as he introduced himself.

"Nick Marchant." He offered his hand.

I took it.

Truth is if I'd had that second cup of coffee and hadn't been in a sugar fog from the giant cinnamon roll, I might have made the connection. But in my caffeine-deprived condition, I wasn't firing on all cylinders.

With everyone in town talking about him, I should have been quicker on the uptake. I'd wondered when our paths would cross. The eye color should have been the giveaway. The brothers shared coloring and height and some facial features.

However, though Nate was nice-enough looking, somehow the very same features were arranged in such a way that Nick was head-turning handsome. Sharper cheekbones, chiseled jawline. The same recipe, slightly different ingredients, and a strikingly different result.

"I wondered if Spicy was around." He held my hand just a little too long.

Spice was a nickname for Dixie that she said had originated in high school. People around town who had known Dixie a long time occasionally still used it. She claimed it was based on her last name and her red hair. I'd always thought her temperament might have come into play as well. She was outspoken to a fault. It was one of the many things I loved about her.

"Dixie is out running some errands, but I can let her know you stopped by."

With most visitors I'd offer a cup of coffee and a chair to wait, but Dixie had made it clear they'd had some sort of history. Though I would have loved to pump him for information about their past, it felt like that story was hers to share. Or not share. In any case, because of her reaction when Disco had mentioned him, I didn't think she'd appreciate a surprise visit.

"Disappointing." He lifted one broad shoulder in a half-shrug and looked around the shop. "But I'm sure we'll catch up with each other eventually."

"Dixie will be sorry she missed you." Even as I said it, I thought to myself, I wasn't totally sure Dixie would be sorry she missed him.

Just as he turned to leave, I heard the back door open.

"Sugar, can you get the door for me?" Dixie called.

Hearing her, he turned.

Shoot. He'd been almost out the door. Not that Dixie could avoid him forever in a town the size of St. Ignatius, but I knew she'd want it to be on her terms.

"Sure," I answered back. I walked quickly to the backroom and held the door for her. Her arms were full of bags of groceries.

"Dixie, there's, uhm, someone…." I struggled to get the words out. And then as I saw the tension in her face and felt the prickles on the back of my neck, I knew Nick had followed me.

"Hello, Spicy." He stepped around me and gave Dixie a kiss on the cheek.

A gentleman would have taken the bags from her arms.

"Hello, Nick." She eased around him and me. "I need to put these down."

"I'm sorry. Can I help?" I reached for a bag.

"Thanks, Sugar. I've got it."

When he moved to follow her to the back room, I blocked his way. "Why don't I get you something to drink? Would you like coffee or tea? Or maybe a soda?"

Wanting to give Dixie a chance to compose herself, I took his arm and turned him toward the front.

"Have a seat if you like." I indicated the stools at the counter. "I'll start some coffee."

"No thanks." He didn't sit but did stay put.

I heard the bell over the door ding and looked up to see Lark Travers from Travers Jewelry next door. Lark had graying hair and wore thick glasses that he often misplaced and then couldn't find them because without them he couldn't see to look for them. Sometimes he'd call and Dixie or I would go over to help him locate his glasses. If that's what he'd come for today, it was going to be easy. The glasses were perched on top of his head.

"Have you heard?" Lark stepped through the doorway and looked around. "They've found Alma Stoller dead?"

"Oh, no." Alma dead? I'd bet that had been where the sheriff had been headed earlier when he left us at the Good Life.

"What's going on?" Dixie had come out from the back.

"Alma has been found. She's dead." I felt my throat tighten. Though I hadn't known her that well, she was an important part of Greer's group of ladies. I'd just seen her a few days ago. She'd seemed fit and feisty, albeit forgetful. What could have happened? Clearly something sudden. Stroke?

Poor Greer. I hoped there'd been some care taken in informing the ladies at the Good Life. They were like family to one another.

"Thanks for letting us know, Lark." I suddenly remembered Nick was there. "I was just making some coffee. Would you like a cup?"

He nodded to Nick. Obviously, they knew each other.

Next through the doorway was Tina. "Did you hear? Alma Stoller has been found dead in the city park."

"I hadn't heard that part, just that she was deceased." Lark took a sip of his coffee. "What happened?"

"I don't know any more than that," Tina swept blonde hair off her forehead with the back of her hand. "Other than I heard it was a car accident."

That's how it works in a small town like St. Ignatius. News spreads like a prairie fire and like a prairie fire sometimes you don't know what hop or turn it's going to take.

Just then I heard my cell phone ring. I'd left it in the office tucked in my bag. I hurried back to grab it. It was Greer.

"Alma's dead," she said without preamble.

"I just heard. I'm so sorry, Greer. I know this must be hard."

"Run over." Greer spoke clearly but there was a quiver in her voice.

"Are you okay?" I asked. "Are you with the other ladies?"

"They're all standing outside chattering like magpies." She took a deep breath and I heard the catch. "Anyways, I just wanted to make sure you heard. We're headed over to the community center, maybe someone will know more."

"All right, hon." I was a bit worried about her. Alma was a friend. A close friend. "You call if you need anything."

When I headed back out to the main area, I saw that we'd collected a bit of a crowd. In addition to Lark, Nick, and Tina, we now had Disco and Pat, our mail carrier. I made a quick U-turn and started another pot of coffee. Dixie had cut the remaining cinnamon rolls into small bite-sized pieces and put them on one of our serving platters.

Setting out coffee cups and napkins, I thought about Alma. What could have happened? Had she stepped out in front of someone driving through the park? And, if so, why hadn't they stopped to see if she was okay? But I was getting ahead of myself—I'm an Olympic jumper where leaping to conclusions is concerned. Maybe someone had stopped. No, wait. If she'd been missing since last night, whoever had hit her must have taken off.

If our storefront had become the place to congregate on this side of the square, I was sure that across the way, the Red Hen Diner was probably also abuzz with people hearing the news for the first time and wondering what had happened.

Once I made sure everyone had coffee or water and something to eat, I poured myself a cup of coffee. Heaven forbid anyone not be offered food and drink. My southern etiquette card would be in danger of being revoked.

The stools were all taken and in fact Dixie had pulled out a couple of folding chairs. I took a breath and leaned against the counter.

I noticed Nick Marchant standing not far from me. His eyes were on Dixie as she moved from person to person. He noticed me staring and turned on a high-watt smile.

"Did you know her?" I asked. "Alma Stoller. Did you know her?"

"Everybody knows everybody around here."

That was true, but it didn't really answer my question. I'd wondered how well. Most of our visitors had an Alma story.

Before I could press further, Dixie walked up. "I'm going to make some more coffee. We've already gone through that second pot."

"I can do that." I headed to the back room for more filters.

After a while, people slowly trickled away. Some had businesses they needed to get back to and others needed to get on with whatever personal business had been interrupted with the tragic news about Alma.

Nick Marchant stayed.

Dixie ignored him, gathering up coffee cups, carrying the trays to the back. I picked up trash and grabbed a sponge to wipe down the counter.

He didn't interrupt, nor offer to help.

I made myself scarce but stayed within sight in case Dixie gave me the high-sign. Not that we had a prearranged signal or anything. But I would know if, for instance, she asked him to leave and he was uncooperative. Which there was absolutely no reason to think he would be. He'd been nothing but charming, right? I just didn't like the tension between them.

Dixie finally finished her cleaning and straightening and went to stand next to him. "So, what do you want Nick?"

"I just wanted to catch up." He spread his hands in an open gesture. "We could go for a drink this evening. I hear the Trading Post has been all refurbished into a fancy sports bar."

"We can do our catching up here." Dixie crossed her arms.

I couldn't hear what Nick said next and I was leaning as far as I could out of the pantry without actually falling out and giving myself away.

"Married, widowed, not interested." Dixie responded to what must have been a question about her marital status. "Let's talk about you, Nick. What are you doing back in town?"

"Back to visit the old stomping grounds."

"That's great," Dixie responded. "We're done. Great chat. See you around, I'm sure."

I really wanted to see his face but I couldn't from where I stood so I grabbed a can off the shelf and stepped out.

"I wanted to ask you about this—" I began.

But just then the bell over the door dinged and in walked Sheriff Griffin.

He stopped, looked at Dixie. His eyes slid to Nick, and then landed on me, holding my can from the pantry. Then, red staining his handsome cheeks, he looked back at Dixie and Nick.

You know the cartoons where steam comes out of someone's ears when they're mad. Yeah, we could've roasted ears of Iowa sweet corn, Sheriff Terry was so steamed.

"Sugar." The sheriff used his official voice. "I need to talk to you. Privately." He cast a searing glance at the two across the room.

"Sure." I gestured with the can I still held. "Come on back to the office."

He followed me and once we were out of earshot said, "What's he doing here?"

"He stopped by and then a bunch of people collected as the news about Alma Stoller spread. You know how it is when something happens." I cleared off a chair so he could sit down.

"Uh-huh." He continued to stand.

"Lark Travers from next door stopped in to tell us about Alma and then as people heard they continued to come." I didn't care if he was going to stand; my feet were tired and I was going to sit. I pulled out my desk chair and sat down. "I'm guessing the call you got when you were at the Good Life was about Alma, right?"

He nodded and finally sat. "That's what I wanted to talk to you about."

"Go ahead."

"How were you involved in looking for Alma? I can see why the women who live there were, but what on earth were you doing?"

I filled him in on Bunny having been missing a couple of days ago and then it turning out that Alma had forgotten her. And Greer's concern regarding Alma's recent forgetfulness.

"Greer was upset that they'd apparently been told by you or someone at your office that Alma hadn't been missing long enough for the sheriff's department to look for her." I leaned back in my chair.

"That's not quite true. My deputy told them she couldn't be considered officially as a missing person, but that didn't mean that we weren't looking for her. I'd called her daughter and we'd looked up the information on her car so we could issue a BOLO."

I hate to tell you, but due to a previous situation I knew a BOLO meant "be on the lookout" for someone.

"The impression that her friends got was that you weren't going to look for her until more time had passed. The ladies were sincerely worried about her." I tapped my finger on the edge of the desk. "I hope they're not going to be in trouble for uhm…being…uhm, in Alma's place." Yikes. I'd almost said breaking into Alma's place.

"They, and you, certainly didn't help matters but we'll deal with that later." He leaned on the hard wooden chair that sat beside my desk. "Anything I should know before I head over there to talk to the women?"

"The women who were with Greer were Bunny Hopper and Nellie… Oh, gosh, I don't think I know Nellie's last name, but she lives right next door to Alma. Nellie Kaufmann, that's it."

He jotted down the names.

"Right now, though, they're all at the community center."

"And you know this how?"

"Greer called me when she heard."

"Of course, she did." He turned to leave.

"Terry." I stopped him. "Do you know what happened? Was it a hit-and-run?"

"I can't give a whole lot of details right now, Sugar." He rubbed a knuckle across his chin. "But it doesn't look like a hit-and-run. It looks like she was run over with her own car."

"With her own car?" Holy Moly, how could that even happen? "Still an accident though, right?"

"We're treating it as a suspicious death." As he stepped to the doorway, Dixie walked in.

"What's the news?" she asked.

"Sugar will fill you in." The sheriff didn't even hesitate a beat before walking out.

"Wow." I sat back down. "He was miffed."

"At you?" Dixie picked up the can of soup that sat on my desk like an Andy Warhol–themed paperweight.

"No, no, sweetie." I held out my hand for the can. "At you and Still-Hot-Nick."

She looked at the can before handing it to me. "You had a burning question for me about cream of chicken soup?"

"No, I just couldn't see or hear very well from where I was eavesdropping and so I needed an excuse to come out of hiding."

She laughed. "Well, at least you're honest."

"So, spill." I took the soup can from her. "What was he waiting around until everyone left to talk to you about?"

"He wanted to go out for drinks and catch up." She rubbed her hands. "I told him thanks but no thanks. What on earth would I have in common with him? Our lives since high school have been nothing alike."

"But he is hot," I pointed out.

"I'm sure Nick Marchant simply wants an audience so he can talk about himself. I'll bet that hasn't changed."

"Still, you'd get to ride in the Jag." I smiled.

"Not worth it." Dixie headed back to the kitchen. "I'm going to get my things and head home. You should too. We've had enough excitement for one day."

"You're probably right." I opened the drawer where I kept my handbag. "I'm trying to decide whether to go by and check on Greer. I'm sure this has been an awful shock. Those four ladies went everywhere together."

"I'm sure she'd welcome the company."

"I don't suppose you'd want to come along."

"Sure, I could do that," she responded. "Let me run home and let Moto out and then I'll meet you at your house. It won't take me more than fifteen minutes."

Moto was Dixie's adorable and smart-as-a-whip dog. A part Cairn Terrier rescue, he sometimes came to the shop with her, but hadn't in a while. I wondered what Moto would make of Nick Marchant. I've found dogs are often a better judge of character than we humans are.

I kind of hoped Dixie would give Nick a chance. She hadn't dated at all since losing her husband and it might do her good.

* * * *

True to her word, in just under fifteen minutes Dixie was at my door. I'd taken advantage of the time to feed Ernest and freshen up a bit. I'd given Greer a call and asked if it was okay to stop by and, as Dixie had thought, she said she'd be happy for the company.

"Shall I drive?" I asked.

"That would be great." Dixie stood just inside the door. "The cab of my pickup is full of some more things my mother thought needed to be shifted from her house to mine."

"Anything fun?" I asked.

"Mostly old high school yearbooks, stuffed animals I should have tossed years ago, and things like that."

"Yearbooks, huh?" I raised a brow. "I'd like to see those. More than that I'd like to hear stories."

"One of these summer evenings we'll get together and I'll tell you stories," she promised. "And then you'll realize just how boring my life was."

"I'm game whenever you are. Just name the night."

Dixie had parked in the street and so we didn't have to move her truck to get out. As we climbed into the Jeep, I noticed Mrs. Pickett near the fence between our properties. She had a hoe and was hacking at something.

I nudged Dixie and pointed. "What do you think she's doing?"

"I'd say killing a snake but if that were the case, he'd be snake puree by now." She leaned forward in her seat and peered out the window. "I guess she could be digging up weeds. There are some stubborn ones you have to dig up to get rid of completely."

I slapped my forehead. "White vinegar."

"What?"

"I forgot to get more white vinegar. It's supposed to work on thistles. Come on. I'll tell you on the way." We needed to get out of my driveway before we were spotted by Mrs. Pickett.

The Good Life retirement center was on the eastern edge of town. But even so, it wouldn't take all that long to get there. On the way I filled Dixie in on my errant Creeping Charlie and my multiplying thistles that were a plague on humankind. Or at least on the neighborhood according to Mrs. Pickett.

"I swear she acted as if I had willfully caused my weeds to spread over into her yard."

"I wouldn't worry about it." Dixie shifted in her seat.

"I know I should have taken care of them earlier in the summer, but sometimes I don't know which things are weeds and which ones are not. And it's not my property. Yet."

"Any more from Greer on her interest in selling?" she asked.

"None." I sighed. "She told me she would let me know before she listed it."

"If something happened to her, her son wouldn't be so kind though. You'd be out on your ear and he'd take the highest bidder."

"Don't say that. I can't even think about something happening to Greer."

We drove in silence for a few minutes. I guess something had happened to Alma, though, hadn't it?

I parked in the visitor area and we walked to Greer's unit. She answered the door almost before we knocked so I figured she might have been watching for us.

"Look at this." She clapped her hands. "I have not one but two beauties visiting me this afternoon."

"You're sure it's okay?" I asked. "We just wanted to look in on you. I know that Alma's death had to be very upsetting."

"You got that right." Greer led the way inside. "I keep thinking it can't be true. That she'll show up and say, 'Fooled you!' and we'll laugh.

She's been a good friend to me since I moved here. Always busy, doing something, giving rides, organizing things. Like working on the breakfast club cookbook project."

"Did the sheriff come and talk to you?"

"Not yet." She shook her head. "He called and we arranged a time for tomorrow. I told him I could have Bunny and Nellie here and he could talk to us all at once, but he said he wanted to talk to us separately. Seems like a waste to me, but it's his time."

"He told me it wasn't a hit-and-run." I didn't want Greer to be shocked when the sheriff mentioned it. "That Alma was run over with her own car."

"She's been so forgetful lately she probably left it running or something." Greer let out a long slow breath.

I hesitated about what I should say. "I don't know if that's what they think happened."

"It would have to be in gear for that to happen wouldn't it?" Dixie settled into one of Greer's easy chairs.

"I guess so, or she could have left it in neutral and it could have rolled." I'd thought about it and hadn't come up with a reasonable scenario.

"Freda Watson's son works for the Parks Department and he said that they had the area around her car marked off and there were a bunch of people out there measuring. So, they can probably tell what happened from that." Greer looked down. "Poor Alma."

There was a quiet knock at Greer's door and she popped up to answer it, grabbing a tissue on her way. The visitor was a woman with a kind face and hair the color of wheat. Her navy pants and matching jacket reminded me of my corporate days.

"Cheri, how are you?" Greer gave the woman a hug and then waved her in. "I know you know Dixie, but you probably haven't met Sugar, her partner in the cookbook business."

I stood to shake her hand. "I'm Sugar Calloway," I introduced myself.

"And I'm Cheri Wheeler," she replied in kind. "I'm Alma's daughter."

"Oh, gosh. My condolences. We were so sorry to hear about your mother."

"Thank you." She ran a hand through her hair. "Do you mind if I come in? Am I interrupting?"

"Not at all." Greer responded.

"We had just stopped by to check on Greer and see how she was doing," I explained.

"How sweet of you." Cheri stepped inside. "Do you live close by?"

"Not really," Dixie answered. "I live on the other side of town."

Dixie still lived in the house she'd shared with her husband. Her family had been nagging her to move to something smaller ever since he died, but she had resisted. She loved her big country kitchen and I also believed that the idea of moving made his passing so final.

"I'm actually renting Greer's house," I explained. "So, I live fairly close."

She looked to be closer to my age than what I would have imagined given that Alma was probably closer to Greer's. I'm not usually someone who gets hung up on numbers, but something about the age difference wasn't right. I tried not to stare at her but kept trying to do the math in my head to make sense of the age disparity.

Terry," she said, and then paused. "Sorry. I still can't get used to the idea that Terrance Griffin is the Jameson County sheriff. Anyway, Terry called me about Mom and he said you and a couple of the other ladies had been looking for her the morning after she disappeared. As it turns out she may have already been gone at that point, but I wanted to tell you how much I appreciated your concern for her."

"It was nothing." Greer waved her hand. "It's just what we do for each other. I'd want someone to look for me if I disappeared."

"Did Terry know any more about what happened?" Dixie asked.

"He said they'd know more after the forensic people, who came out from the state crime lab with all their equipment, get back to him. Measuring equipment," she clarified.

"I guess we'll know more then." Greer made eye contact with me. Cheri confirmed what Greer had heard from Freda Watson.

"I guess you two are in charge of the cookbook project Mom was so excited about?" Cheri shifted her gaze to me. "I hadn't realized that."

"We are." I paused. "In fact, we were talking with Greer about the recipes that had been given to your mom for the cookbook."

"The truth is, Cheri, when we were over there looking to see if we could figure out where your mom had gone, I took this folder of recipes," Greer admitted, reaching for the folder.

"Are you comfortable with us keeping it?" I asked. "It does appear that these were the ones intended for the cookbook. At least at first look anyway."

I took the folder from Greer and handed it to Cheri. She flipped through it.

"No problem." She handed the folder back to me. "I'm sure she had notes and things about the project as well. Like I said, she was very excited about it. But I have to tell you that I probably won't get to her place for a few days. I'll set aside anything I come across that has to do with the retirees' cookbook project."

"Thank you so much." I was relieved. I'd been worried about how we were going to take possession of the files about the project. "You can call us and I can come and get them from you anytime."

Once Cheri Wheeler left, we flipped through the folder. The recipes were kind of disorganized. Like they'd fallen out of the folder and been picked up and just shoved back in.

"We'd better get going." Dixie stood and stretched.

"Thanks for coming by." Greer stood also.

"Not so fast." I stopped Greer and Dixie. "Either that woman has found the fountain of youth and I need the name of her face cream, or there's something a bit off in the ages here. How old is she?

"I'm not sure. I think Cheri was a few classes ahead of me. Maybe in my brother's class. She might have been a senior when I was a freshman."

"So only slightly older than you." I'd been right, there was something off. "How can she be Alma's daughter?"

"Alma had Cheri when she was in her mid-forties, I think," Greer explained. "Not like me; I had Spencer when I was young and foolish. Maybe that's what's wrong with him."

"Greer, you don't mean that."

"I sure as heck do." She shook her head. "I love him but he's a poop sometimes."

Greer's son had been a bit of a problem for me a few months earlier, but I didn't hold it against him. Spiff lived in the Twin Cities, not all that far away, and rarely visited his mother. That, I did hold against him.

Glad to solve the age puzzle that had occupied my brain, I gave Greer a hug and made her promise to call me if there was anything she needed or even if she just wanted to talk.

As we crossed the courtyard to where we'd parked, I noticed Sheriff Terry talking to a tall older man with a full head of white hair who stood near one of the wrought-iron benches that dotted the complex.

I nudged Dixie. "Do you know the guy the sheriff is talking with?"

"I don't, but believe it or not, I don't actually know every single person in town."

"No…I'm pretty sure you do."

Sheriff Terry had his notebook out so it was clear the talk was more than a casual conversation. I'd already begun to move in the direction of where the two stood, when Dixie grabbed my arm.

"I don't think Terry will appreciate us interrupting when he's questioning someone."

"We don't know he's actually 'questioning' the guy," I argued.

"Yes, we do," she said quietly. "Besides, we've already been spotted. And given the look."

Dixie was right. The tall, dark, and handsome sheriff had spotted us and was giving us a "don't even think about it" look. It couldn't have been clearer if he'd sent us a text.

"Shoot, what do we do now?" I really wanted to know why he was questioning the guy. Maybe it had nothing to do with Alma's death. But maybe it did.

"It's really none of our business who the sheriff is or is not questioning." She took my arm and turned me toward the parking lot.

Just then we passed Pat, the mail carrier, on the sidewalk.

"Hello, ladies," she said. "Why is Sheriff Griffin questioning William?"

Dixie gave me a look. "Is that who he's *questioning*?"

"We didn't know who the man was." I didn't think I'd seen the guy before.

"Yup, William Harold." She pushed her sunglasses to the top of her head. "He's fairly new here. Widower. Just moved in about a month ago. Has all the ladies in a tizzy."

"Why is that?" Dixie asked.

"Not many single men around here." She grinned. "I'd bet he had ten pies the first week he was here. Not sure what he did with them. He's diabetic."

"I guess pies were not a great choice for him then." Dixie took my arm and tugged me toward the car.

Back at my place, I pulled into the drive and waved to Dixie as she headed toward her pickup. I glanced toward Mrs. Pickett's house but whatever she'd been doing in the yard she must have either finished or given up on.

As I stepped forward to unlock my front door, I tripped over something on the porch. Glancing down I could see there was a bag propped against the door. Easing open the top, I could see it was a bag of weeds.

A gift from my neighbor. What was up with the woman? Surely she knew it wasn't my fault that weeds spread into her yard. I set them to the side and went in shaking my head at her logic. Or lack of it.

I fed Ernest and then looked for something for myself. I didn't want to go back out to the grocery store but frankly there were not a lot of options. I knew I needed to plan better but that was one of the problems with living alone.

Finally settling on a grilled cheese sandwich, I grabbed the fixings from the cupboard. Not a stand-out in the healthy dinner effort, I know, but I just wanted it over with.

I sat down with the book I'd been reading but I soon nodded off in the middle of a chapter. The ringing of my phone woke me up.

It was Greer.

"The breakfast club is getting together tomorrow to talk about the park shelter project," she said without preamble. "You should probably be there."

"Thanks for the heads-up." I noted the place and time.

"Also, I heard Alma's death is now a murder investigation."

"Who did you hear that from?" It seemed too soon to know from what the sheriff had said.

"According to Freda's son, the crime scene folks say someone else had been driving her car when she was run over. Someone taller than Alma."

Holy cow. I couldn't wrap my head around the idea that anyone could deliberately run down an elderly woman and leave her for dead. Let alone that woman being Alma Stoller, who was a much-loved, long-time member of the community.

Sheriff Terry and his crew had their work cut out for them with this one.

Chapter Four

The Crack of Dawn Breakfast Club had assembled in the community room at the old firehouse and seemed a little adrift on what they were supposed to be doing. Folding chairs had been set up, and I'd slipped in the back and found a seat near Greer and the Good Life crowd. I had a moment's pause wondering how they'd gotten there as Alma had always been the only driver in the group. It wasn't far to the firehouse but probably too far for the ladies to walk.

Though it wasn't a large crowd, the acoustics were lousy and the chatter was loud.

"Complete disaster." Greer indicated the room with a wave of her hand.

Looking around, I had to agree. People milled about, chatting, wandering into the attached kitchen for more coffee. I'd been to only one of their meetings before this one and Alma had been very much in charge of things.

Just like last time, I knew most of the people, but there were a few I didn't know. I noticed Jimmie LeBlanc, a couple of rows in front of where we sat. He was a retired history teacher turned local history fanatic. I thanked my lucky stars there was no history section planned for this cookbook. I loved including local color but Jimmie LeBlanc did not believe in brevity and he didn't always understand that we needed room for actual recipes.

"Who's the man with Mr. LeBlanc?" I asked.

"Stanley Marchant," she responded. "Used to be the bank president, but his son Nate took over about a year ago."

"Right. I know Nate." I didn't remember ever having met his father. "Met his brother Nick for the first time yesterday."

"Yep, all the talk right now." Greer nodded. "They're twins. Nothing alike, the two of them, though."

"I knew they were brothers but hadn't realized they were twins. Nick hasn't been around since I've been in St. Ignatius."

"Probably not." Greer agreed. "He's been busy making his fortune off in New York. Hometown hero, local boy made good. Maybe we can get him to give some money to the shelter house project."

"Looks like Leela is trying to get people's attention," Bunny leaned over and said to Greer.

A short, round woman with salt-and-pepper hair stood at the front of the room, reading glasses perched on the end of her nose.

"I guess she thinks she's in charge now, with Alma gone." Greer's nose crinkled.

"Who is she?" The woman must have been at the previous meeting, but I didn't think I'd met her.

"Leela Harper," Greer replied.

Leela clapped her hands and tried to get the group to quiet down but they kept talking. I wanted to ask Greer more questions about Nick, but I didn't want to add to the din. No one seemed to be paying attention to the poor woman's attempts to create order.

Just then there was a shrill whistle and everyone stopped talking.

"Thank you." She nodded to a tall silver-haired man who leaned against the cement block wall near the exit.

It was William Harold, the man with two first names, whom the sheriff had been questioning. He gave a slow smile and a slight nod. I guessed he'd been the source of the whistle. He definitely was the source of a few sighs from the older women in the room.

Leela smiled at William. She had a vivid pink scarf wrapped around her shoulders and matching pink earrings bobbed as she looked from one side of the room to the other.

"I know we're all discombobulated by Alma's death and she has…" she paused and looked down for a moment, "…had always helped keep us organized. We'll miss her and her little book of notes. But we all know she'd want us to continue on with this project."

There were nods of agreement all around the room. I wasn't sure they knew how to continue on.

The retirees who were part of the breakfast club weren't like most of the clients we dealt with. They weren't formally organized with a chair and specific committees. They'd met for breakfast on the first Tuesday of the month and had decided to take on renovation of the St. Ignatius City Park shelter house. Their monthly all-you-can-eat breakfasts had gotten them part way to their renovation budget and they were continuing those along with the cookbook project.

"Stanley, do you have a report on what our balance is?"

Stanley Marchant stood, cleared his throat, and pulled a paper from his breast pocket. "We've got $2,468 in the bank. That's with the last breakfast and a couple of direct hundred-dollar donations to the project." He sat down.

Wow. I'd say they'd done pretty well.

"Bertie, when's our next breakfast?" Leela's gaze landed on Bertie Sparks, Dixie's aunt, whom I hadn't spotted up to now.

"We're set for next Saturday morning. The shelter is reserved and we're good to go, unless Alma's services are on Saturday, then we're going to want to postpone. Anyone know what the plans are?" she asked.

A lady in the front row spoke up. "I heard from Opal, who works with Cheri, Alma's daughter, that they haven't released Alma's body yet, and she isn't going to make plans until they do."

"That's what I heard, too," Greer whispered to me.

"Well, we'll plan on Saturday unless we hear something different then. There's a sign-up sheet being passed around."

"Let's hear an update on the renovation estimate. William, I understand you're helping us with that." She looked to the whistler, who hadn't moved from his spot by the exit. "Anything new there?"

He stepped forward and lifted a hand to shove his silver locks out of his eyes.

"I talked with the stone company, and it looks like we can get a good price on the limestone benches you wanted. We can always start with two or three and then add additional benches as we're able to afford them." He took a breath and smiled at the room. "Much of the carpentry work is being donated by the local Carpenters Union, which means our cost there is just materials. There's a lot of wood rot and we'll have to replace a few timbers, but most of the façade is fine so we'll be able to refinish that wood."

"I guess he used have a construction company before he retired," Greer whispered.

"Okay, then." Leela nodded. "Alma had been working on the cookbook. Had anyone else been working with her on that?"

There was silence for a couple of beats. I waited to see if anyone from the group had been working with Alma. It didn't appear that was the case, so I stood.

"Hi, I think you all know me, but for those of you who don't, I'm Sugar from Sugar and Spice Publishing, and we'd been working with Alma on the recipes. I'd given her a rough idea of costs and can give you a better estimate once I have all your recipes and know how many pages we're talking about."

"Thank you very much, Sugar." Leela peered at me over the top of her reading glasses. "If you all can get your recipes to Sugar as soon as possible that would be great. How do want us to do that?"

"You can drop them off at the office or email them to us." I gave our business email. It didn't look like anyone was rushing to write it down so I expected we'd get a lot of in-person recipes, which was okay because we also had a release form for them to sign.

"I gave mine to Alma last week," a guy in overalls and a ball cap behind me said.

I'd been afraid we were going to run into that problem.

"I'll see if I can get the files from Alma's daughter, but to be safe you probably should resubmit." I turned and smiled at the guy.

Oh, dear. On closer inspection, I realized that was not a guy but rather a very muscular woman in overalls. "If you'd like to give me your name, I can see if we already have it."

"It's the Cat Shed Biscuit recipe." She pulled out a handkerchief and wiped her face. "If you don't have it, call me. Jeri Beetles."

"Okay, if we don't have any other business, I think that's it." Leela dismissed the group. "Hope to see you all on Saturday at breakfast."

The crowd began to disperse. I stood and reached for my bag. "Do you need a ride back to your place?" I asked Greer.

"Thanks for asking. You are such a sweetheart." She brightened. "They brought us in the Good Life van, but they were taking a bunch over to the library so we were going to have to wait on them. If you're okay with taking us home, I'll cancel them coming back for us."

"It's no problem at all."

As we walked to the parking lot we passed Stanley Marchant, who was moving slowly down the walkway. Greer stopped beside him.

"Stanley, have you met my friend Sugar?" she asked.

"I don't believe we've met formally, but I know who you are." He stopped on the sidewalk. "You are in business with Dixie Spicer, right?"

"That's right." I held out my hand. "Rosetta Sugarbaker Calloway, but everyone calls me Sugar."

"Nice to meet you." He griped my hand firmly. "Stanley B. Marchant." Very formal, no nicknames for him. I guessed I wouldn't be calling him Stan.

* * * *

It was a beautiful morning and the Good Life entrance was ablaze with colorful bright red and white petunias. I pulled into the visitors' area, parked, and helped the ladies out. While Bunny hurried off on her own, Nellie asked if we could walk her the short distance to her unit.

She and Greer chatted about plans for Alma's funeral. It seemed Alma had only one daughter and the burden would be on her to make plans and sort everything out. As an only child myself, I could only imagine the stress.

As we approached Nellie's unit, we noticed a man peering in the windows at Alma's place.

"Hey, you. What are you doing there?" Greer yelled.

The man turned but didn't answer. He was youngish, at least in comparison to the average age of the residents at the Good Life, and was dressed in a gray suit with a bright pink shirt and a gray and pink checkered tie.

A relative? Someone from out of town?

"Do you know where Mrs. Stoller is?" he asked.

I crossed relative off my list. A salesman, maybe?

"I do know where she is, but clearly you don't," Greer challenged. "Who are you?"

He stepped forward and extended his hand. "Greg Cheeters, from Ross & Cheeters Development Corporation."

Hmmm. If I were in business I'd think of a different corporate name, but maybe that was just me.

None of us took his proffered hand and he eventually dropped it to his side.

"I was to meet Alma Stoller here at eleven o'clock and she doesn't seem to be home."

"That's because she's dead," Nellie spoke up.

"She's what?" He blanched, seemingly taken aback by the news.

"Are you hard of hearing?" Greer hadn't softened her stance. "She died two days ago."

"My condolences." He straightened his tie. "Are you family?"

"No, we're neighbors," Greer answered. "What was your business with Alma?"

"I'm not at liberty to say." He began to move away. "That is, since you're not family."

* * * *

Back at the Sugar and Spice office, Dixie sat on a low stool pulling things out of the bottom cupboard. Cutting boards, muffin pans, cookie sheets.

When Dixie has had a stressful day, she cleans or cooks. If only that were true for me.

People getting on her last nerve? She bakes brownies.

When I'm stressed I eat brownies. And any other chocolate I can find.

"How did it go?" she asked.

"You owe me." I pulled up a chair and sat, wondering what we were going to do about the missing recipes. "Things were pretty disorganized. A lady, Leela Harper, Greer said her name was, tried to take charge. At first no one was listening, but eventually she reined in the chaos. Bottom line, it seems no one had copies of the recipes except for Alma. I gave them our email, but no one wrote it down. So, I'm pretty sure we'll have people stopping by to drop off recipes in person."

"I guess that's okay but we aren't always here." She shook a box of rice and then peered in the package. "Maybe we should let them drop them in the mail slot."

"I'm afraid that might create a problem with mixing recipes and contact information."

"You're probably right. We can check with Cheri and see if she's found any more files at her mom's." Dixie set the box of rice aside. "It seems a bit too soon though, doesn't it?"

"It does," I agreed.

We were in a pickle. I certainly did not want to bug a woman who'd just lost her mother, but we were already a week behind according to the schedule we'd laid out. I'm big on schedules.

Dixie looked at me and shrugged. "How many are we missing?"

"It's hard to say. Alma hadn't given me the full list of contributors. If I had that list, I'd know which ones we don't have."

We sat in silence for a few minutes.

"I meant to ask you about this woman who was there." I leaned back in the chair. "Her name was… just a minute and I'll remember it…" I pictured her talking to me, her overalls, her ball cap. "Beetles, Jeri Beetles. That was it."

"Jeri and her husband farm near my folks. Not much of a fashion statement, but, man, that woman can cook." Dixie smiled. "What recipe was she sharing? Did she say?"

"I wanted to talk to you about that too. I think she said, 'Cat Shed Biscuits,' but that can't be right. I mean, are they furry-looking or what?"

"Cat's Head Biscuits, you goof." Dixie tried to hold back a laugh but couldn't contain it.

"That's a little better than Cat Shed Biscuits, but I still think it's a weird name."

"Good grief, Sugar, you've never heard of Cat's Head Biscuits?"

"Cat's Head? I can't say that I have." I made a face at her. "Nor does that make any more sense."

"They're called that because they're drop biscuits that are as big as a cat's head. I thought they were a southern thing."

"Probably are, but apparently one that I missed. Remember my crazy mixed-up childhood."

"That's right. I keep forgetting that you're City Southern."

We heard a ding and I walked out front to see that it was Pat with a stack of mail for us.

"Hi, Pat."

"Hello, Sugar." She handed me a bunch of envelopes and a slip indicating we had a package at the post office. Then she was back out the door. No dawdling for her today.

I looked at the slip. More samples from our printer. Those were always bulky and heavy. I'd have to stop by the post office and pick up the package.

Speaking of which, I wondered how soon my package from Daddy's agent would arrive. I had no clue what might be coming, but I was curious to find out. Daddy had done well with a couple of major books but then had also had a flop or two. From bestseller to hardly selling any copies at all.

When I was old enough, much to my mother's chagrin, I'd read everything he'd written. The books were mostly coming-of-age-type stories with a protagonist who triumphed in spite of his terrible childhood. I wondered if my dad's life had been like that.

The few background facts I'd gleaned from my aunts (Mama didn't talk about him) were that he was an adopted only child of an Iowa couple who moved to Atlanta. He and Mama had met in college at Emory University. His adoptive parents had passed away shortly after my parents were married. Living in Iowa now, I hoped one day to do some investigation into his Midwest roots, but I had very little to go on. Again, according to Cate, there was no one left. He'd been the last in the line.

I filled Dixie in on my conversation with my mother and the boxes that were coming.

Flipping through the mail, I noted an envelope for Jameson County Realty and laid it aside. It had been stuck between a couple of pieces of junk mail.

"Anything of interest?" Dixie asked.

"Most of it is junk." I tossed several envelopes and advertisements into the recycling. "One invitation, two bills, a cooking magazine, and one letter that doesn't belong to us." I dropped the stack on the desk.

"Let me have the magazine." Dixie held out her hand.

Pulling out the magazine, I handed it to her. "I'm going to run this over to Jameson County Realty." I held up the letter that had been mixed in with our mail. "I need a walk anyway. Then when I get back, I'm going to give Max a call about the photography on the Crack of Dawn cookbook."

"Still haven't heard from him?" She raised a brow.

"Not in a couple of weeks." I didn't make eye contact. "I'm sure he's busy."

"You could call *him*," Dixie pointed out.

"I intend to. Just as soon as I get back from delivering this." I waved the envelope.

"I think you're just looking for an opportunity to question Tina about her mystery man." Dixie smiled.

"Maybe." I grinned.

* * * *

When I walked into Jameson County Realty, Tina was the only one in the office, and she was on the phone. She poked her head up over the partition wall of her cubicle and then, seeing it was me, motioned for me to join her.

I headed to where she stood and slid into a faux leather side chair. The wall was covered with eight-by-ten photos of houses, businesses, and farms for sale. Not wanting to eavesdrop on her call (unless it was her boyfriend and unfortunately it sounded more like a client), I got up and walked to the nearest wall to look over the listings.

It didn't take Tina long on the phone. When she finished up, I handed her the envelope.

"This was mixed in with our mail. I think it got stuck to one of the other envelopes in our stack."

She turned it over and looked at it. "Thanks Sugar. I'll give it to Ethan."

"How are things going in the real estate biz?" I pointed to the posted listings. "Busy?"

"Always busy this time of year." She nodded. "If people are making a move, especially families, they want to do it before school starts. I have two couples that I'm showing houses to this afternoon."

"That's great." I was happy for her. She'd had a tough time earlier this year.

"Do you know anything about this development firm that's buying property north of town?" I asked. "I ran into a guy from the company earlier when I dropped Greer and her friends at the Good Life."

"I haven't personally talked to anyone from Ross and Cheeters Development but Ethan has." She brushed a strand of platinum hair off her forehead. "What did you want to know?"

"Sounded like this guy had business with Alma. I was curious what type of a development project they have planned."

"I don't think it's big. They'd have to connect to city utilities to attract any city folks."

"Meaning?"

"You know, water and gas, that kind of stuff." Tina waved a manicured hand. "Most of the farms have rural water, used to have wells, and use propane for heat. But for city folks you're going to need regular gas and water hookups."

"Do you know who owns all that land they were interested in?"

"I thought they had closed on all the land acquisition." She shrugged. "The Garman farm, the former Weaver place, now owned by your guy, Max. A section of the Beers family land and then a few acres that belonged to Alma Stoller."

"Hmmm." I ignored the "your guy, Max" comment.

"Do you want me to ask Ethan about it?" She pulled forward a notepad. "I don't know what he'll know since we're not directly involved, but I think Ethan may golf with one of the investors."

"I'm curious if they've actually completed everything." I'd noticed a crystal frame on Tina's desk. "Is that your new friend?"

"It is." She handed me the photo, grinning widely. "It's not a very good picture though."

It was a lousy picture. I take that back. It was a wonderful photo of a lake. The man not so much. In the photo he was waving from a dock. The far end of a dock. He was totally out of focus. You could tell that it was a guy but that was the extent of it.

"What a beautiful lake." I handed the picture back to her. "Where was it taken?"

"It's at his lake house." She sighed. "I can't wait to see it."

I wouldn't hold my breath on that one. I hate to be such a Debbie Downer, it's not usually my style. But I have to tell you I'm pretty sure that was a photo she'd found online, printed off, and framed.

Thanking Tina for the info, I headed back to the shop to fill Dixie in on Boyfriend-Gate and make my call to Max about the photos.

Chapter Five

I sat at my desk and prepared to make my call to Max Windsor. Dixie had nailed it. Max and I hadn't talked in a couple of weeks. Radio silence after several months of what I had thought were good times together.

All the possible reasons had run through my brain. He'd been sick, he'd been out of town. Maybe he'd had out-of-town company. But the truth was that if any of those had been true, I'd have heard. Remember that news in town spreading like prairie fire I talked about?

I'd finally landed on the idea that he must have just decided we needed to cool things a bit. We'd been doing lots of things together over the summer. Things like dinner or a movie. And when we didn't have something planned, we'd still talked on the phone.

People around town had begun to treat us like a couple. Including Max when they invited me to a function. I had to assume they'd done the same with him.

Maybe that was the problem. Maybe he wasn't ready for whatever that meant. Heck, I wasn't sure that I was. I liked Max as a friend. Whether it became anything more was not anything I wanted to rush. I told myself I was probably just making a mountain out of a molehill, but the dropped contact had brought to life all sorts of insecurities in me.

Still, personal relationships aside, I needed to find out if Max was interested in doing the cookbook. He was a talented photographer and we'd worked with him on a previous project. But he was also in demand and might not be available.

If not, I needed to get started right away on finding someone else. I had contacts from my days of working at the magazine, but I knew others would be more expensive. The sooner I knew what the situation was, the sooner I could plan the cost into the budget.

I took a deep breath and made the call.

Max picked up on the first ring. I tried not to sound awkward about the fact that we hadn't talked in a while.

"Hey, Max." Deciding to go with all-business, I launched immediately into the reason for my call.

He listened and then asked a few questions about the number of recipes we'd need pictures for and what we had planned for the other interior pages and the cover.

"It sounds like something I can fit into my schedule without too much trouble." I could picture him on the other end of the line, jotting down notes as he spoke.

"We're looking at a pretty short timeline so I wanted to make sure. With Alma Stoller's death I've got some work to do to figure out where she was with gathering all the recipes for us," I explained.

"I'd heard about her accident."

"They're calling it a suspicious death at this point."

"Really?" He paused. "I hadn't heard that."

"By the way, when I dropped off Greer today after the breakfast group meeting there was a guy at Alma's, looking for her. Actually, he was looking in her windows. Dixie mentioned that development group he works for was trying to acquire some land near you. Maybe actually *from* you." I let my voice rise a bit, hoping he'd want to fill in some info.

"They are. Still working on it, I think. I had agreed to sell them a portion of my property. And the Potters had also agreed. They're adjacent to me on the east. But as far as I knew, Alma was still a holdout."

"That's interesting." Now it was me jotting down notes.

"I can see those wheels turning." He chuckled. "Do you think her accident had something to do with the land deal?"

"I don't know. It just seems to be quite a coincidence that she was the holdout keeping them from moving forward on their big development."

"Hmmm. What does the sheriff say about your theory?" I could hear the amusement in Max's deep voice.

"I haven't told him about it." Max knew me well. "But I will. No holding back any info from Sheriff Terry." I smiled to myself. "Well, I'd better get busy here. I've kept you longer than I intended so I'll let you go."

This was the place where he was supposed to say it had been too long. Or maybe that he'd missed talking to me. Or maybe we should get together for coffee.

"Great to hear from you," he said. "I'll put the Crack of Dawn cookbook on my schedule."

"Thanks, Max," I said "That will be great."

I put down the phone and sat for a few minutes trying to decide if everything was okay between us or not. He'd sounded fine. Didn't seem distant but also didn't make any effort about getting together. I was at a loss. Standing, I headed back out front to let Dixie know we had our photographer booked.

As I walked down the hallway, the bell out front chimed, announcing a visitor.

"Hi, guys." Disco strolled through the door. Today's look was jeans with an orange and purple paisley vest over a ruffled shirt. Not that I have anything against paisley, mind you. Or a nice retro look. But this was one of those looks most of us had hoped wouldn't make a comeback.

"Hi, Disco. How are you?" I asked. "How's business?"

"Good," he answered. "Kind of slow today."

I was convinced most of his days were slow, but he seemed to be making enough to stay in business. A few months ago, we'd worried that he might actually be sleeping at the store, but Tina had confirmed that she'd helped find him an inexpensive rental. Still, I was guessing there wasn't a ton of markup in the memorabilia he stocked. I should stop by and see if there wasn't some item I could purchase. Maybe a gift. Maybe some random item I could use in staging the pictures for the cookbook.

Yeah, right. Like what? Psychedelic biscuits? Okay, maybe not staging for the cookbook, but surely I could find some trinket to purchase.

Dixie slid off the stool where she'd been working. "Be right back."

She returned a few minutes later with a dish of chocolate chip cookies. She'd been holding out on me.

"Where did those come from?"

"It's a new recipe I'm trying. The recipe made more than I thought it would." She shrugged. "I would have offered some to you, but you've been complaining about all the calories."

She held the plate out to Disco.

He took two.

"Let me know what you think." She placed the plate on the counter.

The door dinged again and this time it was Sheriff Terry. Sharply dressed in official attire, he nodded at Disco, said hello to Dixie and me, and eyed the plate of cookies.

Disco reached out a ruffle-clad arm and pulled the plate out of the sheriff's reach.

Sheriff Terry was undeterred. He reached a light-gray uniform-clad arm over Disco and snagged a cookie. The sheriff couldn't resist chocolate chip cookies. Especially Dixie's.

"Anything new on Alma?" I couldn't resist questions.

"No, not really."

"I'm assuming you know about the real estate deal?"

Sheriff Terry stopped with a cookie halfway to his mouth. "No one mentioned a real estate deal."

Dixie sat back down at the counter and propped her chin on her hands.

I recounted the earlier event with Greer and the ladies when we had spotted the guy peering into Alma's windows.

"And then when I talked to Max a little bit ago, he mentioned that as far as he knew Alma was the only holdout and that if she didn't agree to sell, everyone was out. Cheeters only wanted to buy the land if they could get the whole batch."

"Cheaters." Disco snickered.

"Cheaters?" Sheriff Terry asked. "That's the name of the real estate company?"

"Ross and Cheeters, spelled C-H-E-E-T-E-R-S. I looked it up," I explained. That's the development company. I can't think the name gives people a lot of confidence."

"I'll check it out."

"So why are you here?" Dixie asked. "I don't imagine you just stopped by for a cookie."

"Well, these would be worth the trip but, no, that's not why I stopped in." He eyed the cookie plate, which Disco continued to guard with a fringed arm.

We waited.

The sheriff looked pointedly at Disco.

If he was attempting to telegraph that Disco should move along, it wasn't working. I knew from experience that subtlety didn't work with our fringed friend.

"Would you like me to grab a bag for those?" Dixie asked Disco. "You could take them with you."

"Sure," he mumbled around a mouthful of cookie.

She walked back to the storeroom and returned with a quart-sized plastic bag, dumped the plate of cookies into it, and handed it to Disco.

"Thanks. See you later." He was out the door in two shakes of a lamb's tail.

"I guess we're both out of luck." I turned to the sheriff. "At least you got one cookie. I didn't even get a taste."

"Way to go." He frowned at Dixie.

"So why are you here if not for cookies?" I asked.

"Sugar, you seem to know the ladies at the Good Life pretty well, and you interact with them on a regular basis."

"That's me." I rolled my eyes. "I have quite the exciting social life." That came out a little sharper than I intended, and Dixie gave me a funny look.

"I wondered if you'd noticed whether anyone had a problem with Alma recently." He brushed cookie crumbs from his uniform. "Of course, when I ask, they all say they loved Alma and she was the best. Everyone loved her, etcetera, etcetera."

"She *was* well liked."

"I understand, but it's never the case that 'everyone' loves a person. When people live in close proximity like a neighborhood, an apartment complex, or a retirement village, even the nicest person gets on somebody's nerves."

"Like Sugar's neighbor." Dixie got up and started a pot of coffee. "We all know Sugar is the nicest person ever, but Mrs. Pickett can't stand her."

"Kind of strong, don't you think?" I gave Dixie a look.

"You said she hates you." Dixie put her hands on her hips.

"Well, there is that." I shrugged. "But I still think I can win her over."

"Back to the Good Life crowd," the sheriff prompted. "Anyone you can think of who might have had a problem with Alma?"

I thought back over the times I'd observed the residents who lived there. Mostly Greer, Nellie, and Bunny hung out with Alma. Occasionally, Freda of the flying wig. I didn't know her as well. And there were many other people. I guessed there were probably ten to twelve of the resident buildings, and those were mostly fourplexes. Some couples, but the vast majority were single men or women. Mostly women.

I tried to do the math in my head. "I would guess there are at least fifty people who live there and I only know a handful. Do you think someone from the Good Life had something to do with Alma's death?"

The sheriff sighed and leaned against the counter. "We're not sure, but we don't have a lot to go on. This is only one of many areas we're looking into."

"Are you still treating Alma's death as suspicious?" Dixie handed him a fresh cup of coffee.

"We're not sharing this publicly." He paused and took a sip. "But the info from the forensic team tells us it wasn't a hit-and-run. More likely intentional. She was run over more than once."

I winced. "How awful. The poor woman."

"That would lead me to believe that whoever did this had a problem with Alma Stoller."

"You think?" Dixie raised a brow.

"Was that why you were questioning Harold, the new guy?" I asked. "Did he have a problem with Alma?"

"William," the sheriff corrected. "William Harold."

"Right. That's what I meant, William." I'd known the two-first-names thing was bound to trip me up at some point.

"He's the one who suggested that someone got into a fight with Alma. He heard an exchange of words." Sheriff Terry drained his cup and set it on the counter. "But he doesn't know everyone yet. All he could give me was a description, and not a very good one."

"Let me guess." Dixie tapped a finger on her lips. "An older woman with gray hair?"

"Pretty much." He bobbed his head. "Not thin. Not fat. Medium height. Slightly stooped."

"Good grief." I couldn't believe Mr. New Two-First-Names couldn't be more specific. "That's at least eighty percent of the residents of the Good Life."

"Right." The sheriff tapped his fingers on the counter. "I've tried talking to them, but 'everyone loved Alma' is all I get."

"The Senior Squad closed their ranks."

"They're stonewalling me." He shook his head. "Except for William, who is too new to have become one of them."

"I'm not aware of any problems that any of the ladies had with Alma. I mean she was kind of bossy with the others, but nothing major." I truly couldn't come up with a soul. "Sorry I can't be more help."

"If you hear anything, would you let me know?"

"Sure thing."

"I know you have my number, but in case you've lost it, here's my cell." He handed me a card.

After the sheriff left, Dixie got up from her stool. "What do you think about someone from the Good Life being involved.?"

"It's hard to believe that anyone would mow down Alma, and then run her over again, and leave her for dead." It really disturbed me. "I can't think any of the people at the Good Life are capable of that."

"Besides which, most of them don't drive," Dixie noted.

"That's right. There's only a handful who do. How would someone even have gotten to the park?"

"Maybe they went there with her." Dixie began cleaning up, wiping down the counter as we talked.

"You're brilliant. That has to be it."

"That is, if it was someone from the Good Life," she added.

"Okay, not so brilliant." I frowned because I truly didn't think anyone from the Good Life would murder Alma. "What if it was an accident and one of them is afraid to come forward?"

"Maybe," Dixie shrugged. "Terry seemed pretty convinced it was intentional. She was run over twice."

"I'm going to stop by and talk with Greer on my way home. I'll bet she knows who it is they're covering for."

"The sheriff did ask you to check things out." A corner of her mouth lifted. "Sort of," she added.

"He did and I'm going to take full advantage of that fact." I smiled back. "I'll let you know what I find out."

* * * *

I pulled into the parking lot and looked around at the Good Life with new eyes. The complex wasn't an assisted living arrangement. Everyone who lived there was independent and able-bodied. Most, like Greer, had made the choice to move to the Good Life because they didn't want to deal with home maintenance or have the chore of taking care of a yard anymore.

The majority were female, widows mostly, but there were a few men. Looking around at the grounds and the one-story fourplex units, I totaled up the potential residents. My earlier guess had been pretty accurate. Ten buildings, so forty-plus people.

I'd brought a bag of sweet corn for Greer. What Dixie had brought from her folks to share was far more than I'd use. As I grabbed my bag and the corn and headed toward Greer's unit, I noticed Cheri Wheeler walking toward the parking lot, juggling two cardboard boxes.

I slipped my bag over my shoulder. "Here, let me help you with that."

"Thanks." She let me take the top box. "I thought I could get them both because neither was very heavy but they were bulkier than I realized."

"No problem." I shifted the box to one hip. "Where's your car?"

"It's the white minivan just across the parking lot." Cheri pointed.

I walked with her to the van and then waited while she opened the back. It was already packed with other boxes. I hoped these two would fit.

"How are you coming with going through your mom's things?" I asked. "It must seem overwhelming."

"You've got that right." She rearranged the boxes to make room for more. "My mom claimed to have downsized when she moved here from our house. But I'm afraid mostly what she did was jam as much as possible into this small two-bedroom unit."

"If there's anything I can do to help, please don't be afraid to give me a call. I moved a lot growing up so I've got some well-honed packing skills and would be happy to help."

"Thanks so much for the offer. I may take you up on that." She was able to make room, took the last box from me, and slid it in. "There we go."

"Well, let me know. I'm headed to Greer's."

"You know," Cheri closed the back door, "I found another folder with recipes. They aren't my mom's; I'd recognize her handwriting. I wondered if they might be part of the cookbook project. If you want to walk back with me, I'll give them to you."

"That would be great." I hoped the folder contained the cookbook recipes. "I've been going through what we've got, and I know we are still missing a bunch."

We walked along the sidewalk toward Alma's place. There were people outside on their patios and others out for a stroll. The peacefulness of the setting made it seem highly improbable to me that anyone who knew Alma had run her over. But like the sheriff said, they needed to follow any lead they had.

Cheri opened the door, and I stepped inside. The place looked so different from the day Greer, Nellie, Bunny, and I had been looking for Alma. The furniture had been moved around and the curtains pulled back to let in as much light as possible.

"Here you go." Cheri handed me a bright yellow file folder. "I'll let you know if I find anything else related to the cookbook project."

"Thanks." I tucked the folder into my bag. "And seriously, if there's anything I can do to help, let me know."

"Thanks." Cheri cleared her throat. "My son is coming later to help me with some of the bigger boxes. I'm afraid a lot of it I'm just boxing up and taking to my place to sort out."

"Well, here's my number." I reached in my bag and handed her one of my business cards. "Don't be afraid to call."

Heading to Greer's next, I noticed Silver Fox William, the new guy, out for a walk. A group of three ladies flanked him, chattering as they went. I'd bet he hadn't been prepared for being the object of so much attention when he'd moved to the Good Life. When the girl gang was the Silver

Ladies rather than the Pink Ladies, a single guy with his own teeth could be in serious trouble. This gang had experience.

I tapped on the door at Greer's and could hear her holler for me to come in. She was in the kitchen working at the counter.

"What are you making?" It looked like all the ingredients for a pie. I hoped Greer wasn't one of the women offering pie to poor diabetic William, who couldn't have it.

"We're having dessert after our Roomba class tonight, so I'm making a cherry cobbler." She stirred the dry ingredients together and then added the milk.

I didn't know what a Roomba class entailed. I thought a Roomba was one of those robots that vacuumed your floors. But I was impressed with the dessert Greer was making. The cobbler looked like something I could make, unlike the recipes Dixie was always giving me that required way more time and patience than I had.

"It looks good."

"I hope you don't mind, but I want to get this in the oven." Greer continued stirring. "It takes nearly an hour to bake."

"No problem at all." I sat down at the nearby dining table. "Is there anything you need help with?"

"Not at the moment." She pulled a cake pan sizzling with melted butter from the oven, poured the batter on top, and then heaped it with cherry pie filling from an opened can. "Sounded like you were on a mission when you called."

With Greer it was always best to get right to the point. "I'd heard that someone had words with Alma before her death, and I wondered if you knew who that was."

"The sheriff sent you, huh?" She slid the cake pan into the oven and turned to look at me, her face pink from the heat.

"Yes." I rubbed my temples.

"The new guy, William, was the tattletale, right?

I didn't say anything.

Greer put the mixing bowl in the sink, wiped her hands on a dish towel embroidered with owls, and came to sit down across from me.

"The sheriff doesn't really think any of you here at the Good Life would have deliberately hurt Alma, but in his words they've 'got to follow every lead' because they don't have much to go on."

She sighed. "Well, if he has to know, it was me."

You could have knocked me over with a feather. "What do you mean?"

She looked out the window, seemed lost in thought for a moment, and then looked back at me. "What I mean is, it was me that had words with Alma."

I waited, knowing it had to be difficult for her to talk about it.

"If I had it to do all over again, I wouldn't have been so rough on her, but I was upset that she'd forgotten Bunny the other day."

"Oh." I waited for her to go on.

"I got pretty mad at her and she got mad back and then lit out of here like a house a-fire." She blew out a breath and looked down at her hands. "It's not like we haven't fought before. We have, and then we both regret it, and then we're friends again."

"But this time you didn't get the chance to do that."

"No." She looked up at me. "We didn't."

"I'm so sorry, Greer." I got up and gave her a hug. "Alma knew it was only out of concern for Bunny that you were upset with her."

"I know."

"Are you okay with me letting the sheriff know it was you?"

"Sure." She walked to the kitchen, picked up a dishrag, and wiped down the counter.

"What time is your class?" I asked.

"Not until six-thirty." She rinsed out the mixing bowl and stacked it and the utensils in a dish drainer that sat by the sink. "Do you know if they found Alma's little notebook from her purse?"

"I don't know, but I could ask Sheriff Terry about it."

"She kept everything in that book. That's why I was so baffled by her forgetting Bunny." Greer eyes were watery. "I mean there it was in black and white."

"I ran into Cheri when I first arrived," I said, trying to give Greer time to compose herself. "She found some additional recipes as she's been clearing out Alma's place. She gave them to me." I patted my bag.

"I had asked her about the notebook, but she hadn't seen it so far." Greer frowned. "If Alma had her pocketbook with her, and I'm sure she did, her notebook would've been in there."

"I guess that's evidence now." I hesitated, hating to leave with Greer upset. "Are you okay?"

"I'm fine." She rubbed the back of her neck. "I'm fine."

Giving Greer another hug, I headed back to my car.

So tough to have harsh words be the final words you exchanged with a friend.

* * * *

After feeding Ernest and myself, I changed into a T-shirt, shorts, and some old tennis shoes. I decided it was time to tackle the thistles and Creeping Charlie that Mrs. Pickett was so worried about. The article I'd read had said to mix white vinegar with liquid dish soap and salt. I looked up the measurements to make sure I remembered them correctly and then after mixing them together in a big bucket, I poured the liquid into a spray bottle as suggested.

I wasn't a huge fan of commercial weed killer, and so an organic solution appealed to me. However, by the time I got the solution dumped into the spray bottle my tennies were squishy and I smelled like a salad. But determined to persevere in my war on weeds, I took the now-full spray bottle and worked my way around the yard. I also pulled a bunch of dandelions and other weeds while I was at it and shoved them in a bag.

The sun was beginning to send out streaks across the western sky and I knew I didn't have a lot of daylight left. Exhausted from the yard work, I packed it in for the night. I went in to shower and get ready for bed. An exciting life, I know, but one that suited me perfectly.

Brushing my teeth, I thought about poor Cheri trying to go through her mother's things. It would be hard enough in any circumstances, but with a murder investigation going on it had to be beyond stressful. I hoped she had family members or friends who were willing to help.

Thinking about family members and boxes of stuff reminded me of the package I was expecting. I speculated on when the package of Daddy's things might arrive. My mother's assistant would have contacted Barry, the agent, right away. Maybe in the next few days.

I fell asleep thinking for the first time in a while that maybe it was time to tackle finding out whether it was possible to track down Daddy's birth family. It seemed odd that he'd never had an interest in finding them. Or maybe he had. When you're a kid, you are sort of oblivious to the things adults are going through. Maybe the box of Daddy's things would give me some direction.

* * * *

The next morning, after dragging my bag of dead weeds to the curb for pickup, I waved good-bye to Ernest, who promised to keep an eye on things at the house.

I'm absolutely certain that's what his green-eyed stare meant.

One of the big advantages of working for yourself, as opposed to the corporate offices I'd worked in over the past several years, was the lack of a dress code. Most days I was able to make my wardrobe choices based on comfort rather than having what I wore dictated by the business environment. Usually that meant a skirt or pants and a T-shirt or casual top.

Today, however, knowing I had an afternoon appointment with a potential client, I'd wanted to make sure I looked professional. After reviewing my choices, I finally pulled out a suit I'd always liked. A straight gray shift with a short black jacket, it was businesslike but not overly dressy.

I had no idea what to expect at the American B&B Association Iowa offices. I'd done a bit of research on them but there wasn't much online about the Iowa chapter. They used the acronym ABBA-IA, which always made me want to belt out "Dancing Queen."

There are an amazing number of great bed-and-breakfasts around the state and Dixie's aunt, Bertie, had alerted us to the fact that the association had been discussing putting together a cookbook highlighting each of their member B&Bs. When I'd called the executive director, she hadn't seemed interested at first. They had thought they'd do the work and publish it themselves. I explained how we could save them a little money and a lot of headaches if they did it through Sugar and Spice Publishing. Not convinced initially, but finally agreeing to see me, she'd given me a date. I'd take along some examples of work we'd done and planned to put together a comparison sheet so she could see costs differences.

When I pulled into the parking lot at the back of Sugar and Spice, it was deserted. We shared parking with Travers Jewelry, Tressa's Tresses, and the real estate office where Tina Martin worked. But none of them opened until nine o'clock. I was a bit earlier than usual.

Yeah, because you were hot not to get accosted by your neighbor.

I confess I did hurry just a bit, hoping Mrs. Pickett was not yet up.

Reaching in my bag for the keys to the shop, I realized I didn't have them. I always put them in the exact same pocket but I'd been in such a rush yesterday to talk to Greer I must have left without them.

I checked the back door, then did a quick check of the nearby flower pot to make sure Dixie had not fallen back on her old habits of leaving an extra key hidden—and by hidden, I mean in plain sight—among the summer petunias.

I could run back home and get my keys. Or I could wait around until Dixie got there. She was an early riser, had probably already been up for hours and finished a bunch of chores, and so it shouldn't be long.

Wait. Or I could walk over to the Red Hen Diner and pick up a blueberry muffin for breakfast. I'd only had coffee at home, and the more I thought about a blueberry muffin, the more I knew I had to have one.

"Cluck," the door announced as I entered. I wondered at the purpose of a door chime you couldn't hear over the conversations and clatter of dishes.

The place was packed with people and I glanced around to see who I knew. Knowing people when I went into a store or restaurant was on my list of things I love about living in a small town.

I noted Jimmie LeBlanc and Grace Nelson. Dot Carson, the postmistress, was waiting at the counter to pay, a to-go container in her hand. Old Wally Nelson was shouting something about the weather to Toy, not because the weather was exciting but because shouting was the only volume Old Wally had.

Toy looked up and made eye contact with me, excused herself from Wally, and walked in my direction.

"I think my eardrums are about done for." She tapped the side of her head. "You looking for a blueberry muffin, Sugar?"

Yes, I was that predictable.

"I am." I nodded. "You're busy today." I glanced around the room, and as I did, I caught sight of Nate and Nick Marchant, who sat at a table near the front. Their heads were close together but if their body language could speak, it would say they were not feeling the brotherly love.

I suppose it could be a heated discussion about sports or politics, but I also thought having your long-lost brother show up unexpectedly would take some adjustment. Though by all accounts Nate, along with the rest of St. Ignatius, had welcomed Nick back with open arms. At least according to the gossip, which was right at least half of the time.

Nick looked up and caught my stare and flashed a *GQ*-worthy smile in my direction. Nate turned to see who Nick had spotted and gave a small wave before turning back to say something to his brother. Heads back down, they continued their discussion.

I turned back to Toy, but she had disappeared. Looking around, I spotted her at the cash register waving a white bag. I could almost smell the blueberries from here.

Reaching in my bag for my wallet, I pulled out some cash and headed to the counter to pay. Handing the money to Toy, I leaned in.

"Not much family bonding going on this morning." I said quietly, tilting my head toward the Marchant brothers. "Too early and not enough coffee?"

"Plenty of coffee, but you know what they say about too many cooks in the kitchen."

"Cooks?" I searched my brain for an Aunt Cricket saying, sure there had to be one about cooks in the kitchen. Apparently, I was the one who hadn't had enough caffeine.

"As in too many cooks trying to run the bank." Toy dropped her voice so it didn't carry across the room.

"Ah, right." It finally came to me. Too many cooks spoil the broth.

"Poor Nate had been doing just fine since his dad retired, but now his brother is back and has his own ideas about things," she said under her breath.

"What kinds of things?" I asked.

"I guess promotions, more marketing, get your car loan here."

"Those don't seem like bad things but change can be difficult." Most of the time I had wished for siblings but maybe it was because I didn't have a brother or sister that the idea seemed so attractive.

Toy handed me the bag, which seemed heavier than usual.

"I put an extra blueberry muffin in there for you. It was lopsided and I can't put it out for sale."

"Thanks, Toy, that's really sweet of you."

"It would've just gone to waste." She dismissed my thanks.

"Now, it will probably go directly to my waist." I laughed. "You know I can't resist your muffins."

"Like you need to worry." Toy rolled her eyes. "What have you heard about Alma's accident?"

"Only that they're continuing to investigate." I answered. I hoped they figured out what had happened soon. "You?"

"Nothing." She adjusted her apron. "Nothing at all."

I headed to the door with one last wave.

"Cluck." The door chime announced my exit.

I turned on the sidewalk and headed back to the Sugar and Spice Publishing office. Stores were beginning to open. As I walked past Disco's shop I peered in the window. It didn't look like any lights were on.

Tina Martin passed by at a race walk pace. She didn't speak but waved her fingers in the air as she went past. The other day she'd shown us a small MP3 player that she said Rafe had sent her for the morning walks. I could see it clipped to her arm as she passed me.

Though I had my doubts, I really hoped the boyfriend was real, because if Tina was making him up, that was a whole other destination on the crazy train. I hated to think that was the case, but there were just so many red flags.

Back at the office, the door was unlocked so Dixie must have arrived. I started the coffee and had already placed my muffin on one of the pretty china plates she kept in the cupboard. She had picked up an assortment at an estate sale and we used them from time to time as props.

Props.

That's what it was. It seemed to me as if all the gifts Tina shared that her guy, Rafe, had given her, seemed like props. Like she was setting the stage to convince us how perfect this guy was. I wasn't convinced he was perfect. Heck, I wasn't even convinced he was real.

Coffee done, I poured myself a cup and sat down at the counter to enjoy the sweet and tangy taste of perfection. Coffee and muffin. It doesn't get much better.

I heard the back door open and called out, "Dixie, is that you?"

"Were you expecting someone else?" she asked from the hallway.

"No, just you." I took a big sip of my coffee. "I have an extra muffin. Would you like to have it?"

"Sure, why not? Let me stash my bag in the back and wash my hands. I've been out at my folks. They have some new residents, and I've got pictures to show you."

I got down another plate and shifted the muffin to it. Sliding the lopsided one on my plate, I set aside the other for Dixie. The imperfection didn't bother me, and it would Ms. Blue-Ribbon-Baker.

She returned to the front, poured herself a glass of milk and joined me at the counter.

"Please tell me your folks haven't taken on more pot-bellied pigs."

"Not pigs this time." She laughed. "Although you have to admit the pigs were darn cute."

Last spring Dixie's parents had temporarily had two pot-bellied pigs, and I had to admit Dixie was right. They were darn cute. They were also very smart and Dixie's mom had leash-trained the two and named them Kevin Bacon and Alexander Hamilton. Kevin had learned how to open the refrigerator and that had become a problem. Her parents had been just fostering the two and eventually they'd gone to permanent homes.

"These characters are way cuter than the pigs."

"I don't know, Kevin and Alex were pretty cute."

"Take a look at this." She swiped to a photo on her phone and then passed it to me.

It was a video, and Dixie was right, these characters were cute. They had three baby goats, and the baby goats were adorable.

"What does Moto think of them?" I asked. Moto was easygoing but it looked like the goats were rambunctious.

"He thinks they're fun to play with."

"Do goats eat weeds?"

"Goats eat everything." She closed the video and rested a hand on her hip. "When I was younger we had a goat for a while and he actually ate my homework. Are you thinking about getting a goat? I know someone who would make you a good deal."

I told her about my evening doing yard work with my homemade weed killer.

"We'll see how this works." I took a thoughtful sip of my coffee. "But if it's not successful, maybe it's time for a goat."

"Can you imagine the fit Mrs. Pickett would have?"

"A goat in my yard might be her breaking point." I pictured Mrs. Pickett's meltdown in my head.

Dixie took a bite of the muffin. "Oh my, this is good. I can see why you like them so much." She tore off a bite-sized piece and put it on her tongue. "Toy must use fresh blueberries. I wonder who she gets them from."

She suddenly stopped with a bite halfway to her mouth and eyed me, top to bottom. "Well, look at you."

"See, if you drank coffee you would have been awake and alert sooner. And you don't have to look so shocked. It's not like I'm normally a total slouch. Or, wait, maybe I am."

"Of course, you're not," She finished off her last bite of muffin. "You're usually a lot more casual is all. You carry off the sophisticated look really well. I'd hate you for being so cute if I didn't love you so much."

"Aw, I love you, too," I said lightly. But I sincerely meant it. I couldn't imagine this adventure with anyone else and I loved Dixie like I would've loved a sister.

"Today's that appointment in Walnut Woods with the lady from ABBA." I'd removed my jacket when I was getting down the plates. "I hope I can stay clean until then. How long do you think it will take me to get there?"

"If you don't get lost, it's no more than a half hour."

"I won't get lost." I popped the last piece of muffin in my mouth. "We're meeting at her house, and I have her address already programmed into my GPS."

"You should be fine then." She tilted her head. I don't think she was convinced.

"Okay, I'm going to work on that comparison sheet so I can dazzle her with my fancy spreadsheets and charts." I dusted crumbs from my hands.

"So glad you love the numbers part of this business, because it's definitely not my thing." Dixie grabbed both of our plates. "I can figure measurements and convert recipe amounts, but don't ask me to calculate ROI."

"That's why we make such a great team." I slid off the stool.

I parked myself at the computer and made short work of the comparison. I plugged in estimates for various sizes and types of bindings, and created simple spreadsheets with the variables.

That done and printed out, I tried to make some order of the recipes from the Crack of Dawn Breakfast Club. The retirees who were part of the club had no hard deadline other than wanting to finish the refurbishing of the city park shelter before winter, so they weren't pushing to get it done. However, we had a couple of projects I'd hoped to bring on board. In fact, I hoped to secure the B and B one this afternoon. We would need to get the breakfast club project finished up before we could move on.

Maybe we could start with what categories the cookbook would have.

Heading back out front to talk over that approach with Dixie, I gathered up all the loose pieces of paper, recipe cards, and notes that had been in Alma's folder and moved everything to the long counter out front.

"Let's try it," she agreed, grabbing some colorful sticky notes.

"I had thought one section just for biscuits." I took one of the sticky notes and wrote "Biscuits" on it. "And maybe one for casseroles."

"There do seem to be a lot of biscuit recipes." Dixie picked another color sticky note. "Maybe that's because of their all-you-can-eat biscuits-and-gravy breakfasts that kicked off their fundraiser."

"How about another for sweet rolls?" I stacked a few pieces of paper together. "You know like cinnamon rolls and that type of thing."

"Sure, I think that could work."

This wasn't how we usually worked. We generally broke the cookbook into the customary Appetizers, Main Dishes, Side Dishes, and Desserts, but this was different.

Also, usually the client had given us input on what particular types of recipes they were looking for in the cookbook.

But then again, usually our point person on the project wasn't dead.

In a short time, we had all the categories figured out, and the few recipes we had placed into piles within those groupings.

"We've got to get the rest of those recipes," Dixie noted. "Or this is going to be one slim cookbook."

"I know." I looked at the skimpy piles. "I feel like in a way we're starting over."

I went to the office to get a folder for each group and ran smack into Max Windsor coming in the back door.

"Sorry." He steadied me with hands on my shoulders, dropping a long tube he'd had tucked under his arm. "I knocked, but obviously you didn't hear me."

Obviously.

I sucked in a breath. Max smelled like the outdoors. He looked good. Jeans and an untucked light blue shirt. A bit of a stubble, dark hair shot with bits of silver, dark lashes, intense blue eyes.

I picked up the tube that he'd dropped and handed it to him. "Dixie and I were working at the counter out front. Feel free to go through. I'm just getting something from the office."

Max didn't move right away. "You look nice." A corner of his mouth lifted into a half-smile.

He had a sharp square jaw, and a dimple that showed up at times. This was one of those times. The guy didn't smile often, and I found that sort of disarming. When he did smile, it was a particular treat.

It took a couple of seconds before my brain, and my manners, kicked in.

"Thanks. I've got a meeting with a potential client this afternoon. It's the Iowa B&B group. They may be interested in doing a cookbook. It's a great opportunity for us, because it would be a statewide project. So, I dressed for the meeting."

His smile got wider and his gaze more direct. "I didn't mean the dress. But it's nice too."

Okay, I had been babbling a bit, but suddenly all the nervousness I'd felt, about having not seen each other for a couple of weeks and what that meant, had surfaced.

"Thank you." I cautioned myself to play it cool. "If you'd like to go on out where Dixie is sorting recipes, I'll be there in a minute."

Feeling my face flush, I grabbed the colored folders from the supply cabinet and carried them out to the counter where Dixie stood chatting with Max.

"I was in the area and thought I'd stop by with these." He opened the long tube and pulled out some prints.

As he spread the photos out one by one, I caught my breath.

"Max, these are great." I was blown away.

He'd had some of the shots from the last cookbook project we'd done printed in a large format. I had wanted to use some photos to spruce up the plain walls of the more public part of the offices. I had asked him if it was okay if we did that with his photos, and Max had offered to take care of getting it done. I believed it wasn't just that he was being kind, but that he didn't trust me to get all the details right for such a big print.

Really, I'm good with details. One of my strong suits. But I'm also experienced at working with creative types, and I'd learned when to let them use their expertise. Our graphic designer, Liz, was like that as well. When she said let her handle it, I did.

We laid the large photos out on the counter so we could see each of them. Each one presented a different type of dish and every single one made your mouth water.

"I can definitely see these on the walls." I was so excited to get them up now that I'd seen them. "What size frames will we need?"

"When you've decided which ones you want to install, let me know, and I'll be happy to look at framing with you." Max stepped back and stared at our wall space.

In others words, he didn't trust me to frame them like they deserved either.

Heck, I didn't trust me either. The photos were stunning. And much, much more than I'd imagined. These were the types of photos that you saw hanging in a gallery, and I felt bad that I'd just casually thought I'd have some copies printed, buy some frames, and hang them on the wall.

"Thank you so much, Max." I looked up from the photos and into those piercing blue eyes. "I *love* them."

"What do we owe you?" Dixie interrupted.

It was a good thing she did too, because I was fighting to talk around the lump in my throat.

"Not a thing." He shook his head. "My gift to you ladies for persevering through the past year."

I was touched. I opened my mouth and then closed it.

"Thank you," I finally got out.

Dixie picked up some of the extra markers and sticky notes that were scattered across the counter where we'd been working. "I'm going to put these away."

Max carefully rerolled the photos and tucked them back into the tube. "I'm glad you like the photos."

"I love the photos." I began gathering the recipes on the counter into folders and labeling them. "You should have told me I wasn't up to the task when I tried to get you to give me the files."

"I didn't want to be rude." He sealed the tube with a tap. "But I'm afraid I'm a bit of a control freak with my photos. Not everyone can take that much honesty."

"For future reference, I prefer honesty, and I'm tougher than I look."

For Pete's sake, where did that come from.

Suddenly it sounded like we were talking about more than photos.

"I imagine you shared your developer theory with the sheriff." Max tucked the tube under his arm and leaned against the counter. "Any more on Alma Stoller's death?"

"Kind of." I finished the last pile of recipes and stacked the folders. "It sounds like they're still looking into things, but don't think it was accidental."

I didn't feel comfortable sharing any more than that even though I knew Max wasn't the type to spread gossip around town. In fact, in the past he'd been the subject of loads of conjecture because like me, he wasn't originally from the area. Most of the locals had thought he must have a mysterious past, because he talked so little about his personal life. I wondered if they had him cast as an undercover spy or a secret agent.

"Hopefully they'll get to the bottom of things soon." He moved to go. "Everyone around town seems on edge about it."

"Before you leave, could I ask you about the property you said Ross and Cheeters were buying out by you?"

"Like I said, they seemed to be buying several parcels of land in the area."

"Feel free to tell me it's none of my business—" I began.

"Like that's going to stop you?" One eyebrow rose.

I gave him a look. "What I'm wondering about is whether the developer shared what plans they have for the property."

"The guy who talked to me didn't give me any details, but I'd have to think they were looking at a residential development of some kind." He rubbed his chin. "I'm not crazy about having neighbors nor the increased traffic that comes with more development. Defeats the purpose of living in the country."

"Must have been a good offer then." Came out of my mouth before I thought about how it sounded. "Sorry. Strike that."

"The piece of my property they were interested in wasn't particularly close to my house."

"According to Cheri, Alma's daughter, her mom was reluctant to sell." I bit my lip, thinking about what Cheri had said. "I wonder why."

"She might have been holding out for a higher price."

"That could be the case." I could see Alma being a holdout. "I guess they must have needed her land, or they would've dropped it. Maybe she knew that."

"I think some of us that sold later got a little more per acre than the early sellers."

"So you were a smart negotiator?"

"Not so much smart as just a procrastinator," he responded, and started toward the back door. "I'll get some ideas on framing and get back to you on these."

"If you're still interested in doing the photos for the Crack of Dawn cookbook, we should talk about a date." I called out.

He turned back.

"I don't mean a *date*, I mean a date to do the photo shoot."

He didn't acknowledge my fluster, just gave me that blue-eyed stare. "My calendar will be relatively clear in a week or two, so why don't you email me your first choice for day and time, and we'll go from there. Unless it's during the week of the Jameson County Fair, I can most likely make it work."

"Oh, nothing that late." The County Fair was generally later in August. I'd have to ask Dixie to be sure of the dates.

"Okay, good." He headed for the door. "Just email me."

I stood, clutching my stack of folders, for a while after he left.

That's where Dixie found me.

"No explanation for his distance?" she asked.

I shook my head.

"No 'let's get together' offer?"

"None," I answered.

"Then forget about him. If he doesn't have the sense to see what's right under his nose, you don't need him." Dixie snapped her fingers.

"I don't need him." I sighed. "But I really enjoyed the time we spent together."

"We don't need his stupid pictures either," Dixie huffed. "And we can get someone else to do the photos for the Crack of Dawn cookbook. Call one of those people from the magazine."

"Whoa, girl." I laughed. "I appreciate your fierce loyalty, but the man has done nothing wrong."

Dixie crossed her arms. "Other than hurt my best friend."

"We enjoyed each other's company, but there was no commitment of any kind," I said. "And even if there had been, we can have a professional relationship. Max is an extremely talented photographer."

She didn't look convinced.

"Did you see those wall photos? Pretty awesome, huh?"

"They were extremely awesome," Dixie agreed. "Who knew food could be so artsy."

"And he works cheap," I pointed out. "We'd have to pay someone else twice as much."

"There is that," Dixie agreed with a little grin.

"It's not a problem," I insisted. "He's not my boyfriend. I'm way too old for boyfriends anyway."

I tapped the folders I still held. Establishing the categories for the cookbook had been good. I felt much less panicked. It was incremental but it was progress. "Besides, if I wanted a boyfriend, I'd simply make one up, like Tina."

"You're still convinced her guy isn't real, huh?"

"Are you kidding me? With a name like Rafe?" I chuckled.

"I'm going to ask Dot the next time I'm at the post office if Tina actually gets packages from Canada."

"Really? She can't tell you, can she?" I furrowed my brows. "Isn't that like a federal crime or something?"

"Of course it's not." Dixie laughed. "What murder mystery have you been reading now?"

"But if not illegal, it's at least unethical to talk about people's mail." I felt guilty already and Dot hadn't disclosed anything yet.

"Maybe." Dixie grinned. "But everyone knows you can bribe Dot to keep quiet about where your letters or packages are coming from. I'll bet you can bribe her to tell as well. Banana bread is her weakness."

"Ahh, the secrets of a small-town postmistress." I twirled an imaginary mustache. "Okay, I'm off to finish my handouts for the ABBA lady and then I need to get on the road if I'm going to be on time for that appointment."

I headed back to the office humming "Dancing Queen" under my breath.

Chapter Six

By early afternoon I was on my way to Walnut Woods, Iowa.

I had carefully programmed my GPS with the address the ABBA lady had provided. Dixie wasn't kidding about my sense of direction. I had none.

All I had to do was follow the directions from the nice British lady whose accent I found soothing. She was much less bossy than the GPS lady I'd had before her.

I reviewed the project in my head as I drove. The Iowa Association of B&Bs was interested in creating a cookbook with specialty recipes from each of their members. There were a number of Iowa bed and breakfasts and they each had a unique ambiance and fare that fit their establishment. This would be a great project for Sugar and Spice Publishing because the association would collect and curate the recipes. No need for testing. They might even have some photos, and though they wouldn't be like Max's, if they were of good quality we could use them. We would only be responsible for the publishing.

I'd already had a short conversation with the executive director about a month ago. My in-person visit was a follow up. She hadn't seemed totally convinced and I hoped my handout would help her see all the benefits of working with us. I knew they could probably get the printing done on their own, but we could do it for less. Additionally, what we could offer was, I believed, a more polished look that would make the cookbook stand out.

I followed my British lady's instructions without any trouble. She was so pleasant and if we were going to travel together frequently, I decided she should have a name. Thinking through the possibilities, I almost missed her prompt that I had a turn coming in a half-mile.

Elizabeth sounded very English but a bit formal. Besides, it seemed a bit pretentious to name your GPS lady after the Queen.

Bronwen. I liked that name but decided it didn't fit her personality. Such a serious-sounding name. I pictured her as a little more laid back.

"Please turn left in five hundred feet and continue."

"Thank you, Matilda." That was it. I liked "Matilda." I could call her Mattie when we got to know each other better.

If you're thinking now I've totally lost it because I not only talk to my cat, but I've resorted to naming my GPS, you may be right.

Maybe Dixie had been right. I needed to get out more.

"Continue one quarter mile," Matilda instructed.

"You've got it." I drove on, enjoying the countryside. Rolling hills of green, a few properties built a distance back from the road. Red barns and tall metal windmills. Native grasses and ditches full of flowers. They might be weeds. As has already been established, I'm not an expert on plants versus weeds, but whatever they were, they were pretty.

"Stop the car," Matilda said in her clipped British accent.

"What?" I slowed.

"Stop the car," she insisted.

"I heard you the first time, Matilda."

"You have arrived at your destination. You will need to walk to your destination from here."

What? I didn't even know my GPS could tell me I had to walk.

I looked around. Following Matilda's directions had brought me into a beautiful wooded area. Large trees towered on each side of the pavement, casting soft shadows, and the ditches along the road were lush with a riot of purple and white wildflowers.

I let the car idle while I tried to figure out what to do. The mapping app had to have incorrect information. Maybe I had put the address in wrong.

Maybe Matilda had gotten too big for her British britches.

I checked. The address was correct. I would have to call the ABBA lady, and ask her for better directions to her house. The problem was, I wasn't sure I could explain to her exactly where I was.

Reaching across the seat to get my cell phone, I noticed a white mailbox barely visible out my side window. Arbor House, it read.

Holy smokes, Matilda, you were right.

I was at my destination. It didn't look like a place where I should leave my car though. Was there something I was missing? I got out, leaving the Jeep running, and walked around the Jeep toward the mailbox. As I did,

I spotted the narrow lane beside it. There was tall prairie grass on each side and the entrance had been hidden.

I climbed in the Jeep.

"Not walking from here," I told Matilda, pushing the off button so she wouldn't freak out. Pulling the Jeep into the lane carefully, I drove at a snail's pace. There would be barely enough room if I met another vehicle.

How on earth could they expect someone to find Arbor House? I hoped they gave guests better directions than I'd received. I crossed a small wooden bridge and then at the crest of a small incline, I spotted the house.

Awestruck, I stopped the car. It looked like a fairy castle. A graceful Victorian was nestled among the trees and framed by a profusion of pastel flowers. The house itself was a soft cream with accents in delicate pink, robin's egg blue, and lavender for its trim.

Where I come from in the South, we have some beautiful plantation houses and elegant mansions, but this little gem lifted your mood just to look at it. I could see curling up with a book on the wide front porch and letting the world pass me by.

Speaking of which, time had been passing as I'd sat there staring at the house. I pulled forward into a parking area that had been concealed behind a hedge of bridal wreath bushes.

Checking my watch, I was glad I'd allowed plenty of time. It meant my time arguing with Matilda, and the additional minutes lost in La-La Land while I fantasized about the house, had not made me late.

Getting out of the car, I grabbed my briefcase and headed to the front of the house. As I approached the steps, a tall, slender woman with short silver curls opened the door. Glasses perched on her elegant nose framed intelligent dark eyes, and her raw-cotton shift and soft charcoal shrug managed to look cozy yet professional.

"You must be Sugar." She held out her hand. "And I'm Gwendolyn Arbor."

"So nice to meet you, Gwendolyn." I shook her hand. She had a strong, capable grip. "You were a little hard to find."

"Gwen is fine." She smiled and held open the screen door. "I should have warned you about the lane. I usually remember to mention it when someone hasn't been here before."

"That's okay," I said. Though it really would have been good to have been forewarned. "I relied on my trusty GPS to get me here, but I'll confess I was a little concerned there at the end. The lane is difficult to spot."

Gwen motioned me through. "One of the features of Arbor House is the seclusion. We have a lot of retreats that book it just for that reason. But that can make it challenging to find if you're not prepared for that factor."

No kidding.

"Your house is amazing." I looked around as we stepped into the entryway set with a warm walnut library table and a vase of fresh flowers. "You operate it as a B&B?"

"We do." She led the way through the living room, which was furnished with solid but simple antiques. The effect was one of comfort and charm. "My husband and I are from New York and began considering a move to Iowa to be close to his family. We looked for a while and when we found this place, I fell in love with it."

"I can certainly understand why you would." The heavenly smell of fresh baking wafted throughout the downstairs, and if the guest rooms were as nice as what I'd seen of the downstairs, I didn't know how they got anyone to leave.

"Jonathan was a Wall Street broker, and we'd originally thought we'd spend a few months a year here and plan for a permanent move later. But that's not a kind of career you can simply take a break from and then go back to. If you're going to take a break, you've basically quit."

"Hmmm." I continued to admire the house as I followed what Gwen was saying. But her comment about Wall Street caught my attention. The way Nick Marchant told it, he was on a short hiatus and would soon return to his high-stakes career. If Gwen was right, and I had no reason to think she wasn't, Nick was done. No wonder the brothers had been so intense over breakfast at the Red Hen. Staying permanently was different than coming back for a visit.

I tuned back into Gwen as she led the way to a large adjoining room.

"If you don't mind," she said. "I thought perhaps we'd sit at the dining room table. It's so much brighter than my office, and we can have some refreshments." Gwen's voice, soft and lilting, fit the house. Though she said they were from New York, I thought I detected a hint of the South in it.

"No problem. That will work fine. I have some numbers to show you."

We settled into chairs at one end of the heavy oak table and I pulled out my samples of cookbooks we'd done and showed off the *St. Ignatius Founders' Day Cookbook* with a swell of pride.

It was our first project and, in my opinion, one of our best. I didn't mention the two murders that had occurred during the course of the project.

A young woman quietly slipped in with lavender scones and tea served from a simple French country white teapot. I'd made up my mind to have only one of the scones, which was still slightly warm, but before I knew it I'd polished off the first and was eyeing a second. What an incredible taste combination. Dixie would be sorry she'd not come along on this visit. I wondered if I could smuggle that second scone into my bag for her.

Reminding myself I was there on a professional mission, I decided it probably wasn't a good move to be seen stashing food in my purse.

After Gwen had a chance to look through the cookbooks, I handed her the one-page proposal I'd put together. There were several options and the price changed depending on the number of pages, the type of paper, and the photos they wanted included.

I let her review it while I sipped my tea and enjoyed the last few crumbs of my second scone.

Sorry Dixie.

"Well, Sugar." She looked at me over her glasses. "This looks very promising. I like it very much, and I love the professional look of your projects. I'm not sure any of us have the time it would take to pull off that kind of polish."

"Thank you." That was the conclusion I'd hoped she'd reach.

"I'll need to discuss this with my board." She laid the paper on the table. "If it were just for Arbor House, I'd be ready to sign on the dotted line, but it's not just me on this project."

"I understand completely."

"I can't imagine they won't agree." She tapped her pen on the paper. "Could you send me this pricing sheet via email?"

"I can definitely do that." I packed up my other folders. "And if you'd like, you can keep that copy of the *St. Ignatius Founders' Day Cookbook*."

I'd found that the best advertisement for Sugar and Spice Publishing was word of mouth. You never knew when someone was working on something or had something in mind for the future. Most of our projects were fundraisers, but some were other types of recipe collections. The more we did, and the more people were happy with the final product, the more likely they were to tell others about us.

The grapevine effect could be a positive thing.

Thinking about the grapevine effect reminded me of Gwen's earlier comment about Wall Street.

"You said your husband helps with the running of Arbor House?" I asked.

"He does some with Arbor House, but I mostly run the business." She adjusted the sleeves on her shrug. "He's developed an interest in rehabbing houses and that keeps him busy."

"That sounds like fun. I live in an older Victorian that I'm currently renting but would love to own. It's been kept in very good shape." Except for that problem with the renter letting weeds overtake the yard, I thought to myself. "But there are others in town that have not fared so well."

"Those properties would be right up his alley." She smiled. "He loves old houses."

"You'd mentioned him working on Wall Street. I'm guessing he's left that life behind."

"Mostly yes, but he keeps in touch with a few people from his old life."

"I know this is really imposing, but I wondered if there was a way to check out someone who had approached me about stocks."

Okay, that was really stretching the truth. I'd recently gotten an email from someone I used to work with at Mammoth Publishing about investing my severance from the company, but no one was beating down my door. And said severance had already been invested in starting Sugar and Spice Publishing. What I really wanted to know was whether Nick Marchant, the guy who continued to pursue a relationship with my best friend, was on the up-and-up.

"How would I know if this person is legit?" I asked. "Is there an association like ABBA for stockbrokers?"

"Not exactly like it." She took a sip of her tea. "I can't remember what it's called, but I know FINRA, that's the financial industry's regulator, has some sort of database. If you do a search for FINRA, you should find it."

"Thank you." I felt bad deceiving her but I was already too far in on this to back out. "I just want to do my due diligence, you know."

"Very wise." She pushed aside a silver curl and smiled. "Also, before you go, I wondered if Sugar and Spice Publishing ever does small projects. You know, like a family cookbook."

"We love to do those kinds of projects." Again, a bit of a stretch because we'd only done one. But in my defense, we *had* loved doing it. "Did you have something in particular in mind?"

"Well, it's my husband's family. As his mother has gotten older she doesn't cook much anymore but she, and her mother before her, were the stuff of legends. According to my husband and his siblings anyway. The family would like to preserve some of those family recipes."

"That sounds like a great idea and a fun project." See, I was right. You never know what project someone might have on the back burner. "If they decide to go forward with it, let me know and we'd be happy to talk through the idea with them."

"Much like this." She tapped the paper. "I imagine it will depend on the number of recipes and what they're looking for in terms of photos. Right?"

"That's right."

I thanked Gwen again and asked if she would mind if I took a couple of pictures of the outside of the house. I was excited to tell Dixie about the place and didn't trust that I had enough adjectives to describe just how amazing Arbor House was.

Gwen gave me free rein to take pictures at my leisure and then excused herself. They were getting ready to host a genealogy group that was arriving later in the day, and she had some preparations to finish.

After a few photos with my phone that I was sure didn't do the setting justice, I climbed back in the Jeep and set off for home. I hoped I had a few that I could show Dixie. What I'd really love would be to get Max to come and do some photos. With his talents he'd be able to capture the stunning house and the whole ambiance of Arbor House.

Before leaving Arbor House, I had programmed my home address for the return trip. Matilda prompted me at each turn and though the route did look vaguely familiar in reverse, I was glad for her guidance.

There was a huge oak tree that hugged a pond. I thought I recognized the tree. A big red barn with one side painted red, white, and blue was another landmark, I remembered. But I never would have remembered I needed to turn right just after the landmark. I'd have probably turned left and ended up in Timbuktu. Matilda and I traveled well together.

With Matilda's help, in no time we were off the country roads and back on the highway that led to St. Ignatius. Feeling like I'd had a very successful call with Gwendolyn Arbor and that we were well on our way to a new client made me even more anxious about the Crack of Dawn Breakfast Club cookbook.

I needed to find some way to collect the remaining recipes that hadn't been in either the initial folder nor in the batch Alma's daughter had given us. This Saturday was one of their all-you-can-eat breakfast fundraisers. It would be great if I was able to get a message to the group and ask them to bring their recipes to the event. They could sign the release forms right then and there, and we'd be back on track.

Wondering who might have a contact list for the group, I turned into the town square. It was early enough that many of the shops were still open. Most didn't stay open in the evenings, other than a few bars and restaurants.

St. Ignatius's town square featured a limestone courthouse that was nicely kept and surrounded by a lush green lawn. The green area was dotted with trees and colorful impatiens that had been planted in large containers earlier in the summer at each of the four corners.

There were no stoplights around the town square. I'd found the lack of traffic controls odd when I first moved to St. Ignatius, but now it seemed natural. People politely waited for merging traffic. Most of the time anyway.

There was one stoplight at the north edge of town. Or was that the west end? Anyway, at one end of town, and it was to control traffic trying to cross the highway.

Planning to park behind the shop, I turned down the side street and spotted Nick and Nate Marchant standing in the alley between Marchant's Bank and Ye Olde Antique Shoppe.

I had to wait for a very small woman in a very large car trying to pull out of a parking space so I got a good look at the two while I waited.

A heated argument was in progress. Both were red-faced, and though I couldn't hear with my windows up, it was clear they were yelling at each other. Nick started to walk away and Nate grabbed his sleeve. Nick turned back with a swing and caught his brother's nose with his fist. Nate bent over holding his face. Nick walked away.

I gasped.

The little lady finally managed to get her big Caddy out of the parking space, I decided to pull in and check on Nate. Walking into the alley, I looked up and down but couldn't see him anywhere. There appeared to be a back entrance to the bank.

I debated about going into Marchants to see if that's where he'd gone and to make sure he was okay, but I didn't want to embarrass him. He'd probably ducked inside to clean up his face. Man, that had to hurt. Both his face and his pride.

I walked back to my car and got in, troubled by what I'd seen. Backing out, I headed to the shop. Dixie's truck wasn't there and once inside I saw a note that said she'd had some things to take care of and would see me the next morning.

I sat at the desk for a few minutes considering our dilemma. The need for the remainder of those recipes weighed on my mind. We had to have them in order to plan out the cookbook. Even though the group was only loosely organized, someone must have a list of all the people who were members of the breakfast club. Look how they'd all shown up for the meeting at the firehouse.

Greer had already told me she didn't know who all belonged to the group. I pictured the firehouse meeting and started working my way around the room in my head. Bertie. Dixie's Aunt Bertie had been there. I looked up her number and reached for my cell phone.

She picked up right away.

"Hello, Bertie." I swiveled in my chair. "It's Sugar Calloway and first, I wanted to thank you for that referral to the Bed & Breakfast Association. I met with their executive director this afternoon and the possibility of us working together is good."

"Glad to do it, Sugar," she said. "You and my niece do a bang-up job with your cookbooks."

"Thank you. Also, I wondered if there was a chance you'd have a list of the people that are in the Crack of Dawn Breakfast Club. Or if you know who would."

I explained my need to reach everyone and make sure I had all the recipes.

"I could probably name them all off for you, but my memory isn't what it used to be. I'd miss someone for sure." She paused. "You know who would have one?"

"Who?" I hoped she wasn't going to say Alma.

"Stanley B. Marchant, that's who. He's Mr. OCD organizer himself and keeps up a list of all the retirees and other seniors. I guess I count as one of those other seniors, since I'm not retired. Heck, he's probably got us color-coded too."

"Do you think it would be okay if I called him?"

"I'll call him for you, hon."

"That would be great."

We ended the call and while I waited to hear back from her, I put together a few notes from my visit with Gwen. I couldn't wait to tell Dixie about the place and show her the pictures. I also wrote a quick note to Gwen thanking her for taking the time to talk to me. I'd post the thank you tomorrow.

I was searching in the desk for the book of stamps I knew I'd bought last week, when my phone rang.

It was Bertie. "I talked to Stanley and I was right, he has names and contact information in a spreadsheet. I told him you'd be by to pick it up. Was that okay?"

"That's great. I'll stop by and get it on my way home." Relief washed over me. With the contact information we could get this project back on track. Truthfully, I'd hoped for an email, but beggars can't be choosers. A paper copy would work. "Thank you, Bertie. You've given me hope."

"No big deal," she responded.

"One more thing," I stopped her before she hung up. "What's Stanley's address?"

"Hold on. I'll get it." I could tell she'd put the phone down.

I continued to search for my stamps, and in a few short minutes she was back. She rattled off the address and added, "It's one street over from my place."

"That's great." I wrote down the house number and street. "Thanks again for the referral and thanks for calling Mr. Marchant."

"Stanley B. Marchant and don't you forget it," she reminded me.

* * * *

Okay, I knew how to get to Dixie's aunt's B&B. I drove there first. From the Jefferson Street Bed & Breakfast, I knew the next street was Washington, and I thought I was supposed to turn right. I turned and perused the addresses. If I didn't spot it right away, I was not above asking for Matilda's help. If she'd been able to find Arbor House, finding the Marchant house should be a piece of cake.

The sun was setting and the large shade trees that lined the streets in this part of town made the curbside seem darker. I peered at house numbers.

Ah-ha. There it was.

I had been so intent on locating the house that I almost missed spotting the red sports car that had pulled out of the driveway. The driver backed out in a rush, did a one-eighty, and then burned rubber a half block down the street. The pause when the car whipped around to change directions was right beside my car and long enough for me to spot a redhead in the passenger seat.

I didn't think Dixie had given in to the dinner offer or been sucked in by the lure of a ride in the Jag, so Nick Marchant must have talked a different redhead into a date. Judging by his recklessness, he was either upset or in a big hurry to get somewhere. Or maybe trying to impress his passenger with his driving skills.

I had to admit that I was a little relieved that he wouldn't be there. The town seemed to be enamored of its returning hometown hero. Granted, they knew him better than I did. But I wasn't really sure what it was that gave me pause. Maybe it was Dixie's reaction to him. In any case, I didn't feel like dealing with the flirt right now. I was on a mission.

I pulled into the drive and got out. The house was impressive and the yard immaculately groomed. Ringing the doorbell, I glanced around, wondering which house had been Alma's. From what Greer had told me, Alma and her daughter had lived next door to the Marchants for years.

On one side there was a nicely kept but smaller brick house and on the other side was an impressive Victorian somewhat similar to Greer's house but a bit larger. Both houses looked to be in good shape.

Hopefully, the Marchant family had better neighbors than I did. I guess that wasn't entirely fair; the couple on one side of me was extremely friendly and, in fact, had brought over keys to their house and asked me to keep an eye on things when they'd gone on a Caribbean cruise. It was only Mrs. Pickett who was a grouch of the first order.

It had been long enough that I began to get worried that Stanley wasn't there. Maybe he'd been in the car with Nick. No, that couldn't be. There wasn't room in the low sports car for three people. But maybe there'd been an emergency of some kind and everyone had to leave. When Bertie had talked to Stanley on the phone, he'd said he'd be home. I reached out and was about to poke the doorbell again, when the heavy front door swung open.

"Hello. Sorry to take so long." Stanley had one hand braced on a cane I hadn't noticed when I'd seen him at the breakfast club meeting. "It takes me a while to get to the door and I'm the only one home right now."

Retirement had clearly not made Stanley lower his standards of dress. He wore dark dress pants, a white shirt, and a striped tie. His shirt looked a little big as if he'd perhaps lost some weight. Fighting family members, even if they're grown sons, can be stressful. And though, as I mentioned before, I didn't understand people who lost weight when they were stressed, some did.

"No problem at all." I held open the glass storm door. Apparently, he wasn't going to ask me in. "I'm sorry to trouble you for the Crack of Dawn Breakfast Club list, but Alma was our primary contact for the cookbook and she did all of the back and forth with contributors."

"She was a good organizer." Stanley noted as he held out a paper. "Here's the list that I have of everyone who is a regular attendee at the breakfast club. Don't know if it will help you, but it's a start."

I took the spreadsheet from him. "I'm sure it'll be helpful, and again I really appreciate this."

Just as I was walking to my car, Nate Marchant pulled into the driveway. Nate drove a very nice late-model BMW sedan. Nice, but not flashy like the Jag.

"I'm sorry." I tucked the paper I'd gotten from Stanley in my bag. "I hope I didn't block you from getting into your garage. I didn't think about that when I parked in the driveway."

"Not a problem." He turned toward me as he shut the car door. "This is where I usually park. Lately anyway. Nick's Jag took my spot in the garage."

"A bit of an adjustment, your brother being back home." In the dimming light, I couldn't see how bad his nose was, but it appeared swollen.

"You've got that right," he muttered as he reached inside the BMW and grabbed a thick briefcase from the backseat.

"I don't have any siblings, but I'm guessing you two were close growing up."

His deep blue eyes clouded, and I realized I probably sounded snoopy.

"We had different paths."

"I didn't mean to pry." I reached in my bag for my car keys. "It's just you all here in town have known each other a long time, and I know nothing about your history together."

Nate shifted his briefcase to the other hand and sighed. "Consider yourself lucky, Sugar. Consider yourself lucky." He disappeared inside.

Lucky?

Not sure what to make of that comment, I stood dumbstruck for a minute or two before I moved toward my car.

Chapter Seven

The next morning, armed with my list of members of the breakfast group, I sat down at my desk and started sending emails. Stanley's list was very thorough and had street addresses, emails, and phone numbers. Bertie had been right; there was some color-coding involved too, though I wasn't sure what it all meant.

I'd decided to start with emails and then make phone calls if I didn't get responses from my email.

My message was short and sweet. They could email me their recipes, or they could bring the recipes to the breakfast on Saturday, and Dixie and I would collect them there. I attached the release form with a reminder to fill it out as well. I really hoped for emails in the interest of legibility but figured realistically only a small percentage would do that. Still, a few, where I didn't have to decipher handwriting, would be a net gain.

Last night I'd cross-referenced the list with the ones I already had and marked those. In many cases, even if I had the recipe, I didn't have the release form.

Soon my spreadsheet was even more complicated than Stanley's.

"Hello." Dixie waved a hand in front of my face.

I looked up.

"Wow, you were lost in number land there."

"Sorry. For such a simple, straightforward project, this one has become way more complicated than I'd ever dreamed. For some I have recipes, but no release forms, for others I have the reverse, and for an added level of complication, there are those for which I have neither."

I suddenly realized Dixie had someone with her.

Leaning to the side, I looked to see who was behind her. "Oh, hi, Tina."

“Hey, Sugar.” Tina was dressed in a bright royal blue today and her nails matched. “You know the other day when you were asking me about that development company that’s been buying land north of town?”

I nodded.

“Well, the Cheeters guy is going to be in our office later this morning. He has an appointment with Ethan. I thought I’d let you know.”

“What time is that?” I glanced at the clock.

“Ethan’s calendar shows a ten o’clock appointment.”

“Thanks, Tina.” I tapped my fingers on the desk, thinking.

“Uh-oh, I know that look.” Dixie pivoted. “I’m out of here and, if you’re smart, you would be, too, Tina. She’s about to talk you into something.”

Luckily Tina didn’t heed Dixie’s advice, and with only a little urging agreed to help me with an opportunity to ask Mr. Greg Cheeters a few questions.

* * * *

Just prior to ten o’clock, I sat in the waiting area at the real estate office pretending to flip through a magazine I’d picked up from the pile on the nearby table. Ethan rushed in carting a golf bag over his shoulder. He didn’t even notice me sitting there.

In less than five minutes, Greg Cheeters walked in.

On cue, Tina went to Ethan’s office to ask him some preplanned questions. Questions about listings that weren’t truly urgent, but that Tina thought could keep him tied up for a few minutes.

“Have a seat, I’m sure they’ll be right with you.” I smiled at the developer. He wore dark suit pants and a bright blue dress shirt.

He sat down a chair away and pulled out his phone.

“Sugar Calloway.” I reached across the empty chair and held out my hand. “Nice to meet you.”

Looking up from reading messages, he finally looked at me. “Greg Cheeters, Ross & Cheeters Development.”

I could see on his face he was trying to place me. I glanced toward Ethan’s office, where Tina was doing a great job of keeping Ethan busy as well as blocking his view of the waiting area. I knew I didn’t have long so there wasn’t time to establish much of a rapport. I would have to dive in.

“You’re the ones doing the development north of town.” I turned toward him, feigning surprise. I could play stupid with the best of them. “How is that going?”

“It’s going well.” He looked me up and down.

“So, Ethan must be helping with the closings, huh?” I gave him a bright smile.

"Hmmm." He was noncommittal and still hadn't placed where he'd seen me before.

"Several properties, I guess. What a complicated project." I glanced over my shoulder and could see Ethan standing. It was clear I only had a little more time.

"Everyone on board with that? No holdouts?" I pressed.

"Everything is coming together."

"I heard," I lowered my voice and leaned in, "that Alma Stoller had been a holdout and others were upset with her. I'm sure you know who those people might be."

"Ms. Calloway. Sugar, is it? Mrs. Stoller had come to terms with us. The deal was done. Signed, sealed, delivered. But I can't talk to you about someone else's business. Surely you understand that." That's what he said out loud anyway, but his tone said, "Surely your little female brain can grasp something that simple."

Maybe I'd poured on the playing stupid a bit too heavy.

"Sugar, what are you doing here?" Ethan appeared in front of us. "Ready to stop renting from Greer and look into a buying a house? Those trips to the Good Life have to be getting old."

I could see on Greg Cheeters's face that he suddenly realized where he'd seen me before. He leaned across the space between us.

"It's best not to ask too many questions about things that don't concern you," he said, low enough that only I could hear the words.

"I'm waiting to talk to Tina." I stood and walked away quickly.

"Come on back, Greg," I heard Ethan say, but I didn't turn around.

I quickly said my good-byes to Tina and scooted back to the shop. Once safely in the office, I did an info dump and repeated the whole conversation for Dixie.

"He sounds like a jerk." Dixie made a face.

"Agreed. And the worst of it is that I didn't really get any information other than according to him, they had 'come to terms.'"

It had been worth a shot but I'd hoped for more.

"If they really had, Cheri must have the details," Dixie noted. Which is exactly what I'd been thinking. Cheri Wheeler must know whether there were any problem and if, in fact, the deal had been "signed, sealed, and delivered."

I spent the rest of the day working my email list, glad that Stanley was such a stickler for detail. With any luck most of the group would read my email and come on Saturday with their recipes and we could get this project back on track.

Chapter Eight

When Dixie and I arrived at the Crack of Dawn All-You-Can-Eat Breakfast on Saturday morning, things were in full swing. They had planned this one in the city park shelter house they were raising money to restore. I parked the Jeep in the gravel lot beside the shelter. The lot was full of vehicles but I managed to squeeze in between a ten-year-old Buick and an old rusty pickup that had seen better days.

"The location doesn't seem to have hurt their attendance any," I noted as we walked across the gravel.

"I wondered if it would, given this is where Alma was killed." Dixie carefully carried the basket of Mile-High Biscuits she'd brought along to contribute to the effort. "Maybe it actually worked the other way around and more people came."

"You mean people have such a morbid curiosity that more people turned out than the usual?"

"No, I mean because the location is related to Alma's death, they may feel like coming to the breakfast and supporting the fundraiser is sort of a tribute to her."

"I like that explanation much better." I was sure relief tinged my voice and probably showed on my face.

Under the large canopy, the picnic tables had been pulled together to create one long buffet. I could smell the hot coffee and it mingled with the aroma of food and damp green grass, making my stomach growl. There's something about eating outside that makes good food taste even better.

Greer sat at a folding table right at the entrance, selling tickets for five dollars each. I paid for two tickets, one for Dixie and one for myself, while Dixie dropped off her biscuits to Freda Watson, who was accepting all the donated food items. Feeling bad because I hadn't brought anything to donate, I dropped another five-dollar bill in the cash donation jar.

Thinking I should have grabbed one of Dixie's biscuits when we were in the car, I checked out the piles of biscuits that were being refilled. They looked good, too, but Dixie's had looked (and smelled) exceptional. She joined me in line, and I handed over her ticket.

I smiled at the irony of paying for food you'd just brought, but who was I to question? It seemed to be working out for the breakfast club.

We each picked up a paper plate and plastic silverware at the first station and then started our progression down the line.

Biscuits first.

I guessed it would be rude to ask for a couple of fresh ones out of that basket Dixie had just handed over.

Next stop, two ladles of gravy on top.

In my head I added two miles to my morning run for all the calories I was about to consume.

Who was I kidding? My morning run was really more like a monthly run lately. I'd fallen into some bad habits and I knew I needed to shape up.

But not today.

With my paper plate loaded with biscuits and gravy, I headed to the next station, which was the drinks table. I looked at Dixie, but she shook her head, so I poured a cup of steaming coffee for myself. Spotting small cartons of milk, I handed one to her. I spied a table with a couple of seats open and headed in that direction.

Sliding my plate onto the table before it buckled under the weight of the gravy, I took a sip of the coffee and set it down beside my plate. As I dug in, I decided these might be the best biscuits I'd tasted in my life.

"These are even better than the Red Hen Diner's biscuits," I said under my breath to Dixie.

"You'd better not say that within earshot of anyone who will tell Toy," she cautioned.

"Do these fundraisers hurt her business when they have them?" I'd wondered about whether that was the case.

"I imagine they do cut into her breakfast crowd some," Dixie pushed a forkful of gravy onto her last piece of biscuit. "But it's a limited time. Once they have their money for the shelter house improvements, they'll be done."

"They must be getting close to their goal." I remembered the total Stanley had shared at the breakfast club meeting.

Once we finished, Dixie carried our trash to the receptacle and I went to locate a folding table and set up off to the side so we could collect recipes from anyone who'd gotten my email.

I had the spreadsheet from Stanley Marchant, a stack of release forms, and a folder to collect the recipes people handed us. Once Leela made the announcement about where the cookbook table had set up, there was a steady stream of people who handed me recipes on notebook paper, recipe cards, and one on the back of a grocery receipt. Remembering the ones in Alma's folder that were a challenge to read, I was careful to make sure I had contact information for each and every recipe I accepted.

The line finally slowed and Dixie had gone to find us some water. I was sorting through the pieces of paper, making sure I hadn't lost any in the flurry of activity.

"What happened to your face, Nate?" I heard from behind me.

I looked over my shoulder. Jimmie LeBlanc and Nate Marchant were helping to clean up and Nate held the trash bag while Jimmie gathered up used paper plates and dropped them in. The area around Nate's eye was bruised and his nose was indeed still swollen.

"Nothing." He shook his head dismissively.

"Looks painful," Jimmie noted.

"Not so much anymore." Nate shrugged. "I bumped into the vault door at work. Ellen was coming out while I was going in, and I slammed right into it. Hurt like heck at the time."

Why had he lied? I knew exactly how he'd gotten that injury and it hadn't been a vault door. It had been his brother. Pride, I supposed.

"Are we still on for skeet shooting later this afternoon?" Jimmie asked.

"Absolutely," Nate answered.

"See you there then." Jimmie moved away.

I sat still, going through the motions of sorting the papers. I didn't think they'd noticed me but if Nate spotted me, I didn't want him to think I'd overheard. It was apparently important to him to maintain appearances and if he didn't want the world to know his brother was responsible for his messed-up face, that was his prerogative.

"Sugar, can you grab the other end of this?" Dixie had jumped in to help with the cleanup and was holding one end of a gingham tablecloth.

Setting the papers aside, I caught hold of the other corner and looked around. Nate and Jimmie were nowhere in sight. I folded my section of the tablecloth in half and then we met in the middle. In short order, we had that one done and then started on another. Flattening them in a plastic tub when we were done, we'd soon finished the rest of the tables.

"Hey, Sugar." Greer waved from across the shelter as she made her way toward me.

"Hi," I responded. "I meant to get back over to talk to you, but it seemed like you were always busy. How did you do? Good sales today?"

"We did great." She had the zippered money bag tucked under her arm, and I wondered about the safety of that. "Best turnout we've ever had for one of these events."

"That's great." I hoped Dixie was correct and that it was because people wanted to help out on the project in Alma's memory.

"Say, I wanted to catch you and ask if there was any chance we could get a ride back to the Good Life with you." She shifted the bag to the other side.

"Absolutely," I said. "But Dixie and I rode together so I can only fit three more people in my car. Who all needs a ride?"

"Nellie didn't come. Her arthritis was giving her trouble. It's only Bunny and me."

"In that case, no problem."

"I've got to give this money to Nate first, though. I don't like to have it over the weekend, and Stanley said Nate could lock it up at the bank until Monday when we can put it in the shelter house account."

Good. I felt much better about that. I hadn't calculated how much money it was, but it sure didn't seem like a good idea for Greer to have it at her place.

"There you are." She'd spotted Bunny, who looked even more bunny-like this morning dressed in a gray sweatshirt and sporting a pink headband to hold back her silver hair. "You wait here with Sugar. I'm going to take this cash to Nate and then Sugar is going to take us home."

I sent Dixie a text. If she wasn't ready to go, I could always run the ladies home and then come back for her. She sent back a text that she'd just be a few minutes.

Bunny adjusted her pocketbook and sighed.

"Have you been here long?" I asked.

"Since seven-thirty." She shifted her pocketbook to the crook of the other arm. "You know Greer, always raring to go. We didn't need to be here that early, but if Greer has to wait she gets as antsy as a kid in church."

"I do know that about her." I smiled. "Did you want to sit in the Jeep?" It suddenly hit me that she might be tired after being at the breakfast for a couple of hours already.

"No, thanks," she answered. "I'm fine."

Dixie and Greer appeared just then and Dixie opened the passenger door and helped Bunny climb in. Greer walked around the rear of the Jeep and got in the back seat on the other side.

It was a short trip to drop the ladies off at the Good Life and then I swung by to drop off Dixie and headed home myself.

My shoes were wet from walking around in the damp grass at the shelter, so when I got home I slipped them off and set them on my front porch to dry. Dixie had been smarter with her shoe choices and had worn boots to the breakfast.

Note to self: Function, not fashion, is paramount for eats in the park.

I carried the folder full of recipes inside, excited to get started on them. Once I had these recipes in order, I could merge them with the most recent ones we had from Cheri. On Monday, Dixie and I could work on which ones to use. Each of the contributors had been asked to provide their favorite recipe, but still we needed a variety of dishes in the categories we'd decided on. So, there would have to be some curating.

This was the crux of what we did. Some people thought you could create a cookbook just by throwing together a bunch of recipes, but with each cookbook you were really telling a story. For me, this was the fun part of the process. Dixie and I worked well together in creating a vision and I felt like the Crack of Dawn Cookbook was finally shaping up.

The weekend passed without incident. I got the recipes from the breakfast event sorted out. I also did a few errands, some grocery shopping, and caught up on my reading. No emergencies, no frantic phone calls, no neighborly complaints.

Nice, but I should have known it wasn't a trend.

* * * *

Monday morning, I was up early, fixed a healthy breakfast, had a nice chat with Ernest over my coffee, and got dressed for the day. I was looking forward to getting to the shop, figuring out where we were, and forging ahead.

Once at the office, I jumped in. With all the papers that we'd collected on Saturday in order and cataloged on a spreadsheet of my own, I moved on to the group of recipes from the folder Cheri had given me. Trying to interpret the handwritten notes proved challenging. Some of them might very well be duplicates of recipes we'd been given at the breakfast, but it was going to take painstaking sorting, touching each one, to know for certain.

"What do you think this means?" I held out a card to Dixie, who had just walked in. "It looks like it says two-thirds cup sour, but that can't be right."

"Hmm." Dixie took the three-by-five file card from me. "I'm not sure. Sour what?"

"And what's this name?" I could barely make out the person's name on the faded recipe card.

"That's June Travers." Dixie pointed at the writing. "Lark, from next door. June is his mom. Maybe we can find out from him."

I set the card to the side with a note to talk to Lark and continued flipping through the papers. There were several interesting possibilities and I hoped Dixie would try out some of them. My mouth was watering, my healthy breakfast long forgotten.

A particular brunch casserole from Alma's own collection sounded appealing. It was named Heart Attack Hot Dish. I was pretty sure it wasn't destined for a spot in our category of healthy options. I guess all those ladies at the Good Life had survived Alma's casserole, but it seriously must be a zillion calories.

As I pulled the casserole recipe out of the pile, a light blue piece of paper fell to the floor. I picked it up. It must have been stuck to the recipe card. Having been through enough of the notes, I knew it wasn't Alma's handwriting.

It began, "Grams, I know you're mad at me and that I made some bad choices. I need help this one last time. Don't cut me off!" It was signed with a big D.

I flipped it over. The words on that side of the note were in Alma's handwriting. In bold dark print, they said, "No more."

Good grief.

I handed the note to Dixie. She read it, and her eyes got wide. As far as I knew, there was only one person in the world who could call Alma "Grams" and that was Cheri's son, Dustin. A disagreement over money perhaps? An argument that turned violent? I hoped not.

"What do we do?" Dixie asked.

"Let me talk to Greer." I took the note back. "Maybe this is old."

"In the folder with the recipes for the cookbook?" Dixie raised a brow. "Not likely."

I knew I was only buying time, but maybe the note didn't mean what I thought it did—that Alma and her grandson had fought. I'd been around Alma, but knew nothing of him. I didn't want to think about what it could mean.

We continued sorting recipes, but the mood was much more somber.

The sheriff had said they didn't have much to go on. My money had been on the developer. Probably because I thought the guy was smarmy. But just because he was obnoxious didn't mean that he was also a killer.

And by the same token, just because Dustin Wheeler had left an angry note for his grandmother didn't mean that he'd run over her, I reasoned. Still, it wasn't a normal exchange for a grandparent and grandchild.

I tried Greer's number but had to leave a message. When I still hadn't heard from her by the end of the day, I was beginning to get worried. I tried to remember if she'd mentioned an all-day outing. If she didn't call me back soon, maybe I'd drive over to the Good Life.

Or maybe I'd just be patient and wait for her phone call.

* * * *

I called Greer again as soon as I got home but got her voicemail again. After I changed clothes, I fed Ernest, warmed up some left-over pasta for myself, and paced. Greer might not have any knowledge about Alma's relationship with her grandson, but they'd been friends a long time. I believed she would know if there had been problems.

It was a warm but mild evening. A good night for a date with Creeping Charlie and his thistles while it was still light out, but I didn't want to miss Greer's call. I finished the dishes and paced some more. Moving to the living room, I picked up the book I'd been reading, sat down, and tried to pick up the storyline. It was no use.

Greer would call me back. I knew she would. But I hadn't said anything in my message about why I was calling. Nor had I said it was urgent. What if she didn't call me back until morning? Yikes. I would never get to sleep.

I decided I'd dig out some pants with pockets and take my cell phone outside with me. That way I could make progress on my yard and still make sure I didn't miss Greer's call.

I went upstairs to hunt down some jeans that weren't too tight for me to squat in. Dixie's cooking experiments, and especially those cinnamon rolls, were destined to force me to buy a new wardrobe if I wasn't careful. I found a pair and pulled them on. They were jeans that had been loose on me in the spring.

No more tasting for me. Or maybe if I would limit my tasting to one bite.

Yeah, like that was going to happen.

As I started back down the stairs, my phone rang. I picked up right away.

"Hello, Greer. I'm so glad you called me back."

"Hi, Sugar. You sound a little breathless. Were you climbing the stairs?"

No, I was trying to fasten my jeans.

"You see why I felt like I couldn't do them anymore?" Greer asked.

"No. Well, yes. I was on the stairs," I admitted.

"Did you need something, dear?" she asked. "I had my phone off because I was over at the community center. It was movie night. I don't always go but it was *Die Hard*, and I love that movie. Then, of course, everyone sat around for a while afterward talking. We're all still in shock about losing Alma."

"That's sort of why I'm calling." I took a deep breath and told her that I needed to ask some questions.

"Oh, my." There was silence for a few minutes.

"I know you won't tell anyone else about this, but I need to ask you about Alma's relationship with her grandson." Continuing down the stairs, I walked through to the kitchen.

"She has always doted on Dusty, since the child was born. His dad died when he was pretty young so Alma's daughter raised him as a single mom."

I could relate to that situation, having been raised by a single mom myself.

"Do you know if Dusty has been in some sort of trouble?" I paced back and forth while I listened, still not sure what I'd hoped to hear.

"A while back he got into his head that he wanted to be a musician. His mother was totally against it. Alma paid for voice lessons for him. Some teacher from one of the colleges."

"That doesn't sound like Alma and her grandson had problems." I stopped pacing and stood, staring out my kitchen window at my backyard. From here the stretch of green looked good. How had Mrs. Pickett even spotted those weeds?

"Recently, since he graduated I think," Greer continued, "Dusty had gotten wrapped up with a bunch of boys from a band he was in. Those kids were bad news. They were involved in some vandalism. Alma didn't want to talk about it, but I know she was awful upset over the whole thing."

"Do you think she and Dustin might have had a big fight over it?"

"Sugar, I don't think I like where this is going. But, yes, I suppose they could have had a fight about him running with that crowd of kids."

"Hmmm." I moved to where I'd set my purse on the counter and pulled the note from my bag. Dixie and I had put it in a plastic bag. We didn't know if that was the right thing to do or not, but it seemed like we ought to do something to preserve any fingerprints.

"He used to be a regular visitor at his grandma's but hadn't been around much lately," Greer said. "I can ask Nellie if she's seen him lately since she's right next door to Alma."

"Okay." I tucked the bagged note back in my bag. "If you wouldn't mind. Can you do that without telling her what this is about?"

"Sure, I can. I'll ask her at coffee tomorrow morning and call you after."

I thanked Greer and headed outside to do battle with thistles and Creeping Charlie, and hopefully burn off some worry as well.

Burning off a few calories wouldn't hurt either.

They were difficult opponents but according to the article I'd read, I needed to give the white vinegar concoction a couple of days to work. I doused each weed and gave the big ones extra drinks just to be safe. Satisfied with my work and no less worried about what Greer might find out from Nellie, I headed inside for a shower.

Chapter Nine

The next morning, Ernest and I were enjoying a leisurely coffee and a toasted bagel. Actually, I was enjoying the bagel and coffee. Ernest had already wiped out a bowl of kitty kibble. He had situated himself on my lap for a cuddle while I watched the morning news and munched on my very tasty breakfast.

Suddenly the front door shuddered with several loud bangs. Ernest and I both jumped as if we'd been shot. My cinnamon raisin bagel went airborne, flying out of my hand. Ernest skittered across the room and under the coffee table, leaving a cloud of fur behind. I hurried to the door to find out who, at this time of the morning, could possibly be making so much noise.

Throwing it open, I nearly passed out at the sight of the knife-wielding apparition who blocked my way. I took a step back and stifled the scream about to burst from my mouth.

When my heart stopped pounding in my ears and my eyes focused, I realized it was Mrs. Pickett.

Her gray hair covered by a flowered scarf, she wore her standard pink chenille bathrobe, and black clunky boots that looked as if they were intended for a snowstorm. She held a wicked-looking blade aloft like some fierce Viking granny.

"You scared me," I said, sharper than I'd intended.

She eyed me but didn't move from her Viking pose.

"What are you doing with that knife?" I asked, backing up.

"Pouring stuff on the weeds doesn't work," she declared, waving the steel blade in my face.

I backed up a little more. "Uh-huh."

"You gotta cut them out. Roots and all." Her bathrobe clad arms sliced back and forth with the blade and then she held it toward me again.

I reached out and gingerly took it between two fingers.

Apparently satisfied with having imparted sufficient weed wisdom, she turned and left.

I stood staring at her pink chenille covered back as she clomped her retreat across my side yard to her house.

Well, for cryin' in a bucket.

Dixie was right, the woman was crazy. I closed the door and carried the weed knife to the kitchen and put it in the sink.

Shaking my head in disbelief, I coaxed Ernest from under the coffee table and retrieved my bagel from where it had rolled under my chair. It no longer looked appetizing—I didn't think all those specks were raisins. More like dust bunnies and cat hair. I dropped it in the trash and headed upstairs to get dressed for the day.

I could hardly wait to share this latest episode in the "Won't You Be My Crazy Neighbor" show with Dixie.

* * * *

I'd just walked in the Sugar and Spice office when Greer called.

"How are you this morning?" I asked, putting my bag down on the floor and dropping into the chair at my desk.

"Properly caffeinated," she answered. "How about you?"

"Working on it," I answered with a smile.

"I had a cup before we got together for coffee. Then once there I kept chatting and Nellie kept pouring. Now I'm extra wired." She hesitated. "I do have some things to share with you."

"About Alma and her grandson?" I picked up a pen from the clutter on my desk.

"Yes." She paused and, in my mind, I could see her taking a sip from her favorite yellow coffee mug, which said "Cup of Happy" on the side. "I wish I had different news to report, but it is what it is. I hope and pray it doesn't mean anything."

"I guess there was a problem between him and Alma then?"

"There was. Nellie says she had gone by Alma's to return a cake plate she had borrowed for a fiftieth anniversary party her family had a couple of weeks ago. And when she went to the door, the window was open and she could hear Alma and someone arguing loudly."

"Could she see who it was?" I clicked the pen in and out, a nervous habit.

"She couldn't see who but she felt awkward and so she went back to her place."

"She can't actually confirm that it was Dustin?" I bounced the pen on the desk.

"She can't be sure that's who it was, but she says she kept glancing out her window so she could take the plate back when whoever it was left."

"And did she see who was there?" By now I drummed the desktop with my pen, anxious for a direct answer.

"It was probably thirty minutes later when she saw a young man that she's pretty sure was Dustin, leave Alma's."

"Oh, dear." I let out a sigh.

This didn't look good.

"I hate to keep things from you, Greer, but I don't feel like I can share the details until I know more. I'll let you know as soon as I can."

"I understand, sweetie." I knew it was killing her to not be in the know but she was gracious about it. "I have to assume that you've uncovered something that makes you think Dusty must have been somehow involved in what happened to Alma. Is that much right?"

"I hope that's not the case, but until we know, let's keep this between us, okay?"

"Of course," she said.

I hung up and sat there for a while, head in my hands. I couldn't imagine what might bring someone to harm their grandmother. I hadn't met the boy, but from all accounts Alma had loved him, and had done her best to help him.

I looked up to find Dixie standing in the doorway.

"Was that Greer?"

I nodded.

"And?"

"Nellie confirmed that she heard someone—a guy—arguing with Alma. And then shortly after that, she saw a young man, she thinks it was Dustin, leave Alma's."

"I guess we need to turn that note over to Terry then," she confirmed with a tinge of regret.

"It doesn't necessarily follow that Dustin was the one who ran over Alma." I hated to think that a kid could run over his grandmother.

"It doesn't," Dixie agreed. "But it does mean that with the note we found, plus the fact that Nellie saw him, there are unanswered questions. Right?"

"Right." I tapped my pen on the desk. "When do you want to tell him?"

“We have an opportunity right now because the sheriff is sitting out front drinking a cup of our coffee at this very moment.”

“No kidding?” I must have really been in my own world because I hadn’t heard either of them come in.

“No kidding.”

“I can’t believe you two were in a room alone and behaved civilly to each other.”

“Well, we weren’t alone.” Her mouth twitched. “Disco was there too.”

“Gosh, and we had nothing to feed him.” Before she could say it, I held up a hand to stop her. “I know, not our job.”

“Since I didn’t have any treats, he moved on. Terry is still there.”

“Okay, let’s get this over with.” I gathered the pile of recipes and the note we’d found and followed Dixie to the front.

Sheriff Griffin sat staring into his coffee but looked up as we joined him. “Good morning, Sugar.”

“Hi, Terry.” I placed the papers on the counter.

“Dixie tells me you two may have something you believe might be of interest to me in *my* investigation into Alma Stoller’s death.” There was a slight emphasis on “my” but when I looked at his face, he showed nothing in his expression.

“That’s right. We were going through these recipes that Alma’s daughter, Cheri, had given us.” I spread the papers about a bit so he could see.

“When did you get those?”

“I don’t know, maybe a couple of days ago.”

Sheriff Terry rubbed a spot between his brows. “I asked Cheri to let me know if she found anything when she sorted through her mother’s things.”

“That’s just it.” I pulled out the baggie and handed it to him. “She didn’t find this. It was mixed in with the papers and she probably wouldn’t have seen it. She knew we needed the breakfast club’s recipes in order to move forward with the project.” I didn’t want to out Greer about taking the recipes the first time we were at Alma’s.

“We found it because we were trying to bring some order to the recipes we got on Saturday and the ones that Alma had already collected for the Crack of Dawn cookbook,” Dixie explained.

I handed the note to Sheriff Terry. The man had blue-ribbon control. His expression didn’t change; if anything, he became even more motionless as he read through the note.

Finally, he looked up, his expression grim. “You haven’t told anyone about this?”

“No, we haven’t,” Dixie responded.

"But I did ask Greer about Alma's relationship with her grandson," I admitted.

"The kid has been in some trouble." Sheriff Terry's jaw tightened.

"It sounds like they'd always had a good relationship, though," I said. "Alma helped pay for his voice lessons and all."

He looked at me closely. "But there's more isn't there?

I nodded. "Greer also told me that Nellie heard an argument the day before Alma went missing. And then a little bit later she saw someone that could have been Dustin leaving Alma's."

The sheriff folded the note, put it back in the baggie, and slipped it into his pocket. "I'd really like to point out that the right thing—the smart thing—" He stopped here for emphasis just in case his steely glare didn't make the point.

I mentally squirmed.

"The smart thing to do," he repeated, "would have been to call me the minute you found that note. And the right thing would be to leave the questioning related to Alma and her grandson to those of us who are investigating Alma's death." He paused and looked hard at the two of us.

"I'd like to point that out." He stood and took a final swig of coffee before setting the cup down with a click. "But that would be a total waste of my breath."

Sheriff Terry moved to the front door of the shop. "If you find anything else among Alma's notes, call me immediately."

Dixie and I looked each other. In my defense, he had asked me to help him break through the Silver-Haired Solidarity over who had had words with Alma. I could tell Dixie wanted badly to make that point. We both held our tongues.

"I'll talk to you later." He started to go.

But as he held the door open to make his exit, Nick Marchant walked through it.

The sheriff said something under his breath, turned and came back inside, letting the door close behind him.

He and Nick eyed each other.

"What are you doing here?" Sheriff Terry finally broke the silence.

Nick let his silence stand a little while longer as he maintained his Shootout-at-the-O.K.-Corral stance.

"I don't know why it would be any of your business, but I'm here to talk to Sugar and Spicy."

I don't know what it was about his delivery of Dixie's nickname that rubbed me wrong, but it did. Others in town called her "Spicy" and the moniker from her youth seemed to be said with affection. But with Nick, there was some undertone I couldn't quite identify, but I didn't like it.

Now it was the sheriff's turn to lengthen the silence before he replied. He stared at Nick and waited. Finally, he said, "Marchant, I don't think I like your attitude."

"What are you going to do about it?" Nick smirked. "Shoot me?"

The sheriff said something I couldn't hear and then turned, yanked open the door, and walked out.

"Did you hear that?" Nick's handsome face was incredulous. "He threatened me."

"I'm sure you're safe." Dixie turned and walked out of the room.

I heard her get her keys, heard the back door open, and then slam as she left.

"I don't think she wants to talk to you." I said to Nick.

He stood looking at me. "Is that coffee still warm?"

"Would you like a cup?" I could've kicked myself the minute the offer was out of my mouth. It was that darn southern hospitality gene rearing its head again.

"Sure." He smiled and gave me a once-over.

Great. Now he thought I was interested in him. And not in the are-you-good-enough-to-date-my-friend way.

"Have you lived in town long?" he asked. His tone made me think he already knew the answer to his question.

Stretching to reach a mug on the shelf, I answered. "I haven't lived in St. Ignatius that long."

Suddenly, Nick was beside me, his starched white shirt brushing my arm. With his height, he easily reached the cup and handed it to me with a smile.

What a flirt. A handsome flirt, but seriously?

I filled it with coffee and set it in front of him, then stepped back to put some distance between us.

He took a sip and studied me. "You worked as a big shot at a fancy magazine before moving here, I heard."

Bingo. He did already know my story.

"I wouldn't say I was a big shot, but, yes, I worked for Mammoth Publishing."

He cradled the mug and took another sip. "Nice."

I wasn't sure if he meant my publishing gig or the coffee.

"You've not been back to St. Ignatius since you left after college." I phrased it as a statement rather than a question because I, too, knew the answer. "I heard," I added for good measure.

"That's right." His dark blue eyes followed me as I found a cup and poured some java for myself.

"You all—Dixie, Sheriff Terry, and you—have the advantage of having grown up together." I wondered at the tension between him and the sheriff.

He leaned a hip against the counter and watched me. "I don't know that I'd necessarily call it an advantage."

"Are you the only one from your crowd who left St. Ignatius for bigger opportunities?" I sipped coffee from my cup.

"Me. Bigger opportunities were definitely my goal. Terry left to escape his scumbag family." He pulled a face.

No love lost there. But then I'd already known that.

I wondered if it was an old football rivalry. I'd seen that type of competitiveness carry on for decades. When I was at Mammoth, there had been a big competition between those who attended one or the other of the two state universities. Once a year, they played each other and heaven help the losing team who had to survive the ribbing from the fans of the winner. You would've thought, whatever it was between Nick and Terry, it would be history by now. But absence had not made the heart grow fonder in this case.

"Families can be challenging." Though I'd often wondered if Sheriff Terry had any family in town, I had no intention of following this conversational path. "Your family seems close. You, your brother, and your dad."

"As close as heat to fire," he answered, placing his empty cup on the counter and giving it a spin.

I'd never heard that expression to explain closeness, but it didn't give me a warm and fuzzy family feeling. I knew from experience, families could be complicated as well as challenging.

"Like you, I grew up in a one-parent household," I shared. "It was just my mother and me. And sometimes, my two aunts."

Nick continued to spin the cup on the counter top.

The talk about single moms made me think of Alma, her daughter, and grandson.

"Sad about Alma Stoller." I shook my head.

Something odd crossed his face, and I wasn't sure if it was actual pain at the loss of someone he knew or irritation at the turn the conversation had taken. If it were real pain, I felt bad that I'd brought Alma's death up like that.

"Were you friends with Cheri, her daughter?' I asked. "I'm still trying to get straight who was in which class."

Again, something crossed his face for a brief moment before he composed himself. Only a momentary glimpse and then his cocktail-party persona was back.

"You know what they say about small towns: Everyone knows everything about everybody eventually.'"

I hadn't heard that particular phrase, but it was true that secrets are harder to keep in a small town. And between Dixie's reaction and Terry's and now Nick's, something was afoot.

Nick's phone made a beeping sound. He pulled it out and looked at it, but made no move to answer it.

"If you need to get that feel free."

"Just my brother." He slipped the phone back into his pocket. "Probably has some task for me."

Had that been what the fight was about? Had he and Nate come to blows over who was boss?

He left the mug on the counter. "Great to chat with you, Sugar. Let's get together for a drink one of these evenings. I'd welcome some conversation with someone who has traveled farther than the county line."

"I'll let Dixie know that you'll stop by again or give her a call." I said evenly.

I watched him go, thinking there was not a ghost of a chance I would be joining Nick for that drink. Definitely not my type.

Not that I had a type, but if I did…tall, dark, and fun-to-be-with beat out tall, dark and full-of-himself any day.

After washing the coffee cups, I went back to sorting the recipes. I spread them out on the counter and tried to think through how to order them and what the story was we wanted to tell with the Crack of Dawn Breakfast Club cookbook. Maybe some history on the city park could be added.

It seemed like quite a while, but was probably no more than half an hour until Dixie was back. She had Moto with her so she must have run home.

"Sorry to leave you like that," she said. "I couldn't take it anymore. All the posturing, like I'm some prize. And it's very clear, it's not about me. It's about them."

"Nick stuck around for a while." I straightened my stacks of recipes. "He got a call from his brother but he didn't answer it."

"Nate's got to be sick of all the attention Nick's getting." Dixie patted Moto's head.

"I would think so," I agreed. "What's the friction between him and the sheriff?" I asked. "Were they football rivals or something?"

"It's all ancient history," Dixie blew out a breath. "Lots of reasons not to like each other back then, but that was then. You'd think they'd both be grown up enough now to be over it."

"You would think," I agreed.

My phone rang just then, and I stepped back into the office to take the call. It was Gwen from the ABBA group, and she had talked with her board, who had a few questions. They were easy enough to answer, and it sounded like we had a good chance of taking on their project. After we hung up, I made a few notes and then made a call to Liz, with a question they'd had about redoing their logo.

Putting the phone down after talking to Liz, I heard the bell ding out front as someone came in, but I knew Dixie was within earshot so I continued jotting down some details.

But when I heard raised voices, I decided I'd better go check and make sure Dixie was okay.

"You witch!" was what I heard as I came around the corner, only it might have been a "b" word instead of a "w" word. Cheri Wheeler's wheat-colored hair was wild, her face was red and contorted, and the woman was hopping mad. She advanced toward Dixie. "You—"

"Whoa," I interrupted the tirade. "What's going on?"

"Cheri is upset we gave the note we found to the sheriff." Dixie took the opportunity of a break in the action to take a few steps back and put the counter between her and Cheri.

"But you know we had to, right?" I could understand being upset, but we really had no choice.

Wow, Sheriff Terry worked fast. He must have pulled Dustin in for questioning right after he left with the note.

"That was personal property and you had no right," Cheri hissed. "I brought those recipes to you trying to be helpful and this how to you repay me? You sic the sheriff on my son?"

"I'm sure it will all work out." I tried my quiet voice, which usually calmed upset animals and angry humans. Though come to think of it, my quiet voice hadn't worked at all on Mrs. Pickett next door.

"Easy for you to say." She turned on me and I could see her cheeks were streaked with mascara. "You didn't just have to see your son at the jail."

Cheri was so angry it made me wonder if her son shared this kind of instant rage.

Then I heard the catch in her voice. And I realized in that instant, the emotional tirade was fueled by fear.

"Wait." I hadn't expected the sheriff to arrest Dustin. Just talk to him about it. "He's under arrest?"

"No." She looked like tears or swear words could start again at any moment. "Not yet anyway. But no thanks to you two!"

"The sheriff simply brought him in to ask him some questions, right?" Dixie asked.

"Nothing simple about it." Wild Woman was back and looked ready to pounce.

"I'm sure he was able to tell the sheriff where he was and clear up everything." I hoped to heaven he was able to verify where he'd been.

"Dusty was at home," she bit out.

"With you?" Dixie asked.

"I work nights." Cheri's face twisted and she swiped a hand across her forehead. "None of this would have happened if you two hadn't taken it upon yourselves to give the sheriff a personal note that belonged to my dead mother."

When she put it like that, it did make me feel pretty awful. Though I still wasn't sure that we had any choice.

"What can we do to help?" Dixie asked.

"Don't you use that phony sweet act on me, Dixie Spicer." Cheri face twisted in anger. "You forget. I know you. I hope the sheriff remembers what a cheat and a liar you are. Always have been."

That was it, Dixie had lasted as long as she could.

"Get out." She advanced toward Cheri. "I've tried to be nice because of all the stress you're under, but I am not going to let you come in here and pick the scabs off old wounds."

"Gladly." Cheri bit out. Turning, she shoved my neat stack of recipes off the counter and stomped out.

As the heavy glass door shut, Dixie and I looked at each other. She began picking up the papers Cheri had pushed to the floor. I walked to the back, grabbed a bottle of water and took it out front.

"I wish I had something stronger," I said, handing her the water. "But I guess this will have to do."

She twisted off the top, took a big swig, and then held the bottle against her face.

"I would have never expected that from Cheri." I took the papers from Dixie and started resorting them. "She'd seemed so mild-mannered."

Dixie took another gulp of the water. "No matter how mild you are, I imagine all bets are off when your kid is in trouble."

"Do you suppose her son has that kind of temper?" I had to ask.

"I haven't seen him in years," she said quietly.

Neither of us wanted to think about that possibility, but in reality, the message in the note did look bad. But still there were other potential suspects. My money was still on the creepy developer. I hadn't liked him from the beginning, but I didn't think Cheri was going to be forthcoming with any information about what kind of deal Alma had made with Ross and Cheeters.

"Come on," I motioned to Dixie. "I'm taking you to lunch. You deserve it after what you've been through, and I'm hungry because my breakfast was interrupted by a crazed woman with a knife."

* * * *

"Cluck." The chicken door chime at the Red Hen announced as we entered.

We'd arrived before the lunch crowd so there were plenty of spots available. We picked a booth against the wall. The clatter of dishes from the kitchen said it must have been a busy breakfast shift.

Toy George hustled from the back with two glasses of water and slapped a couple of menus in front of us. I picked it up to look, though I wasn't sure why. I'd reached a point where I had the offerings committed to memory. And I'd tried pretty much everything on the menu, except for the liver and onions. Yuck.

So many good things. What to have? What to have? Feeling cheated out of breakfast because my bagel hadn't been salvageable, I flipped the menu to the back page and perused the breakfast choices, which they served all day.

Toy was back, green-lined tablet and pen in hand. "What'll you have?"

"I'll have the Reuben," Dixie announced.

Toy looked at me, brow raised.

"I'm going to go with the pancakes." I handed the menu to Toy.

She jotted down our selections, ripped off the sheet, whisked back to the pass-through window of the kitchen, then clipped the paper on the wheel and yelled, "Order."

In a matter of minutes, she was back with coffee for me and milk for Dixie. She set our beverages down and slid into the booth beside Dixie.

"So, what do you know, ladies?"

"Not much," Dixie responded. "You've probably heard more of the gossip than we have."

“Maybe.” She untied her Chief Chick apron and slipped it off. “Between the gravy stains and the spilled coffee, this thing is headed for the wash.” She folded the apron into a bundle and tucked it beside her on the seat. “The rumor mill was operating at full power today.”

“About what?” I asked.

“Mostly still about who ran over Alma.” Toy leaned in. “Her memorial service is Wednesday at the Methodist Church. But you probably already knew that.”

We hadn’t known about the services. Greer hadn’t mentioned it and Cheri sure wasn’t going to tell us.

Toy leaned in even closer and whispered, “I guess the sheriff thinks it was her grandson, Dusty.”

So much for keeping that under wraps.

“Hmmm.” Dixie shifted in her seat to face Toy. “If it were true, that would be awful.”

“It could have been an accident,” I offered.

I’d been thinking about the possibility. Like a hit-and-run deal. Cheri was insistent that that her mom and her son had a close relationship. What if he really had run over his grandmother accidentally and was too afraid to be honest about what had occurred?

“He doesn’t have anyone to vouch for him. Says he was at home asleep when it happened, but no one else was there.” Toy shook her head. “Heard they’ve had him in for questioning. Sounds like he’s going to need a good lawyer.”

Wow. That was fast. What was it Nick Marchant had said? Something about everyone knowing everything in a small town.

“What else had the gossip mill going today?” Dixie asked. I was sure she hoped to change the subject.

“Well, of course, Mr. Hold-onto-Your-Knickers, Nick Marchant.” Toy grinned. “But that’s no surprise.”

“He’s sure caused a stir since he’s been back,” I noted. “Was he always the talk of the town? Was that the case before he left?”

“Always.” Dixie took a sip of milk and rolled her eyes. “And that jumped both sides of the train track, too. Debate team winner, track star, student council. Also, speeding tickets, underage drinking, and picking fights.”

“Not a model citizen?” I’d wondered about that.

“No, that was his brother, Nate.” Dixie laughed. “But good behavior doesn’t gain as much attention, and all the girls were drawn to the ‘bad boy.’ And heaven forbid, if a girl liked Nate, Nick would move in right away and capture her attention.”

"He was a stinker, all right," Toy said. "Handsome, but a stinker."

"But nothing serious, right?" You could see the remnants of what had been a spoiled high-school charmer in some of grown-up Nick's behavior.

"No, just dumb high school kid stuff," Dixie answered. "And then he left and to all accounts has had a successful career in the stock market. It probably takes that kind of ego to play on Wall Street."

"Is he back to stay or just visiting?" I wondered aloud. He sure hadn't sounded to me like he wanted to stick around.

"From the sounds of it he's been going into the bank every day," Toy commented, and then got up to get drinks and take the order of a couple who had come in.

"Nate's been the heir apparent for years, so I wonder how that's going over," Dixie mused.

I thought about his comment to me when Nate called him. "I'm guessing not very well."

"You dated Nick for a while didn't you, Dixie?" Toy was back and sat down again.

"Yes, I did." Her cheeks turned pink. "Talk about dumb high school stuff. I was flattered that he took an interest in me and broke up with my long-time boyfriend because Nick asked me to the Winter Formal. My folks weren't happy about it, but I'm afraid I was starstruck."

"That boyfriend was Terrance Griffin?" I had to ask.

She stopped and looked at me for a few minutes. Her eyes flickered and she looked down. "Yeah, it was Terry."

I waited.

"Then Nick dumped me right before the dance, and I ended up not going at all." Dixie shrugged. "Afterwards, I'm not sure what Nick said about me, but Terry believed the rumors. By the end of the whole incident, they were both done with me. And I was done with them." She sat up straighter. "Water under the bridge."

"Sounds like since Nick has been back, he's still a carouser." Toy winked.

"What do you mean?" I asked.

"He had a thing for Tressa in high school and seems to think he can pick up where he left off." Toy slipped her apron back on. "She and her husband have separated." The bell at the open window to the kitchen dinged and Toy slid out of the booth.

So Tressa had been the redhead I'd seen in the Jag with Nick.

"Interesting." Dixie pulled a couple of napkins from the dispenser on the table and handed them to me.

"You've obviously seen me eat." I laughed.

"I have." She grinned. "And you're in good company." She plucked a couple for herself.

Toy returned with our plates. I had chosen well; the pancakes were fluffy and golden brown. The syrup was locally produced and had been warmed. I swear, small town diner cuisine is highly underrated.

We dug in and didn't come up for air until Toy stopped back at the table to offer refills on our drinks. She had the water pitcher in one hand and the coffee carafe in the other. Dixie had barely touched her milk. I had nearly completely downed both my water and my coffee.

Toy deftly refilled both. "Who would have known about all of young Nick's shenanigans would have been Alma Stoller."

I halted a forkful of pancake halfway to my mouth. "How so?"

"Alma lived next door to the Marchant family for years and worked for Stanley after his wife died," Toy explained.

Nick had said nothing about them being neighbors when I'd brought up Alma. Maybe I'd been right. He didn't want to talk about it. People deal with grief in different ways.

Dixie swallowed the last bite of her Reuben sandwich. "I'd forgotten. She was sort of a part-time housekeeper. Fixed meals, did some housework, right?"

"Yep." Toy set the coffee carafe down on the table. "If anyone would have been party to his teenaged antics, it would've been Alma."

Thinking about Nick's reaction led me to think about Cheri's meltdown. Suddenly, my pancake felt like a weight in my stomach. I still felt like we'd done the right thing, giving the note to the sheriff. But that poor woman, planning a memorial service for her mother, and dealing with the possibility her own son might have caused her mother's death.

Chapter Ten

The morning of Alma Stoller's memorial service dawned with clear skies and so I gave Big Blue a quick wash before getting dressed. Rinsing the Jeep in my driveway, I saw no sign of Mrs. Pickett. Apparently after the advice on weed removal, her work was done. For now.

Heading inside to get dressed, I wondered how Cheri would react when she saw us at the church. Dixie and I had discussed it and we both felt like we should attend, but neither of us wanted to cause a scene of any kind. Hopefully we'd be lost in the crowd of attendees.

I had several nice dresses from my days at the magazine, but I'd worn my favorite one on my sales call to Arbor House. I tried a couple of others but they were a bit snug. I was really going to have to get serious about getting some exercise.

I finally settled on a dark burgundy knit that wasn't too heavy in case it got warm in the church. Some simple silver jewelry and I was ready to pick up Dixie.

Her house was at the edge of town. Not sure if that's the east or west edge of town. The house was a clapboard farmhouse and probably had once been surrounded by fields, but as St. Ignatius had grown it was now nested between other, more modern houses.

And before you ask, yes, I can drive to it without the GPS. I know you were thinking I would have to rely on Matilda, but I've been to Dixie's enough I can do fine on my own.

She came out as soon as I pulled in her driveway.

"You must have been watching for me." I noted.

"I was. Didn't want to keep you waiting."

She climbed into the Jeep and fastened her seatbelt. Dixie had picked a champagne-colored dress with a deep brown shrug. The neutral colors set off her coloring and especially her fiery red hair.

"Nice colors on you," I commented.

"Not too bad yourself." She gestured to my dress.

"I was down to two dresses that fit." I frowned. "I've got to stop tasting everything you make."

"Don't blame it on me." She wagged a finger. "It could be those blueberry muffins from the Red Hen Diner."

"Maybe." I smiled. "But they are so good."

In a matter of minutes, we'd arrived at the church. I didn't use the GPS but Dixie gave the turn-by-turn instructions that brought us to the brick turn-of-the-century building. I parked in the large parking lot and we made our way to the chapel.

I'd not been in the St. Ignatius Methodist Church before. It was much more traditional than the Lutheran church across town where I'd attended Elsie Farmer's funeral early in the year. The crowd for Alma's services was also much smaller.

There was a table at the front of the sanctuary with an urn. Small easels on each side held a collection of photos of Alma. Cheri sat alone in the front pew.

"Not many people," I whispered to Dixie as we walked down the aisle and slid into a half-full row about midway. There went my idea that we might go unnoticed in the crowd.

"Maybe a product of her age," Dixie whispered back. "My Grandma Ruby is always worried that she'll have a low-attendance funeral because none of her friends will still be around to attend."

"That's not a bad thing." I settled into my seat and looked around. "It likely means you've lived a long life."

"That's what Grandpa always tells her when she says it." Dixie shook her head. "But she's a planner. Grandpa would say 'control freak.' Grandma has everything written down. Arrangements, songs, who should do her hair."

"Still, Alma wasn't that old, was she? Probably way younger than your grandma." I glanced down at the folder we'd been given with information about the service. There was a nice photo of Alma on the front. "You and Greer mentioned she was older when she had Cheri."

Dixie fanned herself with her paper and leaned back. "My mom and dad were talking about it the other night and apparently Alma and her husband had been hoping to have kids for a long time and had finally given up when lo and behold, they find out Alma is pregnant."

“Wow, that would be a shock.” Talk about a menopause baby. Some couples wait until they’re older to have kids, but if you’d been trying and then decided it wasn’t in the cards for you, that would be a game changer.

“That wasn’t the only shock poor Alma got. When Cheri was little, maybe three or four, her dad had a heart attack and died.” Dixie folded her paper over and continued to fan herself.

“My word.” I hadn’t known any of that. Most of the ladies at the Good Life are widows but they don’t talk much about it. “There’s Alma on her own and with a little one to take care of to boot.”

It explained a lot for me. I’d always found Alma to be a little bossy with Greer and the other ladies who were friends. I guess when you’ve been handling things on your own most of your life, you might develop a habit of taking charge.

A few more people filed in and took seats. Cheri sat motionless at the front, shoulders stiff, never turning to look anywhere but straight ahead.

I heard Greer’s group from the Good Life come in. Shifting a little so I could see them, I spotted Greer, Bunny, and Nellie. There were also several other women who looked familiar to me. There were more women than men who lived at the Good Life. Harold, the new guy, trailed behind the group and slid into the pew where Greer and the ladies were seated. He brushed something off the sleeve of his suit, straightened his tie, and winked at me. Caught staring, I turned back around quickly.

The minister entered, stepped to the podium, and placed some papers there. He then sat in a straight wooden chair nearby. A young man strolled down the outside aisle and slipped into the pew beside Cheri. His suit hung on his thin frame as if he had lost weight or had borrowed it from someone a few sizes larger than he was. He must be Dustin, Cheri’s son. Alma’s grandson. His long straight hair brushed his shoulders. Cheri put her arm around him.

I was again struck by her aloneness. With no brothers or sisters or seemingly any other family members, Dustin was it.

I really hoped he wasn’t involved in his grandmother’s death, but it sounded like Sheriff Terry wasn’t ready to rule him out. According to what Cheri had said, he had no alibi. How awful would it be for Cheri if it turned out the last person she had left in the world had done something so terrible?

The minister stepped to the podium again and said, “Let us pray.”

In unison heads bowed. After a short prayer, he shuffled the papers in front of him and then looked up at the seated crowd.

Holding a single sheet of paper in his hand, he began, "Alma Fogle was born in St. Ignatius and lived here all her life. She married Hugh Stoller, her high school sweetheart, and they had one daughter. Alma was preceded in death by her husband, Hugh. She is survived by her daughter, Cheri Wheeler, and her grandson, Dustin Wheeler. She also leaves behind many friends from her time at the Good Life retirement village."

Simple and to the point. Alma would've liked that.

The minister nodded to Cheri and Dustin and sat down. Dustin rose and climbed the steps to the podium. Straightening his shoulders in the ill-fitting jacket, he turned to look at the piano player, who struck a note and then waited.

Dustin swallowed hard, pushed his long black hair off his face, focused deep blue eyes on a point in the back of the church, opened his mouth, and began the most moving rendition of "Amazing Grace" I had ever heard in my entire life.

I was speechless. The enormity of how strongly Alma must have felt about helping Dustin to have voice lessons was suddenly clear to me. Wow. Incredible talent.

When he finished there was absolute silence for several seconds. Tears welled in his eyes, he bowed his head a moment, and then rejoined his mother.

In those few minutes as he walked to the pew, I knew two things for sure. One was that, even though at this point Dustin Wheeler was an awkward kid with clothes that didn't fit and a bad case of acne, when those pimples were a thing of the past and he'd grown into his lanky frame, he would be a striking young man.

The second thing I knew for sure was that there was no way this young man had killed his grandmother.

The minister closed the services with a prayer and people began filing out the back of the sanctuary. Cheri and her son slipped out a side door. The church had arranged for coffee and cookies in the attached community room, but few stayed for the refreshments. Alma's friends from the Good Life stuck around for a short time. Once they'd gone, there were only a handful of people left.

There were four ladies who lingered and I suddenly realized they were probably the church committee who had provided the refreshments. They were undoubtedly waiting for us to leave so they could clean up.

"Very sorry," I spoke to the woman closest to me. "You're probably needing to clear things and get going, aren't you?"

"No rush," the woman said, but the other three gave her a look that I was sure was meant to convey that they didn't have all day. In fact, when I got a good look at the table it appeared they'd already begun packing up some of the cookies.

A man in a dark suit came through from the chapel. "Do you know where Mrs. Stoller's daughter went?"

"She left," said one of the women. "Her and her son."

"I'm supposed to check and see what she wants done with the flowers." The man, who I assumed was from the funeral home, shook his head.

"Pastor said she told him she didn't want them," the woman I'd been talking to offered. One of the others spoke up, "We can take some of them in the sanctuary, but not all."

"If you like, we could take a couple of the plants to the Good Life where Alma lived," I offered.

"That's a great idea." The man's voice reflected his relief. "Come with me."

Dixie and I followed him to the entryway, where he'd assembled the collection of plants and flower arrangements.

"I'll take these back inside." He separated a group. "They'll stay nice for the church's services next Sunday. And if you ladies wouldn't mind taking those." He pointed to a couple of other arrangements. "And perhaps that one as well." He indicated a potted green plant.

"I'll pull the car up," I told Dixie.

The lot was nearly empty. Most of the attendees had been Alma's friends from the retirement center and they had all come in the van. There were only a handful of cars left and I was betting four of them belonged to the four church ladies inside.

I parked Big Blue in front and the man from the funeral home helped load the flowers into the Jeep.

As we pulled out, I shared my thoughts with Dixie on Dustin and my certainty that he could not have been responsible for his grandmother's death.

"I agree." Dixie clicked her seatbelt. "That young man loved his grandma."

"I can handle the flower delivery if you don't want to go. Would you like me to take you home first?"

"No, I'm happy to go along." She straightened in her seat. "I can help you carry in the flowers. Besides, maybe we'll find out something more that might help in the investigation. Terry's investigation," she corrected.

Next stop, the Good Life. Greer and the others had already arrived and, having dressed in their Sunday best for the services, they'd decided to congregate in the community center.

Ah, here was the assembly that hadn't been happening at the church. At the church, everyone had gone through the motions out of respect for Cheri and her efforts to honor her mom. But here was the true tribute to Alma's life.

Some folding tables had been set up and several people had brought snacks to share. It wasn't fancy but it was impromptu and perfect.

Greer sat at a table with a couple of ladies I seen around but didn't know that well. They were passing around photos from Dilly Dally Dayz, a local festival featuring homemade ice cream, and others from the St. Ignatius Centennial earlier in the year. Alma, ever the organizer, had been a big part of both events, taking charge of the Good Life booth at Dilly Dally Dayz and a float in the parade for the centennial.

I sat down in a chair next to Bunny, who was sitting quietly off to the side.

"It must be hard on you and the others. I know you miss Alma," I said quietly. "She was such a big part of your lives and this event."

"At our age, we know we're going to lose friends." Bunny shrugged. "But we don't think we're going to lose them like this."

"I'm sure they'll figure it all out soon."

"Alma was good to drive us. It's not like St. Ignatius has a taxi service and so she took the lot of us where we needed to go. To the grocery store or post office." She stopped and stared across the room.

"Are you thinking about the day she forgot you at the post office?" I touched her arm lightly.

"I am." She nodded. "Understandable though. She told me later that she was all upset and discombobulated, because she'd had a big fight with Stanley."

"Stanley Marchant?"

"Yes. Stanley B. Marchant, he insists on the B." Bunny smiled slightly. "Alma apologized for forgetting me. She felt real bad."

"Sounds like she might have had a lot on her mind."

"That's exactly what Alma said." Bunny nodded. "She said she 'had a lot on her mind.'"

"I wonder what kind of things."

Had Alma been distracted by something to do with the land deal? Had she and Stanley had a falling out about something?

"She didn't say," Bunny continued. "Just said she was hoppin' mad at Stanley. Don't know why."

Interesting. I wondered what the two might have to disagree about and if anyone had asked where Stanley had been when Alma was killed. He seemed an unlikely suspect, but like the sheriff had said, they needed to follow any clue at this point.

After chatting with the ladies for a while, Dixie and I said our good-byes. On the way to the car, I told her about my talk with Bunny.

"What do you suppose they argued about?" She climbed into the Jeep.

"You don't suppose it was something to do with the cookbook, do you?" I'd been wracking my brain.

"Maybe something to do with the Crack of Dawn breakfasts." Dixie mused. "Stanley is very particular about details. All those years in banking."

I dropped Dixie off at her place, still thinking about the possibilities.

When I arrived home, there was a note stuck to my mailbox that a delivery needing a signature had been attempted.

Finally, my package from Daddy's agent.

It was too late to pick it up because the post office was already closed for the day, but I was sure it was the box of my father's things. I hadn't wanted my package to go missing like Disco's brains, or Tressa's hair products, and so I'd thought the signature required was a good idea, but I was disappointed in the delay.

Taking the note inside with me, along with my mail, I said hello to Ernest, who promptly filed a complaint about his empty food dish. He followed me to the kitchen and waited somewhat patiently while I refilled his food and water.

I opened the fridge and checked out my choices for dinner. Not impressed with any of them, I went upstairs to change clothes.

Once changed, I looked again. Same options.

What, did I think the dinner fairy had made a delivery while I was upstairs?

My choices were a microwave dinner, salad, eggs, or PB and J. That bagel yesterday had been the last in the package.

The truth was what I really wanted was comfort food. The absolute truth was I wanted comfort food, but I wished someone else would make it.

If wishes were horses, beggars would ride.

Ernest tipped his ears and gave me a look, so I must have repeated the idiom out loud. When those sayings popped into my head, it was always Aunt Cricket's voice I heard. In this case, my auntie was absolutely right: wishing was not going to make it so.

And, if she were here—which thank goodness she wasn't or I'd be getting a whole bunch of bless-your-hearts mixed in with a dollop of get-over-yourself—she'd be right about that too. Who was I to feel sorry for myself? Think of poor Cheri Wheeler and all she was going through.

I pulled out the eggs, cracked them in a bowl, and added some cheese. I may not be a blue-ribbon baker, but even I could whip up an omelet in a pinch.

After I ate, I cleaned up the kitchen, picked up the living room, and then pulled out a notepad. When we were working on a cookbook project, it helped me to get my thoughts down on paper. Maybe it would work the same way, in trying to think through who might have wanted to get rid of Alma.

After that beautiful tribute to his grandmother, I knew it had not been Dustin. But if it wasn't Dustin who ran over Alma, who was it?

I started jotting down what we knew and what we didn't know.

Where there were gaps in what we knew, there had to be secrets.

And if we could learn those secrets, we'd have our answers.

* * * *

The next morning, I called Dixie to let her know I planned to stop at the post office for my package before I headed to the office.

I reviewed my notes from the night before, hoping they made as much sense in the light of day as they had when I'd been sipping tea and taking names.

The notes still made sense but, as when I'd pondered the situation last night, there were definitely gaps. It seemed like some of the missing pieces were rooted in the history everyone shared. I could hardly wait to share my thoughts with Dixie; although as I'd written everything out, it occurred to me that some of the gaps were areas where it was possible that she was one of the people with answers.

When I arrived at the post office, Dot Carson, the post mistress, was helping someone else. I waited for my turn at the window.

The customer turned and I realized it was Tina, who I could barely see over the top of the large box she had her arms wrapped around. She was dressed for the office and today's color was peach. She coordinated from her peach lips all the way down to her peach-toned toes. She teetered a bit on the heels of her strappy peach sandals that were a perfect match for her dress. I didn't know how she did it.

I stepped aside so she could pass. "Do you need help?"

"Thanks, Sugar." Tina shifted the box to get a better grip. "I've got it."

"A package from your friend?" I asked.

"Yes." Her peach lips drew up in a big smile. "I'm excited to find out what it is!"

I snuck a peek at the package, but the return address was just that, an address. Nothing that said it was actually from anybody called Rafe.

I held the door for Tina, and then returned to the counter and presented my delivery-attempted note to Dot. She took it and disappeared into the back.

Returning with a box that was taped every which way, Dot hefted it on the counter. "Somebody from New York City sent you something." She looked at me expectantly.

"They did." I knew I'd probably create more interest about what was in the box by not explaining, but I didn't feel ready to share. Especially when I didn't even know what the package contained.

"Sign here." She reluctantly pushed a piece of paper toward me.

I signed where she'd indicated and reached to take the box.

"It's heavy," she said. "You should've brought help. You still seeing that Max Windsor?"

I didn't have a good answer to give her.

"I think I can get it," I said, lifting the package and avoiding her question. "I've been working out."

She was right that the box was kind of heavy, but I managed to get it to the Jeep and onto the passenger seat.

Now I had a dilemma. I wanted to open it right away, of course. But I wasn't sure I wanted to cart it to the office and then have to cart it back home.

Deciding that going directly home with it made way more sense, I called Dixie and let her know my delay was going to be longer, and turned Big Blue toward my neighborhood.

Once I got the box inside, I set it in the middle of my living room floor. Ernest was very suspicious of a container that, at least according to his sniffs, did not smell like it belonged in our house.

Retrieving Mrs. Pickett's garden knife from the kitchen, I carefully cut the tape and lifted out the crumpled packing paper from the top.

The first thing I unwrapped was a small framed photograph. Swallowing around the lump in my throat, I ran my fingers over the tarnished silver edge.

It was Daddy and me at an ice cream shop.

Looking at the photo, I remembered the place. I could smell the rich hot fudge that dripped from the spoon in the picture and feel the tickle of Daddy's short, soft beard as he held me close. I'd been maybe seven or eight years old, I wasn't sure which, and missing both front teeth. We were both smiling. I wondered who had taken the photo. I had no recollection of anyone else being there.

I set the photo aside.

Underneath the next layer in the box were a couple of reference volumes that looked interesting. Below the books was a sheaf of printed pages. It looked like a manuscript. Maybe something Daddy had been working on?

I took a deep breath and carefully pried the pages from the bottom of the box. They were held together with a giant rubber band. When I attempted to slip the band off, it snapped, probably so old it had lost its elasticity.

I lifted the first page and looked at the title. *A Fictional Memoir*, it said. I was familiar with the concept, but knowing Daddy and the books he'd written, it was hard to know if that's truly what it was. Was it actually his fictionalized life story, or that of one of his characters? I couldn't resist a skim of the first few pages. The story began:

> *My parents loved me, but not too much.*
>
> *That's who they were. How they approached work, play, and the world in general. Life was solid, pleasant, adequate. No need for extremes.*
>
> *The problem with that was that from the beginning I was wired differently. They believed their mission in life was to set me on an even keel, and I was born wanting to ride the waves.*

Whether fact or fiction—or, as the title would suggest, a mixture of both—I could hardly wait to read more. But I made myself set the pages aside. Tonight, I promised myself.

I carried the silver-framed photo to the fireplace mantel and set it beside the picture of the Sugarbaker sisters—my mom and my aunts. Gathering up the packing paper, I reached for the box and discovered Ernest had taken up residence.

"That's not for you to play in." I told him sternly.

He flashed emerald green eyes, clearly understanding what I said, but disagreeing.

"Okay, I'll leave it there for now." I patted his head and gave a quick scratch under his chin. "It's clear who's in charge of this house and it's not me."

Giving the Cat Boss one last pet, I reluctantly got my bag and headed for the front door. It would be hard to concentrate today, knowing those pages waited for me.

Chapter Eleven

When I arrived at the shop, the odors of nutmeg and cinnamon filled the air. Dixie was in the kitchen working on a batch of molasses cookies. She was trying something different with the recipe, she said. I knew Dixie could have tried out her experiment at home in the comfort of her own kitchen, but I think she liked the company. And, as you know, I am always willing to be a taste tester. Though Dixie insisted these cookies would have to cool before testing, I wasn't sure I could wait much longer. I'd been in such a rush to get to the post office that my breakfast had consisted of coffee in a to-go mug, and now I was famished.

I filled Dixie in on the contents of my package from Daddy's agent.

"I can't believe you didn't bring the photo so I could see it." She tipped her head to look at me. "I'll bet you were cute as a button."

"A toothless button." I rolled my eyes.

"It must have brought back good memories." Dixie continued working while we talked.

"It did." I smiled. I didn't have many photos of Daddy, and before this, hadn't had any of the two of us together.

"I almost forgot." Dixie slapped her forehead. "You are not going to believe this, but Cheri Wheeler called a few minutes ago to thank us for attending her mother's service and for helping with the flowers."

Dixie utilized a metal scoop to make sure her cookies were of uniform size. I was fascinated with how quickly she worked.

"Wow, that's a turnaround after blasting us the other day."

"She also asked if we would be here the rest of the morning because she wanted to stop by." Dixie looked at her watch. "I told her we would be."

"I guess if there's going to be a knock-down-drag-out fight, it's better for it to be on our home turf."

Dixie raised her brows.

"I didn't mean to sound as if I'm expecting a Jets versus Sharks brawl, but Cheri was beyond angry when she was here." I didn't quite trust the quick change in attitude.

"I don't think she wants to pick up where she left off." Dixie seemed a little more comfortable with the turnaround than I was. "She seemed much calmer and with what's she's been through, I think Terry questioning her son was just too much."

"That would push most any mom over the edge," I agreed.

"I need to get this first batch out of the oven." She grabbed her silicone oven mitt and reached to pull out the cookie sheet.

"You're probably right, if she's a bit unstable, who could blame her." I leaned over the cookies and inhaled.

"Five minutes and then you can try one." Dixie waved me away as she put the next batch in. "I didn't know you liked molasses cookies."

"I didn't either." I sniffed again. "I like cookies. Can't think of a type of cookie I don't like, but these smell extra lovely."

We heard the ding of the bell out front.

"That's probably Cheri." Dixie had begun transferring the cookies to a cooling rack.

"If you want to let her know it will be a couple of minutes, I'll finish setting these off to cool and then join you."

"Sure, go ahead, throw me to the she-wolf." I slipped a cookie off the cooling rack and headed to the front. "You keep your ears open in case I need help."

It wasn't Cheri. It was Nick Marchant.

His stopping by was becoming a regular thing, just like Disco. I wondered if he also was after food or if he simply liked stirring things up. My bet was on stirring the pot. Now that I knew he was seeing Tressa, I had a different feeling about him stopping by so often.

"Hey, Nick." I greeted him. "What brings you to cookbook world today?"

He was dressed as if he'd been at work. High-end suit and designer tie, though the tie was loosened. Dark hair artfully tousled. Given the time of day, he probably should still be at the bank.

"Good morning to you, sunshine." He smiled at me cheerfully, but didn't answer my question.

"Good morning. Back again?"

"I can smell that Spicy has already been baking this morning. She always was a great cook. You ladies could make a fortune if you wanted to open a bakery."

"We're busy with the cookbook business." I crossed my arms. "St. Ignatius already has a bakery."

"Well if you change your mind, I'm sure the bank could help with a small business loan."

"Not—"

Before I could finish my sentence, the door dinged again and Cheri Wheeler stepped in. Poor thing. Her face was ashen and she looked even more exhausted than she had at her mother's services.

Just inside the door, she stopped and looked at Nick and then looked at me.

"I'll come back." she said and was back out the door faster than you could say whiplash.

"Was that Cheri?" Dixie had come out of the backroom, her cheeks pink from the heat of the oven, a plate of cookies in her hand.

"Spicy," Nick greeted her with a smile. "I was telling Sugar here, you two should open a bakery."

"St. Ignatius already has a bakery," Dixie noted.

"That's what I told him."

"Are you just here because you're hungry?" She raised a brow. "Because if that's the case, we may have to start charging you."

"No, that's simply my impeccable timing." He held up a glossy blue folder. "I came by to leave this with you. I'm working with the Jameson County Chamber of Commerce and we're thinking of doing a promo in the state tourism magazine."

"We're not members of the chamber," Dixie pointed out.

"Exactly." Nick tapped the folder. "I've brought you all the materials you'll need to fill out to join."

"Handy." Dixie frowned. "Leave it with us and we'll think about it. Sugar is the business brains in this duo so I'm sure she'll have lots of questions."

"I'm sure you'll see the benefits." He handed me the folder and then turned to Dixie.

"I have more stops to make, but I wouldn't turn down one of those cookies."

She reached under the counter for a napkin, used it to pick up two cookies, and handed them to him.

"Thanks, Spicy." Nick headed for the door. "You two should think about that bakery. More mark up in baked goods than in cookbooks."

Once the door closed, Dixie put the plate down and pushed it toward me. "Gah! I hate it when someone doesn't get what we do. I explained it to him the other day, but he obviously wasn't listening."

I laughed. "Obviously."

"I thought I heard Cheri?"

"She was here, but turned around and left." I reached for a cookie. "I don't think she was feeling well. She was extremely pale. She said she'd be back."

"Even though she was horrible to me, I hope she's okay," Dixie picked up a cookie herself.

"Should we try her cell?" I asked.

Dixie nodded and I grabbed my cell phone from the office. When I dialed Cheri's number, she picked up right away.

I explained we were concerned about her and wondered if now was a good time to talk. Cheri said she had gone home but could be back in just a bit.

* * * *

In less than ten minutes, Cheri was back. It looked like she'd freshened up her makeup. She was still pale but not as white as she'd been earlier.

"First off, I want to apologize." Her hand shook as she impatiently brushed a lock of wheat-colored hair out of her eyes. There were times when I saw a bit of Alma in Cheri. "I am so sorry I behaved like I did."

"You were worried about Dusty," Dixie said. "I'm sure given the same circumstances I would have been upset too."

"Thank you for being so gracious, but there's no excuse for the things I said and how nasty I was to you."

"You're under a lot of stress." I pulled out one of the stools and eased it toward her. The woman needed to sit down before she fell down.

"Yeah, I am." She gave a faint smile and sat. "To top things off I need to get everything moved out of my mom's by the end of the month. I can't believe how much stuff she had jammed into that little place."

"That must be tough to go through everything." Dixie pulled out one of the other stools and sat next to her.

"I don't have time to sort things right now, I'm just boxing them and moving them to my house. I'll have to go through them there."

"Do you have someone to help you?" I asked.

"I'm afraid it's just Dusty and me. We don't have any other family around."

"I'd be happy to help you pack things if you'd like the help," I said.

"I would too," Dixie added.

"That's so sweet of you. I just might take you up on it even if it's just to run interference. Every time I'm over there, at the Good Life, the ladies want to stop by and talk. I know they mean well but, boy, does it slow me down." She gave a lopsided grin.

"Just let us know when you'll be going again and we're on it." I couldn't imagine trying to tackle the task of packing up a lifetime of personal items in such a short time. The one box of my Daddy's things had just about done me in.

She hesitated. "If you're serious, I'm headed there tomorrow afternoon and could definitely use the help. Like I said, I'm not sorting anything, just boxing it."

"What time?" I asked.

"Would two o'clock work?"

"Absolutely," I said. "I'll be there."

"I've got an appointment at the vet for Moto, my dog," Dixie explained, "but I could join you later when we're done."

"Perfect," she said. "I can't tell you how much I appreciate your help. Earlier with the flowers and now this. I'm sorry I was so rude when Terry questioned Dusty. I apologize again. I was beside myself with worry."

"It's too bad no one can confirm he was home. Maybe a neighbor saw him?" A situation like this was when you hoped for a nosey neighbor like Mrs. Pickett. "It would go a long way to clearing him."

"No," she sighed. "But we're dealing with it."

Dealing with it? What did that mean?

"Well, that's good," Dixie finally said into the pause.

Cheri dropped her face into her palms and then lifted her head and looked at us. "He's been in trouble before and so this makes it look bad."

That must be the trouble Greer had hinted at and the sheriff had mentioned.

"A few months back Dusty was involved with some kids that were caught vandalizing the school. Seniors like him. He'd been friends with one of the guys since elementary school, they stayed close, used to be in a band together. He says he didn't do any of the spray painting and I believe him. But he was there and didn't turn the kids in."

As I'd suspected, Dustin *had* been part of the group that had spray-painted school buses, buildings, and some houses, mine included.

"Kids make mistakes." Dixie shrugged. "You were ahead of us in school, but you surely remember my brother, Hirsh, and the cow in the school auditorium incident?"

"Oh my gosh, I had forgotten about that." Cheri gave a weak smile.

"It was 'Bring Your Pet to School Day.'" Dixie grinned. "And my brother, of course, couldn't be satisfied with taking our family dog."

She filled me in on Hirsh's leading of his favorite calf, Milkshake, into the school, and how unamused the school superintendent had been. Her story relieved some of the tension and by the time she was done, Cheri had a little bit of color in her cheeks.

She stood to leave and I hated to do it but I needed to ask about what Bunny had told me.

"Before you go, I need to ask you about something before telling the sheriff about it." I could sense Cheri tense as I said the words. "Nothing to do with Dustin," I hastened to add.

"Okay." She let out a breath.

"Bunny, one of the ladies from the Good Life, mentioned to me that your mom had told her she'd had a disagreement with Stanley Marchant. Do you know what that might have been about?"

Cheri shook her head. "I can't imagine. Mom and Stanley have been friends for years. We used to live next door."

"You're okay with me telling the sheriff?"

"Sure." She looped her bag over her shoulder. "Go ahead."

I'd been planning to anyway, but felt better that Cheri knew about it in advance. This way if Sheriff Terry asked her questions, she wouldn't feel blindsided.

"What about the land the development company wanted to buy from your mom?" I still thought Alma standing in the way of them moving forward could be a motive to get her out of the picture. "Have you heard from them?"

"Greg Cheeters contacted me and according to him, Mom had agreed to sell and they had settled on a price." Cheri shifted her purse. "I don't have any reason to hang onto the property so I'm happy enough with that, but I haven't found paperwork. We may be back at the negotiation stage."

Dixie had bagged a handful of cookies to send home with Cheri and I agreed to meet her at the Good Life the following afternoon at two o'clock to help her with the packing.

As soon as Cheri left, I called the sheriff and told him about the argument between Alma and Stanley that Bunny had told me about. I also asked if he'd found out any more about Mr. Greg Cheeters and shared what Cheri had told us.

Sheriff Terry wasn't very open to sharing about his investigation, but he did tell me they hadn't found Alma's notebook. That notebook was a small thing but it bugged me.

It had to be someplace that everyone had missed.

Dixie had planned to have lunch at her folks. She invited me to go along and though an opportunity to enjoy her mother's fantastic cooking and a chance to meet the goats in person was tempting, I asked for a rain check.

I thought maybe a visit to the city park might spark some ideas on where to look for the lost notebook.

Chapter Twelve

That missing black book of Alma's had nagged at my brain. According to Greer, Alma had never been without it. A bit of a list maker myself, I could understand having one place to keep everything. And if, as Greer said, Alma would make a note of any reminder or appointment in the book, it made no sense that it hadn't been found in her purse or in her car.

When I'd talked to Sheriff Terry about it, he'd confirmed that it hadn't been found in the area either. He'd checked the crime scene inventory and assured me no notebook had been found in Alma's purse.

Could the killer have taken it from her? Did the notebook contain some incriminating information?

Alma's cell phone found had been found. The sheriff said it was not far from her body, as if it had been in her hand when she'd been hit the first time.

Alma's handbag had been found. It had been in her car, in the passenger seat.

But where was that dang book?

My lunch today consisted of a chicken salad wrap I'd picked up at the local market. I had also grabbed some already cut-up carrot sticks. My nod to healthy eating.

It was a beautiful day and I decided to take my impromptu brown bag with me to the city park and enjoy the warm weather. All too soon summer would be gone and the chance to soak up some sun along with it. Last winter had been mild but the Farmer's Almanac was saying this year could be a doozy. Enjoying the snow was part of what I loved about the Midwest, so I kind of hoped they were right.

I parked near the shelter house that was the focus of the Crack of Dawn Breakfast Club's project. Then I found a picnic table in the shade and laid out my lunch and the bottle of iced tea I'd brought along.

Across the way a young mom with two kids pushed them in the chain link swings that made up part of the playground area. Their squeals of delight and calls of "again" mixed with the whir from a trimmer, as a guy in a St. Ignatius Parks shirt worked along the nearby fence line. The green of the cut grass smelled like summer. Between two large shady trees a volleyball net had been set up and a group of teens were about to start a game.

I took a bite of my wrap. An idyllic spot.

Except it wasn't.

In spite of the fact that the park had been returned to its normal routine, a woman had been killed. Near this very spot.

Sure, even though it now appeared that it wasn't Alma's grandson, that didn't alter the fact than someone had done it. Someone had run over poor Alma and then, according to the account from Sheriff Terry, run over her again.

I didn't know anything about the crime scene. That wasn't something that the sheriff or anyone connected to the investigation was likely to share.

I polished off my wrap and tucked the bag of carrots in the pocket of my skirt. Walking toward the large basketball-themed can marked *Slam Dunk Your Junk* to throw away my trash, I thought about Alma. I pictured her arriving in the early hours before the sun was completely up, parking her car, meeting someone.

But who?

I looked around at the area. It didn't make sense to imagine that it could have been her grandson. Why would she meet Dustin at the park? They could simply meet at her place.

She hadn't told anyone about the meeting. Not her daughter. Not Greer. Nor any of her other friends.

That made me think she must not have been afraid of whoever it was.

I walked to the other side of the shelter house. She must have parked in the gravel lot and waited. Would she have gotten out of her car?

And why had the killer been in her car? Had he or she come with Alma to the park? That didn't seem logical either. There must have been some reason to meet here. Some reason to meet where prying eyes from the Good Life wouldn't see.

She was meeting someone whom she had no reason to think would harm her. But it had to have been someone she didn't want others to know she was meeting.

I made a loop around the area and then went back to my picnic table and gathered the rest of my stuff. Time to get back to the office and the cookbook. Plus, I wanted to get through the day so I could head home and get back to Daddy's manuscript pages.

And who knew what my new yard advisor, Mrs. Pickett, had on her list of lawn work that needed my attention. I'd found a flyer stuffed in my mailbox about tasks that needed done before your grass went dormant. According to the flyer, you must rake up the leaves and then aerate and fertilize your lawn. I didn't know for sure how to do that—I mean, the raking yes. But aerate and fertilize?

Google, here I come. I was sure the flyer had come from Mrs. Pickett and that she knew exactly how those tasks needed to be done.

I was optimistic—Pollyanna-ishly so, according to Dixie—that we'd made progress. Now that she saw I wasn't a bad person, just a bad yard person, perhaps we could be friends. Or maybe just friendlier.

Back at the shop, Dixie was busy reorganizing her kitchen utensils. She'd brought a new hanging rack from her mom's and seemed to be having a ball sorting out the various tools and getting them ready for the within-arm's-reach display.

"What is this?" I picked up a funny-looking implement.

"It's an herb stripper." She took it from my fingers. "I picked it up at that fancy kitchen store in Des Moines and wasn't sure how much I'd use it, but I find I use it a lot."

"Sounds kinky." I picked up another item and held it up.

"A spiralizer." She answered my unasked question. "You use it to make your veggies into pasta-like strands.

"Do I need my veggies to look like pasta?" I asked.

"Probably not. Now shoo. Go do something with your numbers back in your office. Have we heard from the ABBA lady since you answered her questions?"

"I don't know. I need to check my email." I put the spiralizer down and headed back to the office. I really did want to check in with Gwen and see if her board had made a decision.

Logging into the Sugar and Spice email account, I checked for a message from Gwen Arbor. Nothing. Deciding that if I hadn't heard from her by the following day, I'd send her a friendly status-check email, I made a note on the pad of paper by my desk.

I had a few more things to take care of and made short work of them before checking in on Dixie's progress. She'd sorted out the gadgets and utensils and had set some to the side.

"Those are for you to take home with you." She held out the group. "I'm positive you don't have any of the them in your kitchen."

"I might," I protested.

"I'm betting not," she insisted. "Unless your mother has sent you a Williams Sonoma starter kitchen gift set." She raised her brows in question.

"No." I took them from her. "I'm not sure I'll know what to do with them."

"Keep them around." Dixie turned back to her sorting. "You never know."

"You keep holding out hope for me, but it may be that I don't have any aptitude in the cooking arena."

"Look what you're doing with your yard." She pointed out. "You thought you didn't have any aptitude there either."

"I still don't." I shook my head. "It's a matter of survival. Mrs. Pickett won't take no for an answer."

"Ah, so that's been the problem with my approach. I needed to be more threatening and crazy." She gave me a mischievous grin and brandished a whisk in my direction.

* * * *

Once home I went through the usual routine of feeding Ernest and then trying to figure out what to eat. Maybe Dixie was right, maybe I just needed to buck up and learn how to make something more than my top five go-to meals that I always fell back on.

When there was a knock at the door, I already knew before I opened it that it would be Mrs. Pickett. It's not that I have any clairvoyance of any kind. If I did I'd use it to keep myself out of any number of snafus in my life. It was simply the lady had developed a routine. Not every night, but every few days she appeared. A new complaint or a variation on an old one.

Tonight at least she wasn't brandishing a knife.

Hey, when you have a neighbor like Mrs. Pickett, you take your small wins.

She was dressed in her usual floral print dress. She must have a closet full of them. This number had pink cabbage roses and was buttoned all the way up her wattle-ish neck to her pointy chin. Her wispy gray hair was pinned back and she stood with her arms crossed.

"I hear you keep the books at that cookbook business."

It was more of a statement than a question, but I nodded. "Yes, I do."

"I got a problem with my bank account."

"You should call the—" I started.

"I don't want those busybodies in my business." She stuck her lip out.

Aunt Cricket's oft-used "pot calling the kettle black" saying popped into my mind, but I held my tongue. "What kind of a problem with your account?"

"I got this bill." She handed me a piece of paper.

I unfolded the paper. According to it, Mrs. Pickett had been purchasing some high-end fashions and expensive designer shoes. I looked at her flowered dress and down at her garden boots. I was pretty sure she had not made the purchases noted on her bill.

"Did you call your credit card company?" I asked.

"Don't have their number."

I looked over the statement but didn't see a number on it to call. Weren't they required to list a number in case of disputes? The paper was slightly mangled and looked like the printing on the bottom had been cut off so maybe there had originally been a phone number.

"I don't see it on here, but it should be on the back of your credit card." I explained. "Do you keep your card in your wallet?

"No. I heard that's not safe. I keep it in a secret place."

Okay, then.

"On the back it will have a phone number and if you call that number, they should be able to help you," I explained. "The credit card company can put a hold on your account and most likely will reverse these charges."

"Oh." She plucked the paper from my hand and off she went.

I stood in the doorway for a little while thinking about how angry it made me that scammers took advantage of little old ladies. Even if they were grumpy little old ladies who couldn't be bothered to say "thank you."

Back in the kitchen, I spread out the utensils Dixie had given me and looked at them. Could I do better? Maybe try a recipe or two that stretched my skills? Probably.

But not tonight. Tonight, I didn't want to spend the time on anything complicated. I wanted spend the least amount of time on food and get back to those manuscript pages.

I decided a salad sounded good.

As I stood at the sink rinsing lettuce and cutting up veggies for my salad, I could see some movement outside my kitchen window. Leaning closer to the glass, I could see over the fence to Mrs. Pickett's yard.

Good grief, what was the woman doing now? I watched as she went to her shed in the back and got out a small ladder, which she propped against the tall oak. She climbed it one booted foot at a time. Though it wasn't a long way up, I held my breath hoping, she wouldn't fall. Finally she came back down the ladder with a small box, which she carried to the house.

I had no way of knowing for sure, but I'd be willing to bet that Mrs. Pickett's credit card was in that box.

In a box, in a tree, in your backyard. So much safer than in your wallet, right?

Chock another one up to—the woman was crazy.

Assembling my salad, I jotted down a variety of things I needed to pick up at the store. Ernest commented a couple of times and eventually convinced me I needed to add kitty treats to the list.

After I'd eaten and washed the few dishes I'd used, I sat down on the couch with a glass of milk and the cookies Dixie'd sent home with me. Pulling out the *Fictional Memoir* pages, I read a few more. The story started with the narrator, Gage, as a teen and as I read I wondered if Daddy had gotten into all the scrapes described in the pages. Soaping the windows of cars on Halloween, TPing trees during his high school's homecoming week, skipping school and then forging his mother's name on the sick day excuse, and sneaking out after his parents were in bed. The escapades were detailed so well, I had to believe at the very least he had some firsthand knowledge.

My eyes were getting heavy and so I put the pages aside and went upstairs to get ready for bed. Ernest followed on my heels and waited while I went through my evening routine, his green eyes following my every move.

Maybe it was the fresh air or just plain exhaustion, but in a matter of minutes I was out.

At three o'clock in the morning I woke with a jolt, startling Ernest, who had been asleep against my legs. I sat up in bed.

Ernest meowed and gave me a green-eyed glare that said, "Couldn't this wait until morning?"

"Secret place," I said to him, gathering his furry body to my chest in apology. "Mrs. Pickett keeps her credit cards in a secret place. If Alma thought she was in danger, she might have put her black book in a secret place!"

* * * *

Early the next morning, I was back at the city park. The park was deserted. No one was in sight, not even a park worker.

I parked in the gravel lot like I had the day before and walked toward the shelter house. There seemed to be only two trees of a height where it would be possible for Alma to reach without a ladder.

I approached the first and looked around. Feeling a little silly, I reached my hand up into the vee where the branches met, just above my head.

Nothing. Alma hadn't been tall but slightly taller than me.

Walking quickly to the second tree, I tried again. I didn't know what kind of tree this one was but there was again a limb that branched out, providing the perfect ledge for hiding something as small as Alma's notebook.

But again, nothing.

Shoot. At three a.m. it had seemed reasonable to me that if Alma felt threatened or became concerned about her meeting at the park that she might stash her notebook somewhere nearby.

My hands were filthy from the tree moss and scratched from the branches. I walked back to the shelter house and sat down at one of the picnic tables.

How could it be that the notebook had vanished? I considered the possibility that whoever had run over Alma had taken it. If that were the case, by this point they would surely have destroyed it.

I kicked at the table leg, trying to get some of the wet grass off my shoes. Once again, I should have remembered that early morning in the park you need to have the proper footwear. Maybe I could get some of those fancy garden boots like Mrs. Pickett.

Disappointed with my search for the notebook, I decided this definitely called for coffee and a blueberry muffin at the Red Hen Diner. I'd been so excited about the idea of Alma hiding the notebook that I'd left home without any breakfast. Or more importantly, without any coffee. And, hey, all I'd had last night was a salad, right? Well, except for those cookies.

One last kick to dislodge some of the grass and I turned to head back to my car. That's when I heard the plop.

My heart skipped a beat. I ducked under the picnic table and there on the concrete floor lay a black notebook.

Shivers skittered up my spine.

I grabbed it and raised up quickly, banging my head. Spooked by the fact that I'd been right and that Alma had hidden her notebook, I dashed to my car. Once in the car, I locked the doors. I looked around, not sure who or what I thought was after me.

There was still no one in the park, but creeped out by the whole thing, I sincerely wished I'd called the sheriff before venturing off on my quest.

I put Big Blue in gear and drove directly to the shop. Parking in the back, I took the notebook inside and lay it on the counter. Then I started some coffee and called Sheriff Terry and left a message.

I really wanted that blueberry muffin as well. Remember what I said earlier about stress eating? But I didn't want to leave Alma's notebook behind and I knew once Terry arrived, he would take it with him.

So I settled for my own coffee and once it had brewed, I took a satisfying gulp.

I also really wanted to look in the notebook, but I knew the Sheriff's Department would want to check for fingerprints, though I'd bet they would find only Alma's. I looked around for ideas. On TV they always have those nifty gloves to keep from contaminating evidence. We didn't stock any of those.

Rummaging in the cupboards, all I could find was Dixie's red silicone oven mitts.

I put them on and carefully opened the notebook. The notations seemed to be in mostly chronological order, although there were all kinds of side notes. Like my own notes to myself, many of them were so cryptic that probably only Alma knew what they referenced. I flipped to pages that were around the time Alma had disappeared.

Greer had been right, on the day she'd forgotten Bunny at the post office there had been a specific note about it. And about the pinochle game.

On the day Alma had been killed there was only one entry and it said, "Marchant."

Well, that sure fell in line with Bunny's comment about Alma being upset over a meeting she'd had with Stanley.

But why? I closed my eyes and thought.

"Hello." I heard from the back. "From the looks of all this grass on the floor, you must have been doing some early yard work this morning."

Dixie came through and then stopped as she looked at my face and the oven mitts on my hands. "What's wrong? Are you okay?"

I explained about my three a.m. epiphany, and going back to the park and finding Alma's notebook.

"Oh my gosh, Sugar, you shouldn't have gone by yourself," she scolded. "I would have gone with you."

"I know you would have, but I wasn't sure I was right." I rested my chin on my oven mitt–clad knuckles. "It made so much sense at three o'clock in the morning and then it seemed silly and then this." I gestured toward the book.

"I know you've already looked, so spill the info, cookie." Dixie sat down. "Was there an appointment on the day Alma was killed?"

I nodded. "Just one and it says, 'Marchant.'"

"Nothing else?" She looked at me. "Do you really think Alma's killer could be Stanley? What would be his motive?"

"I don't know."

There was a tap on the front window and we both jumped.

It was the sheriff.

I had come from the back and hadn't unlocked anything because I was so preoccupied with the notebook. Dixie went to the front door and unlocked it.

The sheriff stepped through the doorway with a small smile as he walked past Dixie, and I was struck as I always was by the subtle chemistry between the two of them. Not always big sparks, but they were always there under the surface. They were such a perfect match and it seemed like everyone could see it except them.

My friend was all fire and spice. Fiercely loyal, crazy smart, and with a heart as big as an Iowa corn field. The sheriff, from what I knew of him anyway, was strong, steady, and not easily swayed. I guess that translated to two people who were as stubborn as the day is long.

It had been a crazy summer with all the fuss about the town golden boy being back, Alma's murder, and now this possible connection to the Marchant family. As they walked back toward me, I said a little prayer that somewhere in all the excitement they'd see each other more clearly.

Sheriff Terry stopped when he spotted me.

I stood at the counter, arms aloft, red oven mitts on my hands, and, I'm sure, excitement on my face.

"What've you got?" he asked. "It wasn't clear from your message."

I nodded at the black book that lay on the wooden surface. "Alma Stoller's notebook that has been missing."

He looked at the notebook and eyed me a couple of beats before reaching for it. "Where'd you get it?"

"At the city park. It was stashed under one of the picnic tables." I slipped off the oven mitts and rubbed my head where I'd bumped it scrambling from under that table.

Dixie and I stood quietly while Terry pulled some of those gloves like they have on TV out of his pocket. He slowly flipped through the pages. I could tell when he came to the entry on the day Alma died.

"This doesn't help us." He looked up.

"Why not?" I asked. "The only entry on that day is 'Marchant.'"

"I see that." He closed the book. "That notation could mean that Alma wanted to remember to stop at the bank that day."

"Maybe," I agreed. "But it also could be she planned to meet Stanley."

"Here's the problem with that." A muscle in Sheriff Terry's jaw twitched. "I followed up on Stanley's whereabouts. After you told me about there allegedly being an argument between Alma and Stanley."

His serious brown eyes looked from me to Dixie and back to me.

He leaned a hand on the counter, "Stanley wasn't even in town when Alma was killed."

I stared at him. How could that be? "Where was he?"

"I won't go into details, but he was at an appointment."

"What type of appointment?" Dixie asked.

I thought about the cane Stanley had when I'd gone to pick up the Crack of Dawn Breakfast Club spreadsheet from him. "A medical appointment," I guessed.

The sheriff stopped midresponse and stared at me.

"I'm right, aren't I?"

"Doesn't matter," he said. "We've confirmed where he was. End of story."

"Nate was with him at this appointment?" I asked.

Sheriff Terry nodded.

"Is that who verified where he was?" Just my amateur opinion, but I didn't think your son saying you weren't in town counted as an airtight alibi.

"No," the sheriff said evenly. "An independent source."

The doctor's office must have been able to confirm that they'd seen Stanley and it must have been an overnight trip. My guess was University of Iowa Hospitals or Mayo Clinic. One of those two meant Stanley had a serious health issue. I was surprised no one had known, but I could see Mr. Stanley B. Marchant wanting to keep his medical problems to himself.

"So where does that leave us?" I asked. "Alma's note says 'Marchant' but Stanley's whereabouts checked out, Nate was with his dad, and Nick wasn't even in town yet."

"Exactly." The sheriff rolled his shoulders and reached a hand up to rub his neck. "Has to be a stop at the bank."

"But it doesn't say "Marchants" like I'd write if I made a note to myself about going to the bank," I argued.

"Agreed." He rubbed his eyes. "But some of those notes are pretty cryptic.

He had a point. I'd just been so sure that the notebook held the key. I slumped onto a stool.

The sheriff picked the notebook up from the counter and placed it in a paper bag he'd also produced from his pockets. "I'll take this with me."

We had to be missing something. Something important. I wasn't giving up on the book. If there wasn't a clue in the notebook, why had Alma hidden it?

If the notation was a simple reminder to stop at the bank, the notebook would have been in Alma's purse where Greer said she always kept it.

I didn't know what the Marchant family had to do with Alma's death, but I knew there had to be some reason Alma had made that note.

Chapter Thirteen

The next afternoon, I arrived at the Good Life a bit early and stopped in to say hello to Greer. I explained about Cheri needing to get everything packed and moved before the end of the month.

"Well, aren't you sweet to offer to help." Greer finished up her lunch dishes while we talked. She was getting ready to go to the grocery store via the retirement center's van.

"I could have picked up some things for you." I felt bad I hadn't thought to offer. It'd been a big adjustment for her to have to schedule transportation when she had been used to counting on Alma for shopping and other errands.

"Thanks, Sugar, I appreciate the offer, but I don't always know what I want to get." She shoved a handful of coupons in her purse and set it by the door. "I'm not organized like Alma was and like you are."

Though I appreciated the compliment, I sure didn't feel organized lately. Between the Crack of Dawn Breakfast Club recipes that were all over the place and my forays into weed control, my confidence level was on the low side.

I filled her in on everything that had happened the past few days, including me finding Alma's notebook in the city park and turning it over to the sheriff's department.

"After Bunny told you about Alma and Stanley having words on the day of Alma's services, I talked to a few people who know him better than I do." Greer reached in her pantry and pulled out an assortment of cloth shopping bags.

"Did they have any ideas on what the two might have disagreed about?" I asked. "Cheri said they'd always been friendly as far as she knew."

"No one had heard of a fuss between them, but several people mentioned Stanley hadn't been himself lately." She folded the shopping bags and put them beside her purse. "Not that Mr. Stanley B. is a ray of sunshine on a good day, but I guess he's been extra cranky."

Stanley not being himself would fit with him having some sort of health problem like the sheriff had mentioned. Or rather like I had guessed and the sheriff didn't deny. I hadn't mentioned the medical appointment to Greer, just that Stanley had an alibi.

"Nate was asking around the other day at the breakfast if anyone could recommend someone to do yard work." Greer picked up her cell phone and dropped it into the outside pocket of her purse. "He didn't say why, but Freda Watson told me the reason he was looking for someone was because Stanley was rude to the kid that had been mowing their yard and the boy quit." She glanced at her watch.

I glanced at mine, too. "I won't keep you." It was time for me to get to Alma's place anyway. "But thanks for the info. I'll pass it on to Sheriff Terry. It sounds like Stanley may have something going on."

"Sounds like Stanley needs to take a chill pill." Greer picked up her purse and her shopping bags. "I think it's worth checking out. I mean, who knows what's going on with him." She gave a sigh. "Wait while I lock up and I'll walk with you."

I walked with Greer to where the Good Life van was parked near the community center. Several other ladies had assembled on the curb and the driver was helping those who needed assistance to climb in. After giving Greer a hug and making her promise she'd call me if she needed groceries or had errands in the future, I walked the short distance to Alma's.

Tapping on the front door, I found Cheri already hard at work. Boxes that had been previously packed were stacked by the door. She had made a lot of progress, but she was right, she had a long way to go if she was to clear the place by the end of the month.

She had some empty boxes ready to go and I started with the large curio cabinet. It had quite a few breakables and those items would need to be well wrapped. I grabbed some of the packing paper and began working my way through the shelves.

We made short work of it, sealed that box, and labeled it. Next, we moved to the bookcase beside it.

"Oh my stars, is that Dustin with your mom?" I picked up a framed photo of a much younger Alma holding a toddler. The boy's hair wasn't as dark as Dustin's was today but I suspected black dye had created the current look. His deep blue eyes gazed up at his grandma and she smiled down at him. "What a cute kid!"

"He was." Cheri leaned in to take a look. "They had a special bond from the beginning."

"I'm so sorry for what you and he have been through with your mom's death and then the investigation." I carefully wrapped the picture in packing paper and placed it in one of the boxes.

There was silence and I glanced over at Cheri.

She had paused, another framed photo cradled in her hands, head turned away. I couldn't see her face but knew from the set of her shoulders, she was trying to maintain control.

She turned to me, her eyes full. "I don't think I can do this."

"Sweetie. I'm so sorry." I gave her arm a squeeze.

She opened her mouth, but no words came out.

I hadn't thought. Hadn't intended to make things harder.

"Let's sit down a minute." I lifted the photo she was holding from her hand. "Can I get you a water? Make some tea? Let's take a breather."

"A water would be nice," she finally got out, and dropped to the edge of the couch. "There's some in the refrigerator."

I went to the kitchen, filled a glass with water, and took it to her. She sat with head in hands.

"Cheri?"

"Sorry, I'm overwhelmed by this." She raised her face and looked around the room. "And everything…" Her voice trailed off.

"Don't apologize. This is hard. You raised Dustin as a single mom. Your mom must have played a big part as he was growing up."

"She did." Cheri nodded, and a single tear leaked from the side of one eye and ran down her pale cheek.

I sat beside her on the couch. "I lost my father when I was young. Like Dustin I didn't get a chance to know my dad as an adult. I often wish I could have."

She took a swig of water, took a deep breath, and then let it out in a whoosh.

"My former husband was not Dusty's father."

"I didn't realize that. I assume that Dusty knows."

"No, he doesn't." Cheri shook her head from side to side. "My mom was the only other real family Dusty had besides me."

"Do you know what happened to Dusty's biological father?" I was thinking about the research I'd been considering regarding my own father's family. "Even if he's not interested, Dustin's dad, I mean, there could be grandparents or cousins."

Eventually I stopped talking long enough to notice the silence.

"I know where Dustin's father is." She lifted her head and made eye contact for the first time since the conversation had started.

"Where?" If that were the case, why hadn't she tapped Deadbeat Dad to help her when Dustin had been in trouble?

"He's..." She closed her eyes and then opened them. "Right here in St. Ignatius.

I went through all the possibilities in a matter of seconds, but hadn't come to a conclusion when she dropped the bomb.

"Nick Marchant is Dusty's father."

Holy Smoley! What?

In all the possibilities I'd come up with, none had included Nick Marchant. And yet, now that I knew it, there was some part of me that connected dots that had been unrelated before.

Some reference Dixie had made to all the hearts Nick had broken in high school.

Cheri's reaction when she'd come into the shop and Nick had been there.

Those eyes.

Dustin looked nothing like the Marchant brothers. Except those deep blue eyes.

"Do the Marchants know?" I asked and then regretted the question the minute it was out of my mouth.

"They do not. And they will not." Cheri straightened her spine and looked me in the eye. "My son and I want nothing to do with them."

"Did your mom know?" I asked.

Cheri nodded. "She'd always known."

Wow. Just wow. I couldn't believe all this time and no one but Cheri and her mom had known.

"I'm not sure why I told you." Cheri gave a deep sigh. "But, Sugar, I need your promise you will not take that information to the sheriff."

"I won't tell him," I agreed. "But I think you should."

I didn't get a chance to continue because we were interrupted by a couple of the ladies who stopped by. I let Cheri continue packing while I attempted to move them along. What the poor woman did not need after sharing that revelation was the strain of having to carry on a conversation with two well-meaning but snoopy seniors.

I stepped outside to talk to them, blocking their ability to come inside. We chatted about the weather, we discussed the dearth of anything good on television, we talked about the best shoe inserts for arch support.

Eventually, I successfully sent them off in the direction of silver fox William Harold, whom I'd spotted sitting on one of the wrought-iron benches outside the community center.

Sorry William. Or Harold. Or whatever your name is.

Throwing a mental apology in his direction, I headed back into Alma's place, where Cheri had finished the rest of the bookcase. I apologized for leaving her alone for so long.

"No problem." She rubbed her temples. "Saving me from having to pretend everything is okay was help enough."

"What would you like to tackle next?" I asked. "Dixie should be here in about an hour."

"I truly appreciate your help, Sugar, but I'm going to have to call it a day." Cheri pinched the bridge of her nose. "I've developed a terrible headache and my prescription is at home."

"No problem at all." No surprise the poor woman had a headache. "The call is entirely yours."

"I'd set aside some cookbooks for you and Dixie." She pointed at a stack on the floor. "If you want them that is. I thought they might be something you two would be interested in with you being in the cookbook business."

"Thank you so much, Cheri, Dixie will be thrilled." And she would be. "As you've probably figured out, Dixie is the only cook in this venture, but she will love them."

"Great, I'm glad they'll have a use." Cheri picked up her purse. "I'll help you carry them to your car, and then I'm going to go home and take my headache meds before this gets any worse."

We carried the cookbooks to the Jeep and set them in the back. I offered to drive Cheri home but she assured me she was okay to drive.

It worried me that she had no one checking in on her. I knew she had Dustin at home, but he was still very much a kid. And besides, he'd been through just as much as she had.

"You let us know if you need anything," I told her. "Anything at all."

"I will." She waved as she drove off.

I called Dixie's cell to tell her not to come to Alma's after Moto's appointment, and told her I'd meet her at the shop. I didn't share what Cheri had told me. That news flash needed to be delivered in person.

* * * *

When I arrived at the office, Nick Marchant was just inside the front door talking to Dixie.

Shoot. From what I could overhear it seemed like a civil conversation, but I needed him to move on so I could talk to Dixie.

I carried the first stack of cookbooks to the counter and set them down.

"Do you need help?" Dixie asked looking up.

"No, I'm fine. I've just got a few more." I headed back out to my car.

When I returned, neither had moved. I slid the second, smaller stack on the counter next to the first one.

"You are going to love some of these." I straightened the pile. "I don't think anyone realized how many cookbooks Alma had."

"Those are from Alma Stoller's place?" Nick asked glancing at the collection.

"They are." I turned to look at him, remembering how he'd reacted when I'd talked about Alma the day we learned she'd been run over. Now I was viewing his reaction with a different lens. "Cheri offered to let us have them."

"How's she doing with getting everything sorted out?" Dixie asked. "You said she doesn't need us this afternoon."

"Pretty well, I guess." I gave her a look meant to telegraph that she needed to get Nick to leave. I looked at him, looked at her, and jerked my head in the direction of the door.

It wasn't working. Dixie looked at me like I'd lost my mind.

"That'll take her a while with all the junk her mom had," Nick commented.

"You've got that right." I zeroed in on his face. Those dark blue eyes. Dustin's were just the same. How could I have missed it? How could everyone have missed it?

"I wonder what she plans to do with all the knickknacks and that statue thing," I added.

"The gnome?" Nick asked. "He's creepy."

Oh, man. Nick had been to Alma's. He had lied.

"Where do you want these?" I asked Dixie, reaching for the cookbooks. "On the lower shelves or the upper shelves?"

Maybe I could get Nick to say more. No telling what else he'd lied about.

"Just leave them," she replied. "I'd like to go through them as I shelve them."

"You got it." I looked through the books. I hadn't had much of a chance to look at them when Cheri and I loaded them. There was a quite variety of cookbooks. Some older ones that Alma may have had for a while. Several tea room cookbooks. Two that were specific to bed and breakfasts. My mouth watered just skimming through those pages. I set those aside to look at, thinking they might give me some ideas for the ABBA Iowa Cookbook.

"I'd better get going or Nate will be looking for me." Nick finally moved toward the door.

No wait, I have more questions. I'd gone from wishing he'd move along to wanting to keep him talking.

"Nate was a stick-in-the-mud as a kid and he's even worse now. The guy simply does not know how to have fun."

"That seems a little harsh." Dixie frowned. "Maybe his fun is simply different than yours."

"See, that's your trouble, Spicy. Always defending people who don't even care. Such a lover of underdogs. Too bad you can't focus on a winner."

"You'd better go while we're still on speaking terms, Nick." Dixie cheeks suddenly tinted with color. "Because right now you're skating on thin ice."

"Still so easy to get under your skin, Spicy." Nick grinned and reached over to touch the end of Dixie's nose.

"Nick." Her voice held a warning tone. "You need to go. Now."

Just then Sheriff Terry walked through the door. From the grim set of his jaw, he was not a happy camper.

It doesn't say much about my relationship with our county sheriff that my first thought was to wonder what I might have done now to irritate him.

But as it turned out he wasn't upset with me this time. His gaze went directly to Nick.

"Marchant, you need to move your car." His tone of voice had no "please" in it.

The sheriff pointed to the door and jerked a thumb toward the street. "You've got people blocked in."

"Or what?" Nick peered outside where a small crowd had collected.

I glanced outside. He had two cars blocked so they couldn't get out.

"Don't mess with me, Nick." The sheriff gave him a shove toward the door.

"Do what you have to do, Meter Maid," Nick sneered.

That was it. Terry grabbed him by the scruff of his designer shirt and marched him outside to the Jag.

Dixie and I watched through the window. I don't know what words were exchanged, but Nick squealed off in the Jag. The crowd on the sidewalk parted like the Red Sea, giving Terry a wide berth as he stomped to his Jameson County Sheriff's Department car.

The sheriff drove away with much more control than Nick had, but I'd be willing to bet on the inside he was squealing his tires too. Lucky for Nick Marchant, Sheriff Terry had more discipline than he did.

Dixie and I looked at each other.

"Wow," we said in unison.

"What was Nick doing here?" I asked. "What did he want?"

"He never got a chance to say." Dixie folded her arms. "He'd just come in. Maybe just to harass me. I was working in the back and heard the door."

"Did you catch what he said about Alma's gnome?"

"Alma's gnome?" She frowned. "I'm not following."

"When I mentioned Alma's place and about how much stuff Cheri had to sort."

"And?" she prompted.

"I forgot you weren't there, but when we, the Good Life ladies and I, initially searched for Alma at her place there was this crazy gnome. In fact, now that I think about it, I almost smacked the sheriff in the head with the gnome."

"I'm not sure what that has to do with Nick." Dixie picked up one of the cookbooks and flipped it open.

"When I mentioned it just now, all I said was "that statue," leaving it vague, and right away he mentioned the gnome," I explained. "Don't you see? He lied about having not seen Alma since he'd been back."

"Why would he do that?" Dixie picked up another cookbook and opened it.

"Why indeed."

I couldn't contain myself any longer. We could come back to the significance of the gnome later. I had bigger news.

"Never mind, I have something else to tell you. Wait until you hear this." I walked over and flipped the lock on the door.

Dixie tilted her head and gave me a questioning look.

"We do not need Disco foraging for food, or Tina raving about Rafe. They can come back later."

I took the cookbook she held from her and then, taking her arm, I pointed Dixie toward the kitchen.

"I don't know what you've been baking today, but it smells incredible." I inhaled. "I'm hoping it's something with a tons of sugar, because we're going to need massive amounts of sugar to fortify us for this conversation."

We walked back to the kitchen area. Once there, Dixie opened one of the lower cupboards and pulled out a cake pan.

I looked at her. "You've been holding out on me."

"Made it this morning. I don't know if it's better than Robert Redford or not, but I wasn't about to share it with Nick Marchant." She reached in a drawer, pulled out a knife, and handed it to me. "You can do the honors."

"Sweet." I grinned at her. I sliced two pieces and transferred them onto the plates Dixie slid toward me.

I waited until she'd swallowed her first bite, not completely trusting my first aid training if she accidentally inhaled Better Than Robert Redford cake.

Then I dropped my bombshell.

"Nick Marchant is Dustin Wheeler's father."

"What?!" Dixie screeched loud enough I was surprised Lark from next door didn't come running to our aid.

"Exactly," I agreed.

Dixie'd had the reaction I'd would've had, wanted to have. But couldn't because I was trying to maintain some composure in front of Cheri.

"Did you have any idea about Cheri and Nick?" I asked. "Did they date in high school?"

"No." Dixie blew out a breath. "I don't think so. I don't remember. She dated Nate for a while, I think, but not Nick."

She reached out her fork and took another bite of cake, and then stood looking off into space. I waved a hand in front of her face.

"Sorry. I'm in shock. I can't believe no one knew."

"According to Cheri, only her mom knew."

Dixie shoved a lock of her hair behind one ear and licked the frosting off her fork. "Nick went to college and then moved to New York. Since Cheri moved away right after high school and got married, I don't think anyone would have connected the dots."

I helped myself to a forkful of cake while I let her process. "I don't understand why Cheri kept silent all this time about who Dustin's father really was. It seems like she could have used some help over the years."

"I guess. But by the time she moved back to St. Ignatius, all of that was ancient history."

"I suppose you're right."

"She has to tell Terry." Dixie dipped her fork into the cake pan, this time going directly for the frosting.

"I agree." I nodded. "She has to."

The cake was rich and pulling weeds was not going to work off this much sugar. I didn't know where Dixie had dug up the recipe, but I'd have to let Greer know we tried it.

"If Alma knew and told Nick, I can't imagine that conversation went well," Dixie mused.

"Nor if she told Stanley," I said, thinking about the idea of him not knowing he had a grandson.

"Do you think she told Stanley?" Dixie paused with a forkful of frosting halfway to her mouth.

"I think she wanted to take care of her grandson and his talent," I said. "And she would have done whatever she needed to do in order to do that."

"I still can't believe it." Dixie looked at me. "Cheri kept this secret all this time."

I had a sudden thought. "Maybe that's what Alma and Stanley had words about. Maybe Stanley was mad that Alma had known all along and hadn't told him."

Dixie's brows drew together in a frown. "Nick would not make a good father."

"That's the understatement of the year." I walked around the kitchen, the fork still in my hand, in case I needed more cake. "I feel like we're still missing something."

Dixie watched me, her face serious. "How will we convince Cheri to tell Sheriff Terry?"

"It's not going to be easy." I passed the counter and scooped up another bite of cake as I went by. "Maybe we can bribe her with this."

"I'm serious, Sugar."

"I know." I stopped, the bite of cake stuck in my throat, and looked at her. "Cheri was adamant she wants nothing to do with the Marchants. But what if this, a secret she's kept all this time, is the key to her mother's death?"

Chapter Fourteen

We cleaned up and then both headed out on our own errands. I was sort of glad to spend the rest of the day out of the shop. I felt the weight of the information Cheri had shared and not being able to help in any way.

After a busy day, I'd spent a good part of my evening digging in my backyard. Wearing some gardening gloves I'd found in the garage, I'd used the knife Mrs. Pickett had given me and worked my way through a small section.

But as I worked my mind kept returning to Cheri Wheeler and the secret she'd kept for so many years. Why she'd chosen me, who had no history with any of the people involved, was beyond me. But maybe that was exactly why. Maybe the fact that I had no ties to any of them made it easier.

It was also possible I just happened to be the one who was there when she couldn't take it any longer and her resolve cracked wide open.

I dug at the roots of the thistles and the dandelions and filled a box with them. The thistles were mean and I was glad for the gloves. I still wasn't completely clear on why I needed to send Creeping Charlie packing. He was green and not pokey like the thistles, and didn't seem like such a bad weed. But Mrs. Pickett had been unyielding that if you gave him an inch, he'd take a mile, so I worked my best to dig up the roots as she'd recommended.

Exhausted from my time crawling around in my yard, once I cleaned up I was too tired to pick up where I'd left off with Daddy's *A Fictional Memoir*. When I got back to it I wanted to be able to savor it.

Dragging my box of weeds back to the garage, I called it a day. I showered and crawled into bed, falling asleep almost immediately. But it was a fitful sleep. I dreamed about being chased by large green knife-brandishing aliens who kept trying to steal food from me. It didn't take an expensive shrink to tell me what was going on with that. The weeds, Mrs. Pickett, the investigation, the secrets.

Of course, it also could have been coming down off that sugar-buzz from the Better Than Robert Redford cake.

Whatever the cause, my lack of sleep made it hard to get up and get moving the next morning. I hit snooze more than once.

"Good morning, Ernest." I greeted my feline stalker, who swished his fluffy tail and walked away, appalled that his dish had been sitting completely empty while I languished in bed.

I filled his dish and started my coffee without attempting further conversation. Somehow I knew he wouldn't be impressed with my crazy bad dreams. Maybe it was the head-turned-away, talk-to-the-paw stance that clued me in.

A quick toast and coffee later, I dressed for the day and headed out. Taking my to-go mug with me, I turned Big Blue toward downtown. A quick peek showed no Mrs. Pickett; I had hoped the little crotchety lady was up early and had checked out my handiwork in the backyard.

Crazy, I know, to want praise from someone who was never going to be a fan, but there you have it.

I arrived before Dixie and lined up my to-do list for the day.

My cell rang just as Dixie walked in the back door. Her dog, Moto, was with her this morning, and I reached in my desk for some dog treats I kept stashed in a drawer, as I answered my phone.

"Sugar, honey, I need a favor." Greer sounded out of breath. I prayed for no further drama at the Good Life.

"What do you need, hon?" Moto took the treat from my hand and then proceeded to show his appreciation with slobbery doggie licks. I looked up at Dixie, who just smiled at my dilemma.

"What a sucker you are," she said as she crossed the office to the bathroom and came out with a handful of paper towels.

I mouthed "thanks" and attempted a one-handed wipe of the slobber.

Greer continued, "I have my monthly hair appointment at Tressa's Tresses and the Good Life van is out of service. If I don't make this appointment I'll have to reschedule."

"Do you need a ride?" I asked.

"Yes, if it's not too much trouble. The last time I had to reschedule it took three weeks before I could get in. If I have to wait that long again, I'll be looking like Sasquatch."

I didn't think Greer would ever look like a big hairy woodland creature, but I totally got the not-wanting-to-miss-an-appointment dilemma. I was still making the drive to Des Moines every six weeks to Anna, my favorite Salon W stylist, and would not want to have to reschedule.

"It's no trouble at all."

I finally had my hand cleaned up and patted Moto's head. "What time is your appointment?"

"It's at ten o'clock."

"I'll pick you up." I told her. "Is fifteen minutes beforehand enough time?"

"Yes, it is. Thank you, Sugar, you're a lifesaver."

"See you at about nine forty-five, then." We said good-bye and I pressed the button to disconnect the call.

"Something from the attic? Another missing senior? Some other emergency at the senior center?" Dixie raised a brow.

"No, she needs a ride to her hair appointment." I moved some papers from the edge of my desk. Moto was attempting to get on my lap and my stacks of papers were about to become a victim of his rambunctiousness. "If she can't make today's appointment, she'll have to reschedule."

Dixie smiled. "I have to agree that *is* an emergency."

"You're right it is." I finished up a couple of things, made a call to Liz about the schedule for the Crack of Dawn cookbook, and checked the time. Just enough time to pick up Greer and get her to Tressa's.

* * * *

The salon was busy. There were three chrome-and-leopard-print chairs in the center area and all three were occupied. Tressa was just finishing up with a lady I recognized from the antique shop, though how Tressa worked so quickly with her long glitter-tipped nails was beyond me.

Greer's stylist, Maxine, had the chair in the middle. And in the third spot, Ashley, the youngest of the stylists, placed strips of foil with uncanny accuracy between layers of long dark hair, giving the young woman she was working on the look of a space alien.

Though much more modern, Tressa's salon reminded me in so many ways of the beauty shop my mother used to frequent in her hometown of Searcy, Georgia. I couldn't recall the name of the salon but the smells and sounds were the same. The swish of the water, the blare of the blow dryers, and the chatter of the ladies. I smiled, thinking of how some things change and still stay the same. Though Mama probably didn't go there anymore. She undoubtedly had transitioned to the latest "It" spot in downtown Atlanta.

"I'll be with you in just a few minutes, Greer," Maxine called from the center chair, where she was teasing the life out of a head of blue-toned hair.

"You thinking of a blue-look?" I whispered to Greer.

"Not on your life." She grinned. "Though I did see a commercial where two ladies get purple hair and go skinny-dippin' and it looked like fun."

I laughed. "You let me know if you ladies decide to go that route, and I'll be ready with bail money."

"I'm afraid us old ladies skinny dippin' would give Sheriff Terry a heart attack." Greer giggled at the thought.

"Ready for you," Maxine called, motioning Greer to her chair.

I turned to go, but Maxine's blue-haired customer stopped me.

"Wait right here." She held up a finger. "I've got something for you." And then she was gone.

I looked around to ask who the woman was, but everyone in the place was busy. I wasn't in a big rush. I guessed I had time to wait.

I sank into a plush cheetah-print chair in the waiting area just inside the door.

There was a stack of magazines with teasers to articles like "Healthy Recipes for the Holidays" (it wasn't clear which holiday), "How to Travel Safely with Your Pet" (pretty sure Ernest wasn't into travel), and "Overhaul Your Diet and Your Life" (I was pretty happy with my life, but my diet probably could use some help).

There were also some loose pages from the last edition of the *St. Ignatius Journal*. I picked up one of the sections of newsprint. The weekly newspaper was one of the many things I loved about my adopted hometown. I checked the headlines, which announced a hearing about some zoning issue. Below the fold was an article on the upcoming city council meeting, and another about the baseball team, which had been having a successful summer of tournaments. The Blotter on the next page listed calls to the Sheriff's Department. I skimmed those. In the past week there were multiple traffic stops, a call because of cows blocking a road, a couple of fender benders, one loud party, and a few reports of vandalism.

No elders skinny-dipping in the list. For now.

I flipped to the editorial page, which often was packed with as much drama and angst as a soap opera. There was an op-ed piece about wind turbines. I'll spare you the obvious tilting at windmills references, but suffice to say both pros and cons were long-winded. No anonymous op-eds were allowed, so I hoped the Ms. Pro and Mr. Con, who so strongly disagreed, were more civil when they passed each other on the street.

"Oh my gosh, Sugar." Tressa suddenly swooped in with her usual bear hug and then plopped down into the chair next to me. She must have finished the antique store lady while I was knee deep in local news.

"Your hair is just so classic." Tressa reached over with sparkly-tipped fingers and fluffed the top. "I know you have a girl in Des Moines who does it, but if you ever decide you're ready for a change you just let me know."

"Uhm, thanks." I reached up to touch my feathery bob. I thought "classic" was meant as a compliment.

"Jeepers, I am so tired!" She slumped back in the chair and pushed an errant lock of vibrant red hair off her forehead. "I've been going since seven o'clock. I had an early appointment with Gretchen. She insisted on being worked in."

I hadn't noticed it when she'd been working on the lady, but seeing Tressa up close it looked like she either was fighting a bad cold or she'd been crying. Plenty of eye makeup had been utilized in an effort to cover it up, but the signs were there.

I set the paper aside and touched her arm. "Are you okay?"

"I don't know what you're talking about." She straightened up, smile pasted in place, head held high. "I'm fine!"

"Are you sure?" I held her gaze.

Suddenly all of the bravado went out of her and she collapsed back into the plush of the chair, covering her face with her hands.

I waited.

She dropped her hands from her face. "You're right. I am not okay." She blew out a breath and touched her fingers to the corners of her red-rimmed eyes.

"What's wrong?"

"Man trouble," she whispered. "You see, a little while back I started hanging out with Nick Marchant."

Newsflash, Tressa. Everyone in town knows about you and Nick

"But you're married, right?" I tried to keep my tone nonjudgmental, but seriously she *was* married and they hadn't exactly been discreet.

"Bud and me had already been having trouble and when Nick showed up back in town and was so nice to me…" Tressa's voice thinned and I feared tears were next.

She gulped some air and continued. "We'd always been close, Nick and I. And when he got back, he came to see me before he even went to see his father and his brother."

"He did?" That tidbit was a game-changer. "You two were close?" I prompted.

"In high school, we were like this." She held up two crossed sparkly-tipped fingers.

"I thought he dated Dixie." I watched her face. "And Cheri Stoller," I added.

"Gosh, no." She waved a hand dismissively. "Dixie was just to break up her and Terry. And Cheri was to break up her and his brother. He was never serious about either of them. It was all about the competition."

"But then he left and you married Bud." Tressa was such a sweetheart. How could she not see what an awful comment it was on Nick's character that he'd done something like that?

"Nick was off to college and I was off to beauty school. We decided to see other people and it became clear he was never coming back to St. Ignatius." Her eyes focused on a point in the distance. "But then when he did come back after all these years, the spark was still there and I thought…" Her voice trailed off.

"Things are not working out like you thought?" I never could understand the fascination with bad boys, but maybe it's just me.

"I don't know what I was thinking. He could never stick with anyone for any length of time before. Why did I think he would now?"

"You think he's seeing someone else." I've also never understood the faulty rationale when someone who cheats on their spouse is shocked when someone turns around and cheats on them. But I kept my highly opinionated views to myself.

She suddenly focused and looked around at the busy shop. "I have to get back to work! Thanks for listening, Sugar. I'm sure it will all work out." The pasted-on smile was back and just as quickly as she'd swooped in, Tressa was back at her station, chatting up her next client.

I stood and almost ran into the blue-haired woman who had returned.

"Thanks for waiting." She handed me a typed recipe card. "Lark said you needed clarification on my recipe and I've been meaning to get this to you and I kept forgetting. I hope it's not too late."

"We're still putting everything together, Mrs. Travers." I took the card. "I'm sure this will help."

I let Greer know she could either call me or just walk down to Sugar and Spice when she was done. Then I headed back to the shop.

* * * *

Dixie was at the counter with a vintage cookbook propped open. She looked up as I entered.

"Max was just here. He stopped in with some framing ideas." She waved a hand at the wall. "I told him you were the one with the classy taste in this partnership and so I was leaving all those decisions up to you."

"Sorry I missed him." I was, too. Maybe if we ran into each other more often the weirdness would pass.

"I told him you were at Tressa's and would be back in a few minutes, but he couldn't wait. Something he was doing for the Quilt Guild. I think maybe photos for their catalogue."

"I got held up because Mrs. Travers asked me to wait while she ran to get this typed version of her recipe to give us." I laid the card on the counter by Dixie's reading material.

She picked it up and looked at it. "I think we already have this one, don't we?"

"We do but it was the one where we couldn't read the handwriting," I said. "I think this will help."

That's great." She looked me over. "I see you escaped from Tressa's without being dyed or sheared."

"I did. Still my old self." I touched my hair where Tressa had fluffed it. "It looked like Tressa had been crying."

I gave Dixie the Cliff Notes version of Tressa's man trouble.

"She's right, Nick only dated me to get back at Terry. He couldn't stand that although Terry had none of the Marchant family advantages, he managed to be a standout." She bit her lip. "I was so stupid I couldn't see it at the time."

"We were all stupid in high school." I gave her a hug. "The important piece of information she shared is that Nick came to see her before he even went to see his brother and father. That means he *was* in town when Alma was killed."

Nick is a jerk," Dixie said, "but I can't imagine him as a killer."

No one likes to imagine anyone we know is a cold-blooded killer. But the fact remained that Alma's death was not accidental. Nor was it a random killing. Everything so far pointed to that it had to be someone who knew her. Someone we all knew.

"If he was involved in Alma's death, even if it was accidental, he didn't give aid. He didn't come forward." I pointed out. "And now with what we know about him being Dustin's father…"

Greer walked in while we were talking and we cut short our discussion. Greer was one sharp cookie and I didn't want to run the risk of accidently breaching Cheri's confidence. The secret she'd kept all these years was her secret to keep or share.

After I dropped off Greer at her place, I walked over to Alma's, hoping Cheri might be there working and that we could talk.

She wasn't there and the place was locked up tight. Walking back to my car, I tried her cell but had to leave a message.

I still held out hope that Cheri could be convinced to, at the very least, share her story with the sheriff. He had to have all the information, every single piece, if he was to figure out who killed her mother.

Chapter Fifteen

When I arrived at the shop the next morning, Dixie already had coffee brewing. I started to make a comment about her coming over to the dark side, but something in her face stopped me.

"What's up?" I asked, trepidation creeping up my spine. It was clear something was wrong.

"Nick Marchant was found in the city park this morning"—she stopped and took in a gulp of air—"dead."

"What?" My question echoed in the quiet. "How?"

"Shot." She covered her face with her hands and then rubbed her temples.

"Someone shot him?" I tried to focus.

Dixie ran a hand through her hair. It looked as if she'd been doing that for a while. "They think he may have shot himself."

I thought about that for several minutes.

"Who found him?" I didn't know why that mattered, but I needed details as I tried to make sense of the news.

"Grace Nelson. She was out early this morning walking her dog."

"That must have been a shock." I reached over and put my hand over Dixie's and left it there for a few minutes. "Are you okay?"

"I'm fine," she said with a gulp that told me she really wasn't.

"I've been thinking. Maybe you were on to something with what you'd been saying about Nick. About him being back in town earlier, and lying about being at Alma's place. What if he was the one who killed Alma?"

"You think that might be the reason for his suicide?" It was true, he had lied. But we didn't know why he'd lied.

"There wasn't a note, but I do think it's possible."

"I don't know..." Nick Marchant didn't seem to me like someone who felt remorseful. Look at how he'd used Tressa and then moved on to someone else. To me Nick seemed—entitled.

"How do you know there wasn't a note?" It had suddenly occurred to me that Dixie knew an awful lot about the situation. "News travels fast, I guess."

"Terry called me to let me know about Nick."

The coffee had finished, she poured some, and handed me the cup.

"That was thoughtful of him." He hadn't wanted her to hear it from everyone from the surrounding shops, like we'd heard about Alma. As I said before, our Sheriff Terry is a stand-up guy.

She looked up at me. "It was."

"Did you tell him about the inconsistencies in Nick's story? About when he arrived in town?"

"I didn't go into great detail but I did tell him." She nodded. "He said he'd talk with Tressa."

"Oh, my gosh. Tressa." I set down my cup. Outside of Nick's father and brother, she was probably the person who would take this news the hardest. "I hope he's careful when he tells her."

"I'm sure he will be." Dixie held the heels of both hands against her forehead. "It seems so surreal. Nick was here in the shop yesterday. He seemed like himself."

"If Nick did run over Alma, whether on purpose or accidentally, I guess we'll never know now." I thought about the possibilities. Would there be any way to ever know exactly what had happened between Nick and Alma?

I also thought about Cheri and hoped someone had told her. Though she'd been clear she didn't want anything from Dustin's biological father, and didn't ever intend to tell him, this news meant there would never be a father-son meeting.

"What about Cheri?" I asked.

"I didn't tell Terry anything about Cheri." Dixie looked at me. "I was so shocked by the news. Do you think I should have?"

"I think we should make sure she knows." I stood. "And maybe we can encourage her to call."

I fished my cell phone from my bag and quickly tried her cell number but again she didn't pick up.

She probably knew. Though there was no official word yet about Nick Marchant's death, I was sure everyone in town had heard the news. That St. Ignatius grapevine again.

Unlike Alma's death, which had created a steady stream of people hanging out at the shop, the news about Nick seemed to have affected the town differently. News was discussed in whispered groups or not at all.

We hadn't seen anyone all day. Not even Disco.

Agreeing that it was best to keep busy, Dixie and I decided to lay out our photo shoot plans and so we took some blank paper out front and began jotting down our ideas.

Midmorning, the bell dinged and we both looked up.

A very official-looking guy stepped through the doorway. Though not in uniform, his posture and his expression said law enforcement of some kind.

"Gene Minor, DCI." He handed over a business card.

I'd have liked to have seen a badge but maybe no one did that anymore.

"Sugar Calloway," I replied. "And this is my business partner, Dixie Spicer."

He nodded as if he'd already known who we were.

"I need to ask you some questions about a fight between Nick Marchant and Terrance Griffin you may have witnessed two days ago." He looked from Dixie to me, his face serious.

"No 'may' about it," I responded. "We definitely witnessed it. Why do you ask?"

He ignored my question. "Can you tell me what the fight was about?" He crossed beefy arms across his chest.

"Parking," Dixie answered. "Nick had parked his car blocking in a couple of cars."

"Nick was in our shop at the time, but we didn't know about the problem until Terry arrived," I offered.

"The people who were blocked in must have called the Jameson County Sheriff's Office," Dixie added. "I guess everyone was busy or out, so Terry came and told Nick to move his car."

Mr. Gene Minor from the DCI wasn't writing any of this down so I had to assume that he already knew the story.

"Then what happened?" he asked.

"They exchanged words." I couldn't remember exactly what was said.

"Nick said something like, 'What are you going to do, Meter Maid?'" Dixie added.

Even Mr. DCI couldn't help but wince at that. "I understand that Sheriff Griffin may have gotten physical with Mr. Marchant at that point."

"He grabbed Nick by the scruff of his shirt collar and walked him to his car."

"Could you hear what was said next?" He wanted to know.

"No, others were probably closer," I answered. "We didn't go outside."

"Then Mr. Marchant moved his car?"

"Right." Dixie nodded.

"More like peeled out," I added. "It's lucky no one was in the street or they would've been mowed down." I mentally winced as soon as I said it. The comparison to what had actually happened to Alma was too strong.

"Could he have said something like, 'You're a dead man?'"

"Like I said, we didn't go outside."

Mr. DCI thanked us and left.

Once he was out the door, I looked at Dixie. "Why do you think the DCI is investigating Nick's death?"

She looked as sick as I felt. "I don't know. Whether he shot himself or something else happened, I'd think the County Sheriff's department would look into it. Even if Terry and Nick had words."

The day was endless.

We'd finished our notes on the cookbook photos before lunch and I was about to suggest we call it day and go home, when the chime out front dinged again.

My money was on it being Disco. We hadn't seen him at all and were about due for a visit for some bogus reason so he could see if there were any treats to be had.

It wasn't Disco.

It was Cheri Wheeler.

I could tell from her face that she knew about Nick. And I couldn't for the life of me think what to say to her. There didn't seem to be anything appropriate for this crazy, mixed-up situation.

"Are you all right?" I asked, finally.

"I don't know what I am," she admitted.

"Come and sit down." Dixie scooted a stool forward. "Coffee, tea, water? Something else?"

"Nothing, thanks," Cheri said quietly. "I need to ask you about what I'm hearing."

"We don't know very much." I sat down across from her.

"Still, more than I do, I'll bet." She gave a weak smile.

"We'll share what we know." Dixie also sat.

"What I'm hearing around town is that Nick Marchant may have committed suicide…" Cheri's voice disappeared into a whisper.

"Possible," Dixie answered.

"I see." She sat for a few minutes looking down her hands limp in her lap.

Finally looking up, she spoke. "After talking with you, Sugar," she glanced up at me, "I knew I needed to tell Sheriff Terry what I'd told you. As much as I didn't want to, I knew I had to. If they were to get to the bottom of things with my mom's death, he had to know."

I nodded. That's what Dixie and I had talked about too.

Cheri's information could have led the Sheriff to Nick, and could have explained the notation in Alma's notebook. At the very least it was a part of finding answers.

"So I called Terry." Cheri looked at Dixie and then shifted back to me. "Then I called Nick."

As that sunk in, again I was at a loss on what to say.

I had so many questions, none of them appropriate given what had happened after that call.

"He didn't answer," she went on. "But I left him a message and so my call was the last call on his cell phone before…"

I struggled to say something, anything, of comfort.

Sometimes there are no words. I got up and wrapped Cheri in a hug. Dixie did the same.

When we'd all three recovered enough to talk, I grabbed tissues from the office and Dixie made some tea.

"A DCI agent questioned me," Cheri blotted her eyes. "Just him. I don't understand why Terry and the Sheriff's Department weren't there."

"A Gene Minor?" I asked.

"I think so." She reached for another tissue. "I was so upset that I didn't get his name."

"He was here." Dixie paused to take a gulp of tea. "From what we got, they're the ones investigating because Terry and Nick had a disagreement. Yesterday…before." Dixie couldn't continue.

"We're not sure but we wondered if because of the fight, they're not letting Sheriff Terry handle the case," I filled in.

"That's awful." Cheri twisted the tissue she held. "Wait. They can't think—they can't really think Terry might have had something to do with Nick's death?"

"Hard to know for sure what's going on. The agent didn't share anything." I hoped they didn't really think Terry had anything to do with Nick's death, but I had the impression that Agent Minor was from the everyone-is-a-suspect school of thinking.

"I was confused because I'd heard suicide, but the guy, uhm, agent, that talked to me led me to believe that they are looking at it as a possible homicide." Cheri wiped her cheeks with the tissue she still held.

The silence was so complete as we sat there that I could hear the tick of the clock back in the kitchen.

There were no clear answers. No note. No one who could say exactly what had gone on that day in the park when Alma had been run over.

Two people dead. And perhaps they were the only two who knew for sure exactly what had happened.

Chapter Sixteen

A week later, the Crack of Dawn Breakfast Club had assembled in the community room at the old fire station again. There was a table set up with muffins and pastries and, most importantly, a very large coffee urn. I approached the table and helped myself to a cup.

Though I couldn't hear whole conversations, I caught bits and pieces and the pieces were about either Nick Marchant and his apparent suicide or Sheriff Griffin and the suspicion surrounding him. No one seemed to be aware that Cheri Wheeler had also been questioned.

Stanley Marchant stood near the front of the room talking to Jimmie LeBlanc.

I worried about him overhearing the talk I was picking up. Bad enough to lose your son, but to have to hear all the speculation surrounding his death had to be like salt in the wound.

The snappily dressed Leela, in black-and-white polka dots today, clapped her hands to get everyone's attention.

I scanned the room. No silver-haired senior to give a shrill whistle this time. I wondered where William Harold was today. I really did owe him an apology for siccing those two ladies on him that day I'd been helping Cheri.

"If everyone could take a seat," Leela raised her voice to be heard over the din. "We have just a few items to take care of this morning and then everyone can be on their way."

A few people sat down. I refilled my coffee and took a seat near the front. I had a handful of folks I needed to catch to sign their release forms, and to verify that I had the name of the recipe and the contributor's names spelled correctly in the proofs.

We were close to the finish line on the cookbook. The printing was scheduled. The copy had been reviewed and I only had a couple of details to take care of, and then we could proceed with the photos. Max was coming in later in the week to do the photo shoot.

With this type of a cookbook you don't do photos of all the recipes. You simply choose a few to highlight. The choice for photos never has anything to do with the quality of the recipe or choosing the "best" recipes. Hopefully you've picked all quality recipes.

The ones that would be photographed were totally based on which ones would present well, and which ones would best help us tell the story we were trying to tell with the book. We were using some history of the city park. The *St. Ignatius Journal* had been helpful with providing bits of interest to intermingle with the recipes.

I hoped to give them an update, get the forms signed, verify the spelling, and then get back to the office. At this point in the editing, we didn't want to have to make a lot of changes.

Leela clapped her hands again.

"I'm going to have Stanley give the final report first," she said loudly.

Stanley Marchant joined her at the front of the room.

The room quieted.

"Stanley, I think I speak for all of us when I say how sorry we were to hear about your son, Nick. Our sincerest condolences to you and to Nate." Leela looked across the room toward the back door.

Nate Marchant stood in the doorway. He gave a brief nod of acknowledgment.

Stanley took a paper from his breast pocket and unfolded it.

"Our balance is close to the four thousand mark with the proceeds from last week's all-you-can-eat breakfast." His voice was firm and carried. "With the donated labor and a couple of corporate donations, we can now move ahead with the rest of the renovations."

He refolded the paper, tucked it back into his pocket, and then headed across the room to where Nate stood. Nate followed his father out the back door.

After Stanley left, the buzz in the room escalated again like an agitated hive of bees.

"I don't know that Leela speaks for all of us," a whispered voice behind me said. "I'm sorry Nick is dead but that boy has been in trouble since the day he was born."

"You shouldn't speak ill of the dead," another voice spoke up.

I really wanted to turn around and see who was talking but I didn't want to give away that I was eavesdropping.

"I am sorry for their family," the first whispered, "but I'm sure things will be a whole lot easier for everyone."

Leela was clapping again, trying to get everyone's attention and it wasn't working. I wished I could do one of those piercing whistles like William Harold had done the other day.

Finally banging her hand on the podium at the front of the room, she got the room settled enough to move on to the next topic. They had set a date for the rest of the work to be done and planned an event in a few weeks, weather permitting. This would be another all-you-can-eat biscuit breakfast to show off the remodeling. They were hoping to have Crack of Dawn Breakfast Club cookbooks available and I thought we would be able do that. That was if we could make the printing deadline. Dixie and I had everything done and off to Liz for design. The only remaining task was the photo shoot and that would soon be complete.

We got through the rest of the meeting without Leela losing it, though it looked iffy a couple of times. I managed to catch everyone I needed to.

Stuffing the papers in my bag, I headed to the Jeep.

I never could figure out who had been sitting behind me, but their words nagged me. The idea that the sheriff had anything to do with Nick's death was ridiculous. I felt sure he would be cleared. But whoever had been talking was right; Nick Marchant had created a lot of trouble in St. Ignatius for a number of people, his family included. The family everyone knew about and also Cheri and Dustin, the family no one knew about.

* * * *

Back at the shop, I entered from the back but followed the sound of voices to the front. Terry Griffin sat at the counter chatting with Dixie and munching on a chocolate chip cookie. He wore jeans and a checked shirt. The fact that he was not in uniform and given the time of day, I took to mean that nothing had been resolved.

"How are you doing, Terry?" I asked. "Anything further on the investigation?"

"The DCI is working on it." He looked up. Somehow, the sheriff always looked younger in regular street clothes than he did when he was in uniform. "They're sharing nothing with me. Nothing at all."

"Just because you and Nick had words?" I asked. "That's crazy. He acted like a jerk."

"Not just that." He wiped a hand over his face. "There's more. The night Nick died, I took a call about shots fired in the city park. Everyone was already on a call, so I went."

"Oh." I hadn't heard that part, which was surprising because at the Crack of Dawn meeting and just about everywhere else, people were talking about nothing else but Nick Marchant's death. "But you didn't find him."

I glanced at Dixie. She'd nearly completely shredded the paper towel in front of her.

"I checked out the city park but didn't see anything," he explained. "I figured it was kids. We've had some vandalism at the park."

"Seems reasonable."

He continued, "After looking around a bit, I went home rather than back to the office."

"So no one can account for where you were or when, huh?"

"Right. But I'm not worried." He shrugged. "It will all get sorted out, but in the meantime it's frustrating."

"How will it get sorted out?"

"Even though there was no suicide note, they'll be able to tell from the angle of the shot whether he shot himself or not."

"And they think if it turns out to be a suicide that it's related to Alma's death?" I asked. "Or do they think because of his financial problems?" That's the other theory I'd heard.

"Like I said, they aren't sharing with me, but the research I'd done on Nick Marchant showed that there were some major problems with him, his finances, and the firm he worked for in New York."

My own research, using the site Gwen from Arbor House had directed me to, hadn't told me much. Only that Nick was no longer listed as a stockbroker.

"I understand the Jag was due to be repossessed," Dixie added.

"Where did you hear that?" Sheriff Terry raised his brows.

"Red Hen," Dixie admitted. "Dot Carson said she overheard a big fight between him and Nate. Nick wasn't willing to give up the car, Nate didn't think he needed that type of ride as a small-town banker."

"I hadn't heard that, but it doesn't surprise me." The sheriff brushed at the sleeve of his shirt.

"If they don't think Nick committed suicide, there must be other theories besides the local sheriff had an argument with him and killed him, right?"

Dixie winced and Terry gave me a tone-it-down look.

"Sorry to be so blunt," I apologized. "But it's plain crazy to think you had anything to do with it."

"I appreciate your support, Sugar." Terry smiled for the first time since he'd arrived. "But it really will get sorted out. I have complete trust in the DCI. These people are professionals."

"What about Bud Hostetter?" Dixie asked.

"Tressa's husband?" I asked. I hadn't considered that angle but it seemed like a reasonable one.

"I heard he'd threatened Nick." Dixie plated up some chocolate chip cookies while she talked. "Told him he'd better stay away from Tressa, or else."

"Let me guess. Red Hen, again?" The sheriff reached for another cookie.

"And then there's Cheri Wheeler, right?" I had to add.

"Yeah," Terry rubbed his chin. "I feel bad about that one. Like she needed to be put through anything more? Man, talk about going through a rough time."

The bell over the door dinged, and Tina Martin popped in.

The sheriff stood. "I need to get going."

"Keep us posted," Dixie handed him a couple of cookies for the road.

"I'll do that." He headed for the door. "Thanks for the cookies. And the support," he added.

"Tina." He nodded as he passed her.

"Sheriff." She smiled at him. Tina's signature color of the day was red. Her nails were red, her lips were red, and her black jacket was piped in red trim.

"Oh, gosh." Tina's crimson lips formed a circle. "I hope I didn't interrupt. Are you helping the sheriff with the investigation?"

"We're not," Dixie and I answered in unison.

"Not at all," I added.

"Uh, huh," Tina shook a bright red finger in our direction. "You two…"

I got the sense any further protests would be futile. Telegraphing Dixie a let-it-go look, I asked Tina what we could do for her.

"Right." She seemed to remember why she was there. "I know you said you couldn't make the Looking Pretty party at the salon, but I wanted you to have this."

She handed us each a gift bag with some samples and a small travel mirror with the words "You're Looking Pretty" on it.

"Thank you, Tina." I took the bag from her, feeling awful that I'd made up an excuse for the reason Dixie and I couldn't make the party.

And feeling even worse because it was an excuse that right now I couldn't even remember. Yikes! See, this is why I always try to stick to the truth.

"You are very welcome," Tina beamed. "Rafe is going to be coming through in a couple of weeks and I can't wait to introduce him to you two. I've told him all about you."

"That would be great." I made eye contact with Dixie. "We'd love to meet him. When did you say he'd be coming?"

"I'm not sure of when," Tina hesitated. She turned to go and then turned back. "I heard the Crack of Dawn Breakfast Club has set a date for a breakfast and unveiling of the shelter house remodeling. Maybe Rafe can come to that. I'll email him."

"Can't wait." I gave her a smile that I'm sure was just as lame as whatever made-up excuse I'd used to get us out of the Looking Pretty cosmetics party.

I waited until I was sure Tina was gone and then turned to Dixie.

"What are the odds that 'Rafe' will have a sudden business trip, just like the last time he was supposed to be coming through, and won't be able to make the Crack of Dawn shelter house unveiling?"

"Such a grump." Dixie tossed a chocolate chip cookie in my direction. "Must be a low blood sugar problem."

Chapter Seventeen

The cookbook revisions were complete and photo shoot day had arrived. The sun was shining, which would help with the natural light. And the baking had already begun.

Sheriff Terry walked through the door while we were clearing the space to make room for Max's photo equipment. The sheriff was still not in uniform so I took that to mean he continued to be on leave from the Jameson County Sheriff's Department.

Terry took the wooden chair Dixie was dragging and moved it across the room for her. Then he circled back and reached for the top of the sign I was attempting to tape to the window.

The last time Max had done a photo shoot for us, we'd collected a crowd outside. People peering in wasn't a problem in itself; I could understand their curiosity. Nevertheless, in trying to see what was going on, they'd blocked Max's light for the photos.

This time I'd thought I'd get ahead of the curious and put up a couple of signs.

Terry took the tape from me, finished taping the top of the paper, and then went to help Dixie with a table she had carried from the back.

I heard someone come in the back and figured it was Max.

"We're out front," I called.

"Hello." It wasn't Max but Cheri Wheeler who peered at us from the hallway.

"Sorry, Cheri." I waved a hand. "I thought you were Max here to set up for the photos."

"I don't want to interrupt." She came through to where we were working. "It's clear that you're very busy. But I came across this apron of my mom's.

I thought it would be really nice if maybe you could use it in one of the photos. It was one she wore all the time, was actually in her car…" She closed her eyes. "So, I just got it back."

Cheri handed me the apron. It was an old-fashioned red-and-white gingham with a pocket on the front and long ties in the back to keep it in place.

I looked it over. "It's in perfect shape, hon, and might be a great addition."

The apron actually did fit the feel I'd been going for with the cookbook. Favorite breakfasts, family recipes passed down. It could work.

"If you can't use it, that's okay, but I thought I'd take a chance and bring it by just in case."

"We always defer to our photographer on props," I told her. "And he often has his own ideas, so I can't promise anything, but I'll give it to Max and we'll see what he thinks. Okay?"

I really hoped Max could make it work.

"That would be great." She smiled. "Now, I'll get out of your hair."

"See you later, Terry. Dixie." Cheri waved and headed out the back.

I carefully placed the apron on the table where we'd arranged some of the potential props. There was a vintage white pitcher, an antique biscuit cutter that I'd picked up at a yard sale, a few assorted plates, and some colorful napkins. We had an ornate silver ladle from Dixie's Aunt Bertie and Nate Marchant had dropped off a Wedgewood platter that Stanley had mentioned when we'd talked with the group about including some family items in the photos. We'd been clear with them, as well, no promises, but those types of details would make the cookbook much more personal and unique.

Like I'd told Cheri, Max usually had his own ideas and they were always great ones, so we'd see which of the items he might want to use.

"Hello." A voice called from the back and this time it was Max.

He carried several bags of equipment and had a tripod tucked under his arm.

"Do you need help?" Terry asked.

"No, I think I've got it." Max carefully set the bags on the floor and shook hands with Terry. "Good to see you."

He scanned the room. "I see you're all ready for me. That's great because I have the high school baseball team right after this and I'll be cutting it close. Where are we on the food?"

"Shoot. I've got biscuits baking and I got distracted." Dixie spun around and scurried toward the kitchen. "Let me go check on them."

Max gave Sheriff Terry a look.

"I'm going." He held up a hand.

Dixie would deny it but though Sheriff Terry had been a lot of help, he was also a distraction. Even if he wasn't worried about being a suspect if the DCI couldn't confirm that Nick's death had been suicide, Dixie was worried for him.

I hoped the DCI wrapped up their investigation soon. It sounded like they were waiting on some evidence to be processed. So, hopefully some answers soon.

Then Sheriff Terry could get back to his life. The Marchants, Nate and his dad, could deal with their grief and have some closure. And maybe at some point, Cheri could also have some answers about Alma and she and Dustin could move forward.

And my favorite town could get back to normal.

Nick had brought some excitement to St. Ignatius, but ultimately, he'd also brought tragedy.

Staring at the room without really seeing it, I'd drifted off into thinking about Alma and her murder and everything else that followed. It was natural, I guess, given what a big part of this project she'd been.

"Everything okay?" Max asked, his expression concerned.

"Yeah, I'm fine." I gave myself a mental shake. "Sorry."

Enough with worry. It would all be sorted out and worrying would not make that happen one bit quicker.

Worry casts a big shadow.

Another of Aunt Cricket's bits of wisdom.

"Let's get this party started." I smiled at Max. I had emailed him the list of the dishes we wanted to feature. Showing him the table where we'd put the potential props, I explained about the apron Cheri had dropped off.

"We might be able to work it in." He began setting up, moving quickly, putting everything in place so he could begin.

I absolutely loved to watch this process. Dixie was in her element and Max was in his. In their own ways they were each virtuosos. Or was that virtuosi? Either way they were both highly skilled and I found that fascinating. I'd seen Dixie tweak a recipe until she got a dish just right, tirelessly trying different ingredients.

Max was much the same with his photography. He was never satisfied with a shot that was only "okay." He'd tirelessly keep making changes, trying different light, varying the props, until he got the effect he wanted.

With the biscuits, he wanted them fresh from the oven, butter welled in the thumbprint top and dripping down their sides.

The cinnamon rolls he tried still in the baking pan, then on a plate with a fork, and finally on a cutting board, oozing with glaze and festooned with a little sprig of cinnamon sticks tied together with a bit of string. Perfect.

Alma's casserole was a feast, cut into squares and ready to serve, her red-and-white checked apron off to the side as if the cook had just taken it off. Even though there was not a single person in the photo, you could sense the family, just out of the shot, ready to dig in.

I didn't know how he managed it but Max captured each dish in a unique way. No people in the photo, but still you felt the people.

It was an exhausting process and I began to wonder if the time I'd planned for the photos was enough. But Dixie kept baking, I kept shifting food and props, and Max kept shooting.

Two hours later, we were done. It was a wrap.

Max hurriedly packed up and took off to take pictures of the St. Ignatius baseball team. He'd taken his time with our photo shoot, but that had eaten into his schedule, and threatened to make him late for the baseball team commitment.

Dixie had washed up dishes and pans as she went so most of that was done. She was headed to her brother's house for a birthday party for his son, Theo, who was turning six.

Everyone had someplace to be, except for me, so I offered to clean up and put things away. I couldn't wait to see the photos. I knew we were going to love them. If the process was similar to the other projects Max had done for us, he might have them ready to look at in the next couple of days.

It seemed like everything had been sorted out, at least as far as the Crack of Dawn Breakfast Club Cookbook project anyway.

As far as everything else, there was still a lot of sorting out to be done.

If Nick really had killed Alma, and by all accounts that was still a possibility, then he must have decided he couldn't live with what he'd done. I still couldn't put it together in my head, because based on the stories from Dixie, Tressa, Cheri, and others, Nick Marchant had taken advantage of people all his life. The man seemingly had no conscience.

But like Dixie said, this was a new low even for him. And so perhaps he had felt sorry for what he'd done. Or, more likely in my book anyway, he'd known that his daddy couldn't pull his fat out of the fire on this one and that he was probably going to prison.

I took down the signs and tossed them in the trash.

I guess everything would be sorted out in the end and everyone would be okay. Except for poor Alma Stoller that is. I imagined her confronting Nick and insisting it was time for him to do the right thing. I folded Alma's apron over my arm and carried it into the office, feeling sad for Cheri and Dustin.

I was glad Max had been able to work Alma's apron into the photo of her breakfast casserole. Cheri would be pleased. Maybe we could frame a copy of that particular photo for her. This time I knew better; I'd ask for Max's help in choosing a size and a frame.

I felt sad for Nate and his dad, too. Even if it were true that Nick had been the black sheep of the Marchant family. "A problem since the day he was born," according to the anonymous guy at the breakfast club meeting. Still, Nick had been Nate's brother and Stanley's son and I'm sure they loved him.

I looked for something to put Alma's apron in to return it to Cheri and found a nice box that some of our sample paper had come in. Folding it into a square, I felt a rustle of paper. Probably a recipe. Cheri said her mom was always tucking recipes into her purse or her pockets.

I unfolded the apron and checked the front pockets, which were trimmed in red piping. Nothing. Running my hand down the length of the apron, I heard it again. Moving some books and files, I cleared a space and flattened the apron on my desk. I looked over the front and then flipped it over and did the same.

Ah-ha. There was a small inside pocket at the waistband. With a pinch I pulled a folded paper from the hidden pocket. Must be a super-secret recipe. I smiled as I unfolded it, wondering what secret ingredient this one had.

Holy cow.

It wasn't a recipe, it was a check. A blank check written to Alma and signed by Stanley Marchant.

Dumbfounded, I stood looking at it. Why would Stanley write Alma a blank check?

I'd been thinking about her confronting Nick, but maybe she really had told Stanley about Dustin. Had Stanley agreed to help with Dustin's schooling? If that were the case, good for him. I supposed there could be many reasons for not filling in an amount. But Mr. Down-to-the-Last-Detail Stanley Marchant was not the type of guy who left commitments open-ended.

And Mr. Color-Coded Spreadsheet sure-as-shooting wouldn't be happy with a blank check floating around. A signed blank check.

Whatever it was for, he'd given Alma this check, and if it had to do with Dustin, he'd want to write a new one to Cheri. Maybe he and Alma had come to some sort of agreement and she hadn't had time to cash it before she'd been killed. But why hadn't he contacted Cheri? Something about it bugged me.

None of my business. All that was for them to sort out.

I laid it on top of the Wedgewood platter I needed to return to Nate and Stanley Marchant. I'd planned to drop the platter off on my way home. I'd just drop the check off as well.

Heading back to the kitchen to finish up the dishes, I washed and dried the few pieces Dixie hadn't gotten to and then put the remaining food away.

Luckily Dixie had taken quite a few of the biscuits with her to her brother's house. We'd sent some with Max as well. And I'd reserved two (okay, three) to take home with me. That would be my dinner.

Dixie had supplied me with her Grandma Ruby's sausage gravy recipe to make and put over my biscuits.

Instead, I fully intended to warm the biscuits up in the microwave and eat them with the honey I'd picked up at last Saturday's farmer's market. I'd say don't tell Dixie, but I think she probably already knew when she gave me the recipe. But I promised myself I'd eventually try the gravy recipe.

I checked the front door to make sure it was locked and carefully carried the Wedgewood platter to my car. I had put Alma's apron in the box I'd found and I brought it along as well. After I stopped at the Marchant house, I could swing Cheri's house and drop off the apron. I was excited to let her know we'd used it.

This time I had no trouble finding the Marchant house. It helped to know what you were looking for. I noted that Nate's car wasn't in the driveway and wondered if the Jag still sat in his parking spot in the garage or if he'd reclaimed the space.

It hit me again how mind-boggling it was what had happened in the past few weeks.

I rang the doorbell, but this time I didn't worry when it took so long for Stanley to open the door. I knew to wait. And when he opened the door, I didn't expect to be invited in. I was surprised when he motioned for me to come inside with the platter.

"Thank you for bringing it by. That platter has been in the family for years. My late wife often used it." Stanley said. "Nate can put it away when he gets home."

"I also wanted to give you this." I shifted the Wedgewood platter and pulled the blank check out of my pocket. "I found it in an apron we used for the cookbook photo shoot." I explained about Cheri bringing her mom's apron, how we'd used it, and then how I'd come across the check.

"Anyway, sorry to be so long-winded," I finished. "But I thought you'd want it back."

Just as I reached out to hand Stanley the check, it hit me.

I suddenly knew what had been bugging me. I looked down at the check in my hand.

Made out to Alma Stoller.

Signed by Stanley Marchant.

No "B."

I looked up at Stanley. At that moment, I sincerely wished I'd cleaned up at the shop and gone on home. Minded my own business.

But no.

Ever helpful, that was me.

Help find Bunny, go search for Alma, return the Wedgewood platter, drop off a misplaced blank check. MYOB. Mind your own business, Aunt Cricket would have advised.

This one time, Sugar Calloway, it would have been good to MYOB.

I remembered in Daddy's *A Fictional Memoir*, how Gage had become adept at forging his mother's signature on notes to the school.

"You didn't sign this check, did you?" My voice was calm, but my pulse was racing. My heart pounded in my ears.

Stanley's steely eyes bored into me. He had the dark blue Marchant eyes. Like Dusty. Like Nick. Like Nate. "No, I did not."

He knew that I knew he hadn't, and knew I was on my way to figuring out what that meant.

"No," he repeated. "I did not." His voice even, his eyes never left mine. "I would say, my son signed that check."

"Your son signed it." I nodded and took a step back. I mind racing, my only thought was that I needed to get away.

He was old. I was young. He wasn't that big. I could make it to the front door and out of the house. Call 9-1-1.

Another small step backward.

"Don't move." Stanley lifted a gun from his pocket.

It was small but deadly looking.

I didn't know a lot about guns, but I did know a lot about people. And Stanley did not look like a man who was bluffing.

"You knew Nick was Dustin's father?" I took another step back, thinking if I could get closer to the door. "From Alma?"

Stanley nodded slightly, his eyes narrowed to slits. "Don't move."

He shifted his grip on the gun and steadied it with his other hand.

It was then that I realized the gun wasn't pointed at me.

"Nate," he said. "Put the gun down."

I turned my head slowly and looked over my shoulder.

Nate Marchant stood in the hall behind me. He also held a gun and it was pointed at the middle of my back. With my continued steps backward, I'd nearly backed into it.

"He had to be stopped." Nate had the gun on me but his eyes were on Stanley. "Slinking back here and making all kinds of trouble. It wasn't enough he'd cheated his investors. He had to come back here and ruin everything. Wreck our lives."

"Nate." Stanley's voice held a warning. He steadied his grip again.

"And to find out..." Nate's voice shook, but his hand did not. "To find out he had a son. With Cheri Stoller. That should have been me." He took a deep breath. "He was never going to stop."

Some of the things I had suspected, others I hadn't realized. Nor had I realized the depth of the animosity between the Marchant brothers.

"I'd already had to take care of Alma Stoller."

I felt sick. I could see on Stanley's face that he'd hadn't known for sure.

Had Alma gone to Nate about money for Dustin? She would have had no reason to think Nate would harm her.

"All he had to do was leave. Like he always did." Nate's voice was ragged. "But he wouldn't."

"Enough, Nate." Stanley straightened up and steadied his hand, which had begun to shake. "Enough."

"Father?" Nate swallowed.

I took advantage of Nate's brief hesitation and spun around, smacking his gun arm with the Wedgewood platter. At the same time, I brought up my knee, hoping to connect with parts tender enough to bring him to his knees. But he was tall and I was short. I think I only knocked him further off balance. Still, I gave it my all.

And then I ducked.

I don't know which gun went off first, but I know Stanley and Nate both fired.

Nate fell to the floor with a thud and then Stanley toppled.

The old man looked across at me. His face was ashen and tears streamed down his face. "Call."

Scrambling to my purse, I grabbed my cell phone and dialed.

"What's your emergency?" the woman on the other end asked.

At a loss for words, not knowing how to explain, I just said, "People are shot. We need help."

I looked over at Nate, who lay on his side, moaning. And Stanley, who was losing a lot of blood from his leg.

I kicked both guns away from them with my foot, having seen that on TV.

I had a brief thought that might be the wrong thing to do because the placement might be important later. But right now, not getting shot at again was more important.

"Two people are injured." I gave her the address. "We need help."

Yanking a cloth from the nearby table, I wrapped it around Stanley's leg like a tourniquet, hoping to slow the bleeding. I could already hear the sirens coming closer.

The sheriff's department arrived with the ambulance and paramedics right behind them. There were so many people and so much chaos at first, I just stayed where I was. But then both Stanley and Nate were stabilized and loaded quickly for transport to the hospital.

A young deputy talked to me, jotted down some notes, and moved me to another room.

I could see Sheriff Terry talking to the deputy, and they began securing the area. The sheriff looked in to where they'd put me and asked, "You okay?"

I nodded. My legs had begun to shake, so I'd sat down on an ottoman.

Dixie arrived a few minutes later. I assumed that Sheriff Terry had called her. He motioned her through and she immediately folded me into a hug.

"I had the wrong brother," I mumbled into her shoulder.

"I know." She pulled back to look at me and then hugged me again.

"Come on." Dixie gave me a hand up. "Terry says he's got enough information from Stanley and that you can give your statement tomorrow. Okay?"

I nodded, getting to my feet. I was wobbly but able to stand.

"I hear you kicked Nate in the shin and saved the day." She grinned. "I would've aimed elsewhere."

"I was aiming elsewhere." I smiled back.

"Anyway, it worked and you saved the day." With an arm around my shoulders, she headed me toward the door.

"I didn't save the day." I shook my head. "But I didn't die."

Chapter Eighteen

This time the all-you-can-eat breakfast at the St. Ignatius City Park featured several dishes from the Crack of Dawn Breakfast Club cookbook.

Alma's Heart Attack Hot Dish was popular, as were the Cat's Head Biscuits, and Dixie's Grandma Ruby's Cinnamon Rolls. Greer had set up a card table to take money, and Leela Harper had a table right next to her where people could purchase their very own copies of the cookbook.

Nate Berg, from the *St. Ignatius Journal,* was on the scene interviewing people and taking pictures. And most importantly, the cookbooks were selling like hotcakes.

This time I was better dressed for a walk in the park. Jeans, a lightweight gray cotton top. I smiled to myself, thinking Tressa would have exclaimed that it matched my eyes. I hoped she was okay. I'd heard she was back with her husband.

I'd also gone for boots this time instead of cute but impractical shoes. It was a gorgeous summer day with mild temps and a gentle breeze that rustled through the big oak trees. We couldn't have asked for better weather.

I'd taken a turn around the park trail while waiting for the line to clear out a bit. After my walk, I settled myself on one of the rustic limestone benches that had recently been installed around the perimeter.

There was still a long line of customers and the queue wasn't moving very fast, mostly because Greer chatted with each person as they paid. Out in one of the open green spaces, Dixie chased a frisbee with her nephew. At the edge of the shelter house there was a burst of whoops and laughter as several volunteers chased down some napkins that had blown off the picnic table. I watched the action and savored the scene.

Home. This was home. This was my home.

I heard someone come up behind me and turned to see Max approaching.

"Mind if I join you?" he asked.

"There's plenty of room." I smiled and scooted to the side of the seat. "Aren't these benches great? I love how they blend with the weathered limestone of the shelter house."

He nodded and sat down beside me. His ever-present backpack of photo equipment was missing.

"No camera?" I asked, surprised.

"Not today." He sat forward, his elbows resting on jean-clad knees. He sat for a minute or two looking at his hands, and then looked up and met my eyes. "I owe you an apology."

"For what?" I asked.

"For ignoring you." He took a breath and let it out. "For keeping to myself. For being a jerk."

"Max, you don't owe me anything."

"But I do." He stared off across the park. "I've been alone so much of my life that when stress hits I don't know how to share that with someone else."

"What were you stressed about?"

"Decisions."

I let the silence lie between us.

"My old job called and they want me back."

Before moving to St. Ignatius, Max had worked at a big glossy magazine doing photos all over the world. An injury had sidelined him, but when he'd talked about it, it had always sounded like he loved it. Loved the work. Loved the travel. My head jerked up. "But wait, that's good news, right?" I asked. "That's what you want to do."

"I thought I did." He tilted his head and gazed up at the blue cloudless sky. "The exciting life, assignments all around the globe."

"But?"

"But I've discovered I don't want to do that anymore."

"Hmm, I can't see you doing quilts and baseball teams, or that kind of thing, and being happy with that."

"No, I can't either. But I really enjoyed doing the food thing for the cookbooks and I've looked into some more in that line of work. And I'm very much enjoying the local nature photography I've dabbled with, so I want to do more of that. Iowa is beautiful and doesn't get much credit."

"What did you tell your old boss?"

"I told him thanks but no thanks. I'm staying here."

"Well, in that case, no apology necessary." I bumped him with my shoulder. "But next time you're sorting out major life decisions, I'm a really good listener."

"I know you are." He turned toward me, his bright blue eyes serious. "I simply defaulted to loner mode. I'll work on that."

"And I defaulted to neurotic mode. I'll work on that, too." I laughed.

"Deal." He smiled, the corners of his eyes crinkling. Then turning serious again, he picked up my hand. "I understand you literally dodged a bullet, a couple of weeks ago."

"Yeah, two of them." Sometimes it hit me like a brick just how close I'd come to not being able to enjoy a summer day in the park like this.

"I understand Nate Marchant has been charged in both Alma Stoller's death and his brother's."

Max kept my hand in his and I liked it.

"What a bizarre turn of events." He leaned back to look at me.

"According to Sheriff Terry he went to the park to give Alma the money she had asked for to help her grandson," I explained, "but Nate thought that meant she'd keep quiet about it and that wasn't what Alma had in mind."

"Wait. Nate Marchant knew his brother was Dustin's father, but Nick didn't know that himself?"

"That's right. Alma had contacted Stanley, but Nate intercepted the message and decided to take over as the 'fixer' of his brother's problems. He didn't tell his dad or Nick and must have thought the secret would die with Alma." I shivered in spite of the warmth of the day.

"But to run over the poor woman." Max shook his head.

"I know. Unbelievable." I felt sick at the fear Alma must have felt. "It sounds like he panicked and jumped in her car and ran her down. And then backed over her."

Max laid his other hand on top of mine. "And why his brother?"

"Wanting to help find whoever had killed her mother, Cheri Wheeler told the sheriff who Dustin's father was. And after that she called Nick and told him." I paused thinking about how quickly all that had unraveled.

"And Nick put two and two together and realized what his brother had done." All the pieces had been there; I simply had not put it all together. "Not only was he going to expose what Nate had done, but he was also going to acknowledge Dustin as his son."

"So, Nate Marchant's world was falling apart and, in his mind, there was only one person to blame. His brother."

"Exactly." I suddenly realized I hadn't actually talked about it since everything had happened. It felt good.

We sat silently for a few minutes.

Finally, I stood and pulled Max up with me.

"Have you had any of the Cat Shed Biscuits yet?"

"Any of the what?"

"Come on," I linked my arm with his. "I'll explain."

As we made our way through the crowd in the shelter house and got in line, I felt a tug on my sleeve and turned to find Tina Martin beside me. Her blonde hair was tied up in a sparkly scrunchy that matched her sparkly pink top. Even her jeans had sparkly rhinestones down the sides.

"I'm so glad I found you, Sugar." Tina clamped pink-tipped fingers on my wrist and pulled me beside her. "I want you to meet Rafe."

She turned me around to face a pleasant though slightly pudgy and very ordinary-looking man. In contrast to Tina's sparkles, he wore nondescript khakis and a plain white dress shirt. He extended his hand. "So nice to meet you, Sugar. I'm Rafe and I've heard so much about you and your business partner."

I reached out to shake his hand and as I did, met Dixie's gaze from across the picnic tables. She was grinning from ear to ear.

"Nice to meet you, Rafe." I laughed. "Welcome to St. Ignatius. I hope you're having a good time."

"It's a great town." He glanced around at the shelter house and the crowd.

"Yes, it is." I looked around, too, my gaze taking in Dixie and Greer and Max.

"It's home."

Recipes

Jeri Beetles Cat's Head Biscuits

These are called Cat's Head Biscuits because they are as big as a cat's head.

Ingredients

4½ cups all-purpose flour
¼ cup granulated sugar
2 tablespoons baking powder
1 teaspoon baking soda
2½ teaspoons salt
⅓ cup butter-flavored shortening, cold
¼ cup cold butter
2 cups cold buttermilk
¼ cup melted butter

Instructions

1. Place oven rack in upper-middle position and preheat the oven to 450°F. Grease a 12-inch cake pan. (A deep-dish iron skillet works well too.)
2. In a large bowl, mix together flour, sugar, baking powder, baking soda, and salt.
3. Pour the dry ingredients into a food processor and then add the shortening and the cold butter. Pulse the food processor until the butter and shortening are mixed in.
4. Continue pulsing as you add the buttermilk and stop as soon as everything is blended together.
5. Turn the dough out onto a floured surface and press it flat with your hands. You'll want it approximately 2 inches thick.
6. Using a glass or a three-inch biscuit cutter, cut out your biscuits. If necessary, reshape the dough to get the last couple of biscuits.
7. Place the biscuits in the pan and brush with the melted butter. Place in the oven right away.
8. Bake until golden brown, about 30 minutes. You'll be able to tell if they're done by looking at them.

Tips for great biscuits

Don't over mix the dough. The dough should be fully blended but still have a course texture. In order to get the best rise on your biscuits they should go into the oven when the dough is cold, so if you start with cold ingredients and work quickly, they may actually end up the size of your cat's head.

Alma Stoller's Heart Attack Hot Dish

Not exactly your healthiest breakfast but made to be shared with family and friends, so those calories are negated by the laughter.

Ingredients

1 pound of breakfast sausage
6 slices of white bread, buttered, crusts removed
1½ cups shredded cheese (sharp cheddar works great)
6 large eggs, beaten
2 cups half-and-half
1 teaspoon salt

Instructions

1. Preheat the oven to 350°F.
2. Cook the sausage, crumble, and drain well.
3. Place the buttered slices of bread in the bottom of a 9 x 13-inch baking dish.
4. Spread the crumbled sausage on top of the bread.
5. Sprinkle the shredded cheese over the sausage.
6. In a medium bowl, beat the eggs, half-and-half, and salt until blended.
7. Pour the blended mixture on top of the sausage and cheese.
8. Cover with foil and refrigerate overnight.
9. Remove from the refrigerator fifteen minutes before baking.
10. Bake uncovered for approximately 45 minutes, or until a knife inserted into the center of the casserole comes out clean.
11. Let cool only slightly, cut into squares, and serve.

Tips

You can add extra sausage and shredded cheese, if you like. Alma always did. If you do, you may want to add a little more half-and-half. Pour in just enough so you can see it through the other ingredients.

Greer's Better Than Robert Redford Cake

Greer thinks this cake may be better than Robert Redford but not George Clooney. Just her opinion, of course.

Ingredients

1 box chocolate cake mix
3 eggs
1¼ cups milk
½ cup oil
1 can (14 ounce) sweetened condensed milk
1 jar (11.5 ounce) salted caramel sauce
2 cups heavy whipping cream
2 tablespoons powdered sugar
½ teaspoon vanilla extract
1 bag (8 ounces) Heath candy pieces

Instructions

1. Preheat the oven to 350°F and spray a 9 x 13-inch baking dish with nonstick spray.
2. Prepare the cake mix according to the directions on the package but use milk in place of water.
3. Pour the batter into the baking dish and bake according to the package directions.
4. Let the cake cool.
5. Using the handle of a wooden spoon, poke holes throughout the cake.
6. Pour the whole can of sweetened condensed milk over the cake, filling the holes.
7. Drizzle the cake with half of the jar of salted caramel sauce.
8. With an electric mixer, whip the whipping cream until stiff peaks form, adding the powdered sugar and vanilla while whipping.
9. Spread the whipped cream over the cake.
10. Drizzle with the remaining salted caramel sauce and

sprinkle with bits of Heath candy pieces (small chunks, but not crushed).

Tips

You can use frozen whipped topping, but make sure it's completely thawed before you put it on the cake.

Diane's Blue-Ribbon Made-from-Scratch Biscuits

Diane says these are served best with lots of sausage gravy.

Ingredients

2 cups all-purpose flour, plus ½ cup more for dusting
2 tablespoons sugar
4 teaspoons baking powder
¼ teaspoon baking soda
¾ teaspoon kosher salt
2 tablespoons unsalted butter (chilled)
¼ cup vegetable shortening (chilled)
1 cup buttermilk (chilled)
1 teaspoon butter flavoring
Small amount of melted butter to brush on after baking.

Instructions

1. Preheat the oven to 400°F.
2. Place all dry ingredients into a large mixing bowl and whisk together.
3. Using your fingers, rub the butter and shortening into the dry ingredients.
4. Make a well in the middle and pour in the buttermilk and butter flavoring.
5. Stir with a spoon until it all sticks together.
6. Knead in the bowl until all the flour sticks together.
7. Turn the dough out onto a lightly floured surface and begin folding it over.
8. Knead the dough until it's soft, but don't overwork it.
9. Press the dough into a round, about ¾ inch thick.
10. Using a biscuit cutter, cut out the biscuits and place them on a pan so they just slightly touch. Reroll your scraps, if you have to, to finish out the dough.
11. Use your thumb to make a shallow dimple in the top of each.
12. Bake 15 to 20 minutes or until they are golden and then

remove from the oven and brush with butter.

Tips

It's important not to overwork the dough and it's also important not to overcook your biscuits.

CPSIA information can be obtained
at www.ICGtesting.com
Printed in the USA
LVHW091841081219
639829LV00001B/57/P